THE THICKETY

The Last Spell

J. A. WHITE

Illustrations by
ANDREA OFFERMANN

KATHERINE TEGEN BOOKS
An Imprint of HarperCollins *Publishers*

Katherine Tegen Books
is an imprint of HarperCollins Publishers.

The Thickety: The Last Spell
Text copyright © 2017 by J. A. White
Illustrations copyright © 2017 by Andrea Offermann

ISBN 978-0-06-238139-2

Typography by Amy Ryan
17 18 19 20 21 CG/LSCH 10 9 8 7 6 5 4 3 2 1

First Edition

For the Goffins:
Kim, Vinny, Andrew, Matthew, Hailey

PROLOGUE

Martay grasped the hilt of his cry-sword and waited for death. It would not be long now. The famous glass walls of Ta'men Keep were as strong as stone but couldn't keep the Spider Queen's creations out forever; he could see them milling just outside, testing the building for weaknesses. Colored panes distorted their monstrous shapes, creating impossibly tall silhouettes with curved claws and stalactite teeth.

Or maybe those aren't distortions at all, Martay thought. *Maybe that's their true appearance.*

He wondered—and not for the first time—how he had come to be here. Unlike his older brothers, Martay had never wanted to be a soldier. Since childhood he had dreamed of becoming an apprentice to a Master Glass-blower and learning the secrets that had made Lux the wealthiest region in Sentium. His family had not been influential enough to secure him such a coveted position, however, and with no other options he had enlisted in the city guard. It had not been such a bad life at first. Ta'men Briel was a city at peace, and mindless drills and guard duty seemed a small price to pay in order to provide a stable life for Yonda and their baby girl, Wix. Martay's childhood dreams remained unfulfilled, but he had found a new purpose in his daughter's eyes.

And then the entire world had changed.

At first it had only been rumors, easily dismissed. *A beautiful sorceress with eyes like cracked glass. Hideous monsters. Entire towns destroyed overnight.* As the Spider Queen made her way across Sentium and gathered witches to her cause, however, her existence became irrefutable. Since nearly killing the graycloak leader Timoth Clen in a fierce battle up north, her army had been sighted in the most obscure places: a mining town reclaimed by pines; the last remaining Ice Swamp; burnt remains of an ancient cathedral.

Rygoth was searching for something.

The Curators of Lux had gathered in Ta'men Keep and consulted forgotten texts written in dead languages, desperate to find out what could be so important to this new enemy. As a result of their investigation, a small chest was dragged up from the vaults and placed under vigilant guard. Martay could see it now at the opposite end of the hall, sitting on a tall pedestal. The chest was circular and constructed from red nosidian, a rare, nearly indestructible crystal that took centuries to form.

There was no keyhole, no lid. It was never meant to be opened.

Rumor had it that the chest held one-quarter of an ancient weapon called the *Vulkera*. No one knew the exact nature of this weapon, only that its four sections, when joined together again, would grant the Spider Queen unimaginable power. Just a few months ago, Martay would have scoffed at the thought, but that was before magic had escaped the stories and woven itself into the fabric of their world. Legends and lore, however far-fetched, could no longer be ignored.

They had to keep the chest from Rygoth at all costs.

A thunderous boom shook the Keep as something struck the towering doors. Martay heard the soldier to his right—a mirror-bender's son, if he remembered true—let out a single, involuntary sob.

"Hold steady!" shouted High Swordsman Bellamy, a bear of a man with a beard thick enough to nest a family of birds. "Remember your orders!"

The doors, struck again, rattled in their frame.

Martay tensed with anticipation. He heard the soldier behind him mutter a prayer beneath his breath.

"Draw your weapons!" Bellamy shouted.

Martay's turquoise cry-sword, a marvel of crystal-smithing as strong as steel and half its weight, made a sound like tinkling glass as he withdrew it from its sheath. He was a passable swordsman at best, but a grizzled old veteran called Two-Toes had promised Martay that skill mattered only on the practice field. In a true battle, whether he lived or died would come down to instinct and luck. The words were not reassuring.

Past the mirror-bender's son, whose single sob had escalated into a series of quiet whimpers, Martay saw that new silhouettes, human in appearance, had joined the monsters still pressed against the outside walls of the Keep.

As one, these new arrivals opened the books in their hands.

"Gr-gr-grimoires," said the mirror-bender's son, following Martay's gaze. His eyes danced like sparks off an anvil. "That's what they call 'em. Heard that from a peddler who passed through the ruins of Gildefroid. Told me what happened there, he did—what a book like that can do in the hands of someone with—"

The great doors rattled more violently, as though a

particularly fierce storm had grown hands and learned how to push. Soldiers took fighting stances. High Swordsman Bellamy barked orders. A chandelier of flickering shard-glass swung from side to side, shifting the hall from light to darkness, darkness to light.

Here they come, Martay thought, waiting for the doors to explode open and unleash Rygoth's forces into the hall. He clenched his cry-sword tightly and pictured his daughter's face.

The attack came from the sides.

It was only afterward that Martay pieced together what had happened. While the soldiers' attention had been fixed on the doors, magic had enabled Rygoth's monstrosities to pass through the exterior walls and into the Keep. The subsequent battle, if indeed it could be called that, was over in minutes. The Spider Queen's abominations blanketed the surprised soldiers like a mist of death, leaving behind nothing but armored corpses.

Martay found himself on the floor, a dull wetness

spreading across his stomach. He had been bitten, or clawed, or impaled with a horn. It had happened too quickly for him to make sense of it. He touched his wound and his hand came away an irrevocable red.

The doors yawned open. Rygoth glided into the chamber.

Her beauty—undeniable but frightening—was that of a swooping hawk or raging bonfire. She wore a spotless white gown with gloves that extended to her elbows. Her cracked eyes were a collage of colors, like a stained-glass window that had shattered and then been reassembled by a madman.

Three girls entered the Keep behind her. Two of them were identical in every way, with straight glaucous hair and eyes as cold as polished moonstones. The third girl was younger and had dark skin. When she saw the carnage that filled the hall her lips quivered, building toward a full-fledged scream, but then Rygoth looked her way and the girl's face immediately slipped into an impassive mask. She shrugged, as though the deaths meant nothing to her.

She's pretending to be one of them, Martay thought. *Why?*

Rygoth's eyes locked onto the red chest at the end of the hall.

"I can feel the grim's power from here," she said, starting forward.

Boar-like monsters with obsidian tusks repositioned the bodies that blocked Rygoth's way, clearing a narrow path from one side of the Keep to the other. Martay bit back a scream as something dug its teeth into his calf and dragged him across the floor. He forced his body to go completely slack, playing dead. Once the creature released him, Martay opened his eyes just the tiniest bit and watched the witches through a haze of eyelashes.

"Everyone leave," Rygoth said.

There was a flurry of motion as monsters stampeded through the front entrance. Before the dark-skinned girl could join this sudden exodus, however, the Spider

Queen's prismatic eyes clamped down on her like a vice.

"Everyone except you, Safi. There are matters we need to discuss."

The girl stood with bowed head as the hall emptied out. The twins were the last to leave, every step in perfect sync. Before closing the large doors behind them, they paused to look back at Safi and shared a knowing smile.

A silence like that of a graveside vigil descended over the hall.

"It's unfortunate that it was rumors and whispers that led us here, and not one of your visions," Rygoth said.

Safi followed a few paces behind the Spider Queen. Though she gave the appearance of being deferential, Martay noticed how close the girl's hand remained to the grimoire knotted to her belt.

She wants to be ready in case she needs to use it, he thought.

"I know that I've failed you thus far, my queen," Safi replied, "but—"

"Perhaps if we were searching for a single grimoire I might find your failure—not acceptable, certainly, but understandable. Needle in a haystack and all that. Only we haven't been searching for a single grimoire. The *Vulkera*, as you well know, has been split into four sections, four *grims*. Surely you should have found at least *one* of them by now."

"I'm getting closer," Safi said. "There's a second grim not too far from here. I saw it in a vision last—"

"*Where?*"

"I just need a little more time."

"So you've said. Repeatedly."

"I've never had to *control* what the visions show me before," Safi said. "A few mistakes are to be expected."

"*More* than a few," Rygoth said. "For a year now, you've been leading us to every corner of Sentium. If I didn't know any better, I might suspect that you were lying to me in order to buy time for that meddlesome friend of yours to find the grims on her own."

Martay held his breath as the witches passed right by his head, their boot heels clacking sharply against the stone floor.

"Kara Westfall is *not* my friend," Safi insisted. "I could have helped her at Clen's Graveyard, but I remained by your side. I serve you and no other. You know it's the truth—you've been inside my mind!"

Safi was doing her best to sound confident, but Martay heard a twinge of nervousness in her voice.

"And what a fascinating mind it is," the Spider Queen said. "Not the slightest hint of betrayal—or doubt, even. Every thought is a paragon of perfect loyalty." She stroked Safi's hair with the back of her gloved hand. "And to think you were once my enemy. The change in you is truly . . . unbelievable."

Martay risked turning his head for a better view and found himself face-to-face with the mirror-bender's son. The boy bore an expression of mild surprise, as though dying had been an unexpected but not entirely shocking turn of events. Martay wished he had taken the time to learn his name.

How many Luxians died today? How many more will die if she lives?

Anger anesthetized Martay's wound. He slowly rose to his feet. At the end of the hall, the Spider Queen was examining the nosidian chest, her back to him. She waved her hand over the lid and a shower of translucent worms fell from her fingertips. Black smoke rose as their acidic bodies began to burn through the chest.

Now's my chance, Martay thought, inching closer. *While she's distracted.*

Rygoth slowly removed her gloves. From this distance Martay could see that one of her hands was swollen and misshapen, with a red welt on its palm from a stinger's kiss. She reached through the hole that the worms had created and withdrew a rectangular flap of leather. It was rose-colored, with the petals of a flower embossed into its surface. If Martay had seen the contents of the chest yesterday he might have thought the Curators had made some sort of mistake, for this scrap of leather did not look like a weapon at all. He knew better now.

It's the cover of a grimoire.

"I can feel the power thrumming through it like an underground river," Rygoth said. "And this is just one grim. When I have all four . . ."

She turned to Safi. Her lips contorted into a cruel smile.

"I know that you've been faking your visions, Safi. You might somehow be able to hide your true thoughts, but you can't conceal the hatred in your eyes. You're trying to keep me from my book."

Safi took a step back, both hands on her grimoire now.

"Don't be ridiculous, my queen," she said weakly. "I only wish to be your faithful—"

Rygoth waved her entreaties away.

"It's not your fault. Your entire life has been built upon a foundation of lies. 'Do the right thing.' 'Help your fellow man.' But there is no joy to be found there, only servitude to a false nature. Humans yearn to destroy one another. Just look around you. Do you think these swords and bows are to keep the peace? Of course not! Men invented war so they could kill as they please and call it 'honor.' At least I'm honest about my intentions. I kill because I like it."

Martay took another step forward and Rygoth's head jerked upward, like a deer hearing a predator in the brambles. He paused in midstride, certain that she was about to spin around and end his pathetic assassination attempt, but she continued talking as though nothing had happened. Martay nearly collapsed with relief.

Almost there, he thought, taking another step forward. His arms shook as he struggled to keep his cry-sword from dragging along the ground. He was still losing blood, growing weaker by the moment.

"Once the *Vulkera* is whole again," Rygoth said, "my reach will extend to everyone's mind at once, like the rays of the moon. And what a gift I shall bring them! All people will finally understand that *love* and *compassion* are nothing but lies. They will embrace their desire for violence and become the monsters they were meant to be. A better world is coming, Safi. With your help—or without it."

Martay stepped into position.

Now!

Drawing back his sword, he tensed his arms for a horizontal slash that would sever the Spider Queen's head from her body. It never happened. A cold presence invaded his mind and he froze in place, unable to move. Rygoth looked back at him with an amused expression, as though he were an ill-tempered child who had attempted to kick her shin.

"Why are you trying to be a hero when you are so ill-suited to the role?" she asked him, looking away from the young witch for only a moment.

It was enough.

Sensing an opportunity that might never come again, Safi snatched the grim and ran toward the tall doors behind the pedestal.

Where are you going? Martay wondered. *Rygoth's army is waiting for you. There's nowhere to run.*

Except the girl, he now saw, had no intention of fleeing through a door made by human hands. Still running, she opened her spellbook and read strange words in no recognizable language. A magic portal, hazy with purple light, popped into existence just a few yards in front of her. Safi put on a final burst of speed, leaping through the air at the last moment so she could dive headfirst into the portal. Her outstretched hands vanished into the light.

That was as far as she got.

There was a loud crack, like a tree falling, and the stone floor buckled into a giant hand that snatched Safi from the air. Her grimoire slipped from her grasp along with the rose-colored grim.

From the darkened corners of the Keep stepped the twins. Martay wondered when they had reentered, assuming they had truly left at all. From what he had gathered, this had all been a plan to expose the young witch as a traitor.

"What a surprise," Rygoth said coldly, as one of the twins rushed to return the grim to her. "Our little seer isn't as loyal as she seems. Such a waste of talent." She smiled. "Throw her in the Stinging Cell. Perhaps she'll have a change of heart. If not, there are other ways to find the last three grims."

The stone hand relaxed its grip and Safi slammed to the floor. The twins each took an arm and started to drag her away, but the little witch didn't make it easy. She kicked and scratched with strength that belied her age.

"Kara's going to stop you!" Safi screamed, all pretense of loyalty dropped. "She did it once and she'll do it again! I bet she's looking for the grims right now. Knowing Kara, I wouldn't be surprised if she already—"

The twins dragged Safi through the open door and into the night.

For a long time after that, the Spider Queen stood with

her back to Martay, breathing deeply. Safi's betrayal—or perhaps her final words—had struck a nerve. When she turned around to face him, her fragmented eyes were cold with fury.

So this is how I die, Martay thought. *At least Yonda and Wix are safe. That's all that matters.* He had sent them to a distant aunt the moment he learned that the Spider Queen's forces were heading in their direction. Martay suddenly remembered that it was Wix's fifth birthday next week and he had not yet chosen a gift for her. He hoped that Yonda would find something special and say it was from him.

Picturing them in his mind's eye, a smile crept across his face. He was ready.

"I feel your love for them, *hero*," Rygoth said with disgust. "Your precious family. But don't you understand? Love is weakness. All you're doing is showing me the exact spot to strike."

There was a tugging in his mind and all memory of Yonda and Wix vanished.

The effect on Martay was devastating. His wife and child were the foundation of his entire existence, and without them his interior world collapsed inward like a tent whose poles had been removed. His mind was crushed to scattered fragments, and his heart shriveled to a black pebble capable only of despair.

"What have you done to me?" Martay asked, trembling. He felt frozen from the inside out.

"Wix has such pretty hair," Rygoth said.

Though he could not say why, the name filled Martay with crushing sadness.

"Who's Wix?" he asked, tears streaming from his eyes.

The Spider Queen laughed and left him alone with a dead army and an empty red chest. Though Martay remained a living statue, his wounds continued to bleed. He died just before morning but went mad long before then, his mind snapping beneath the magnitude of all that he had lost.

BOOK ONE
THE HOURGLASS TOWER

*"The seeds of the future
are buried in the past."*

—The Last Days of Kronia
Author Unknown

ONE

Kneeling by the stream, Kara cupped her hands together and splashed water on her face, grimacing as pinpricks of ice stung her cheeks. Her reflection rippled in the moonlight: dark circles under darker eyes, hair lank and wild.

I look like a witch, she thought, chuckling to herself.

The starry night was ripe for introspection, and Kara found her mind wandering to the strange events that had brought her to this place. She could trace the main path of her journey—growing up among the Children of the

Fold, her travels through the Thickety, sailing to Sentium in order to stop Rygoth, regaining her powers in the Well of Witches, the battle in the graveyard—but quite a few of the details escaped her. *Wexari* magic required memories to work, and her mind was littered with blank spaces, like patches of dead grass in an otherwise fertile field.

Behind her, footsteps crunched through a thin crust of snow.

"Evening, Darno," Kara said.

The wolf regarded her with amber eyes. His scorpion tail was curled in a tight spiral, the stinger tucked into a fold of fur.

The night is quiet, Darno thought, and Kara heard the words in her head as clearly as if he had spoken them aloud.

"Quiet is good," Kara said. "Right?"

Not good quiet. The quiet before the leap.

"I don't follow."

Darno sent her a vision of a taloned, apelike creature

swinging silently through the treetops of the Thickety, waiting to pounce upon the innocent paarn below it.

"You think we're being hunted?" Kara asked.

Yes.

"Have you seen someone? Something?"

Not seen. Felt.

Darno had survived for years in the Thickety before Rygoth stole him away, so Kara was not about to dismiss his finely honed instincts. She couldn't justify abandoning a good hideaway based on a feeling, however—not without confirmation.

"Let me see what's out there," she said.

Kara extended her thoughts to dozens of creatures in the vicinity: birds mostly, for these made the best sentries, but also rodents skittering through the undergrowth and even a lumbering bear. Some animals welcomed Kara into their minds, but the stubborn ones required her to spend a memory in order to construct a bridge between them. For a hatchling who had just learned to fly: *lifting*

Taff into the air so he can clothespin *Father's shirt to the line.*
With a hungry squirrel she shared *the taste of freshly picked
hushfruit.*

Once inside their minds, Kara searched the animals'
memories. They hadn't seen anything unusual.

"I think you're just being your overprotective self,"
Kara suggested to Darno. Since she had rescued the
wolf from Rygoth he had been a constant shadow by her
side, baring his teeth at every branch snap. Then again,
she supposed he had good reason to be paranoid: Rygoth
wouldn't rest until she was dead, and now Grace was
loose in the world as well.

"There's a blizzard in the air," Kara said. "Maybe that's
what has you on edge."

Darno nudged her shoulder.

Yes, he said. *Snowfall soon. Go inside. Not safe.*

Kara sighed. At times, Darno's constant vigilance
could grow tiresome. When she had professed these feelings to her brother, his face had brightened instantly:

"Now you know how *I* feel around you!"

"Give me another moment in the cold air," said Kara. "I need my senses about me before I head back inside and give the spell another go."

Not that it will matter, she thought. *We're trying to do the impossible!*

She cupped her hands beneath the surface of the pond, intending to splash her face, and fell backward with surprise.

The reflection in the water was not her own.

Darno rose up on his haunches, scorpion tail uncurled and rattling violently. Kara placed a hand on his flank.

"It's okay," she said. Now that the initial shock was over, she recognized the girl instantly. "That's Bethany. She's a friend."

Darno glared down at the image in the pellucid stream. Kara understood the wolf's doubt. Though they could only see Bethany from the chest up, it was enough to reveal the double-fanged spider sewn into her black robe. She appeared to be a loyal follower of Rygoth.

Kara knew differently.

"I never got to thank you for saving us that night," Kara said. "If you hadn't reflected the twins' spell back at them we'd all be dead right now."

Bethany waved Kara's words away. The motion should have caused the water to ripple, but it remained eerily still.

"You saved me from becoming the monster of Nye's Landing," Bethany said. "You brought me back into the light. I owe you a debt that can never be repaid."

"You're giving me too much credit. All I did was point you in the right direction."

"You know it was more than that."

Kara poked the stream with a single index finger. Concentric circles spread across the water but Bethany's image remained undisturbed, as though she were a solid form floating just beneath the surface.

"How are you doing this?" Kara asked.

"A particularly useful quirk of my grimoire," Bethany said. "I don't know if you remember, but the pages aren't like regular pages."

"They're mirrors," Kara said.

"Mirrors that cast the reflection I choose. All I have to do is look into a page and picture the face I want to see. The grimoire does the rest. The tricky part is that the other person has to touch the mirror in order for me to see them. Or water—any reflective surface will work."

"It's a crafty bit of magic, Bethany," Kara said. "But you have to be careful not to overuse the grimoire. It can take hold of you before you realize it."

"I know. But you helped me resist it once, and that's given me the strength I need to refuse its call."

Kara nodded, remembering her own experience. A grimoire's dark influence was powerful, but it could be subdued by a strong enough will.

"Now that I've created a link between us," Bethany continued, "you can call on me if you need to. Touch any reflective surface with two fingers and picture my face . . . just don't let your thumb touch anything or the spell won't work."

"Why not?"

"I have no idea," Bethany said, throwing her hands into the air. "It doesn't make any sense!"

"I know," Kara said. "Magic is so *weird* sometimes, isn't it?"

Both girls burst into laughter.

It felt so good to talk to someone who *understood*. Kara wished that Bethany were here with her right now. She often longed for the company of witches—the good ones, at least.

"Where are you?" Kara asked.

"I'm not sure, to be honest with you," Bethany said. "We've been traveling the same road for days. I just follow along, keep my head down. Everyone's asleep right now." She leaned forward, peering behind Kara. "All I see behind you are some treetops and Rygoth's wolf.

Actually, I guess your wolf now."

"Darno is not anyone's wolf."

"The point is, you could be anywhere that has trees and wolves. That's about all I *want* to know, just in case Rygoth decides to poke around in my head at some point. In fact, don't tell me anything important at all."

"What if she finds out you contacted me?"

"She won't. I blend in with the other witches so well, I'm not sure Rygoth even knows I exist. All my life I've wanted people to notice me, but I just vanished into the background. I thought I was cursed." Bethany smiled slyly, making her look like a completely different girl. "Now I'm starting to think it's a talent."

"Still, Bethany. You're taking a big risk talking to me."

"I had to. There's something you need to know." She paused, looking away. "It's bad."

Kara folded her legs and leaned against Darno for warmth.

"Tell me," she said.

"You heard about what happened at Ta'men Keep, right?"

Kara shook her head. "Been avoiding towns and people. Makes it difficult to keep up with what's going on in the world."

"I'll give you the short version," Bethany said. "Rygoth attacked the Keep and killed everyone inside it. They were guarding a grim."

"What's that?"

"A section of Princess Evangeline's grimoire—which Rygoth calls the *Vulkera*."

Kara felt ridiculous. All these weeks trying to locate the princess's grimoire, and she hadn't even known it had a special name.

"And she has this . . . grim now?" Kara asked.

"Yes."

"How did she find it?" asked Kara. She leaned forward as a horrible thought occurred to her. "Was it Safi?"

"No!" Bethany snapped. "Rygoth just followed a trail

of clues that led . . . How could you even *think* that Safi would help her?"

Kara could tell, given Bethany's defensive attitude, that the girls had become good friends during their two months together. *More than two months*, Kara reminded herself, forgetting to account for her time-stretching days in the Well of Witches. *Safi has been Rygoth's captive for over a year, which means Bethany has known Safi longer than I have at this point.*

"I hate doubting her," Kara said. "She's my friend, too. But I know how tempting the darkness of magic can be. You understand, Bethany. I know you do." Even in the water, Kara could see the other girl's cheeks flush slightly. "Besides, if Safi was still . . . herself . . . why did she attack me at the graveyard?"

"Because Safi knew that she could do the most good by staying," Bethany said. "By attacking you and remaining by the Spider Queen's side she demonstrated her unquestioning loyalty. After that, Rygoth really started to trust her—which allowed Safi to lead her all over Sentium, following false visions."

Guilt warmed Kara's numb cheeks. She had been so certain that Safi was caught in the thrall of dark magic and required rescuing. Instead, the younger girl, through courage and guile, had done more to stall Rygoth's schemes than Kara.

Taff never lost faith in her. I won't either, after this.

"How did Safi hide the truth from her?" Kara asked. "Rygoth can see into people's minds."

"That was my doing, actually," Bethany said, with no little pride. "I put these *mind mirrors*—that's what we called them—in Safi's mind, so that every time Rygoth took a peek she saw a girl who worshipped her utterly and completely. But of course what Rygoth was really seeing was a reflection of how she feels about herself."

"That's brilliant," Kara said.

"Safi thought so too," Bethany said, a sad smile on her face.

A particularly fierce wind bit through Kara's cloak. She learned into Darno, seeking warmth.

"What's wrong?" Kara asked.

"Rygoth figured out the truth," Bethany said. "She imprisoned Safi."

"But she can't hurt her," Kara said. "She needs Safi to find the rest of the grims."

"Rygoth claims she has another way. And since she found Ta'men Keep without Safi's help, I think she might be right."

Kara thought about this. If Rygoth truly didn't need Safi's help anymore, there was no reason for her to keep the girl alive.

"We're coming to rescue both of you," Kara said. "The grims can wait."

"No!" Bethany exclaimed. "Don't waste your time on us—Rygoth has the first grim already! You need to find the other three!"

"But—"

"Did Safi ever tell you about the vision she had? About what happens if Rygoth uses the *Vulkera*'s power?"

Kara nodded, remembering. *Rygoth, grimoire in hand, standing on a mountain of bones. That's all that will be left of the world.*

"Then you know what's at stake," Bethany said. "The only thing that matters is keeping the *Vulkera* out of Rygoth's hands. Nothing else is important."

Kara knew that Bethany was right. But she hated the thought of leaving her friends in danger.

"I'll find the grims first," Kara said. "And then I'll come for you."

"Don't worry about us, Kara," Bethany said. "Rygoth doesn't even know I'm helping you, and if she hasn't hurt Safi by now, I'm sure that she'll be fine. I'm not scared at all."

Even through the water, Kara could hear the quiver in Bethany's voice. She was a good witch, but a poor liar.

TWO

The stone farmhouse sat on a knoll overlooking several fields and a small pond. In the warmer seasons the view might be worthy of paintings, but for now all she could see was barren sameness in every direction. There were many things about Sentium that Kara enjoyed, but this frigid winter weather was not one of them. She missed earth, the smell of freshly grown flowers, chirping insects.

She missed Lucas.

It had been two months since she last saw him. She was certain that her father, now only pretending to be

Timoth Clen, would do his best to keep him from danger, but Kara had no way of knowing if either one of them were safe, and she worried constantly. The graycloaks were out of their league when it came to magic, and she couldn't fight the feeling that she might never see Lucas again. Rubbing her hands vigorously by the hearth, Kara remembered how Lucas had almost kissed her at the Swoop station and felt a keen regret: *Why didn't I lean forward and meet his lips when I had the chance?*

"Kara!" Taff called from upstairs. "Get up here!"

"Coming!"

She started up the stairs. For the most part, the farmhouse was comprised of features familiar to her: a wood-burning stove, four-poster beds, spheres half filled with water that required only a glorb to swirl them into illumination. Other elements of the house, however, baffled Kara and emphasized the fact that they were still strangers in this part of the world: ridged, metallic discs that adorned the walls like familial portraits; shelves filled with cheaply made chapbooks written in an unintelligible language of dots and swirls; countless buttons, dials, and switches that seemed to serve no purpose whatsoever. (Which of course did not stop Taff from pushing/turning/flicking each and every one, repeatedly.)

Kara still didn't know who owned the house; it had been empty when they found it, like so many other places. The world was in flux, and rumored sightings of the Spider Queen caused people to abandon their homes like animals fleeing a burning forest. On their journey here, Kara and Taff had traveled along roads packed with dusty emigrants, their wagons piled high with a lifetime of possessions.

Why do they bother? she wondered. *There's nowhere safe to go.*

Ducking her head beneath the low doorway, she squeezed along a narrow staircase to the attic.

Though they slept in the downstairs bedrooms, where it was warmer, this was where the Westfall siblings spent the majority of their time. A huge pane of glass set into the sloped ceiling kept the room well lit during daytime hours, and they had pushed the moldering crates against the walls, giving them the space they needed. With no usable paper to be found, they had covered the floor with charcoal drawings and any available wall space with lines of dense script.

Taff was kneeling on the floor, his back to her. He had found a blank space and was rapidly drawing something with a piece of charcoal worked down to a nub.

"Why were you gone for so long?" he asked.

Kara hesitated. She wanted to protect her brother, but she had also promised herself that she would never hide anything from him again, no matter how terrible.

Taff stopped drawing, sensing something wrong.

"What is it?" he asked.

She told him everything. When Taff learned that Rygoth had already acquired one-fourth of the *Vulkera*, he pounded his fist into his knee in frustration. The news that Safi was in great danger hit him even harder, and Kara expected Taff to argue with the decision not to try and rescue his best friend immediately. He surprised her, however, immediately understanding the hard logic of making the grims their first priority.

He's getting older, Kara thought.

"We need to focus on the spell," he said, his voice trembling ever so slightly. "The quicker we stop Rygoth, the quicker we can save our friends."

"Good plan," Kara said, resisting the urge to wrap her arms around him; he was doing his best to act like an adult and needed to be treated accordingly. Instead, she peeked over Taff's shoulder at his most recent sketch. "You've been hard at work. What are those things you—" She paused, noticing crumbs on her brother's shirt, "Hey! Did you eat the last of the cake?"

Taff grinned impishly.

"I got hungry. And to be fair, it *was* my cake."

Two days ago, Taff had celebrated his eighth birthday,

and Kara had managed to scrounge together the ingredients for a pumpkin cake with sweet-cream frosting, his favorite. She had also given him a battered pocket watch purchased from a peddler. Taff had taken it apart the next day and was still working out how to put it back together again.

"Don't worry," Taff said. "As soon as we get this spell to work, I'll bake *you* a cake to celebrate."

"Looking forward to it," Kara said with more confidence than she felt.

She thought back on the conversation that had started it all. Father, no longer Timoth Clen but needing to continue the facade for their own safety, had come to free Kara and Taff from their imprisonment by the graycloaks. In their few precious minutes together, he told his children something useful he had learned while the ancient witch hunter inhabited his body.

"There's a man name Querin Fyndrake," Father said. "He's old—older than Timoth Clen, even—and he should be dead, but he's not. 'A heathen frozen in time, cowering in his Hourglass Tower' was the way Timoth described him, whatever that means. I was going to—I mean, *Timoth* was going to mine this man for information. He knows where the four sections of the princess's grimoire are located. Timoth was certain of it. Even so, he wasn't in a huge hurry to talk to the man. The Clen showed no hesitation running headlong into battle with Rygoth, but this Querin Fyndrake frightened him."

"Then he must be a good guy," said Taff. "Right?"

Father clasped his son's shoulder.

"I think it's more complicated than that."

"We need to talk to him," Kara said. "If he can tell us where the grimoire pieces are, we can keep them away from Rygoth. Where do we find him?"

"That's the hard part," Father said. "See, the Hourglass Tower isn't on any map, because its location is not a *where*. It's a *when*. 'The hour without a toll.'"

"That doesn't make any sense," Kara said.

Father shrugged his shoulders. "I wish I could tell you more, but I don't even think that Timoth knew exactly what it meant."

Taff turned to Kara, grinning madly.

"A riddle!" he exclaimed with glee.

During the next few weeks, they had considered all sorts of theories about the unusual phrase: *The hour without a toll.* Perhaps the "toll" was money that had to be paid in order to gain entrance to the tower. Or maybe Querin was living near a church whose bell was broken.

In the end, however, they had returned to Timoth's description of the elusive man as "a heathen frozen in time."

"A bell tolls every hour," Taff said. "So if it never tolls, it means the hour never ends. Time has stopped. So all we have to do is freeze time and take a look around, see if we can find this Querin guy."

"You make it sound as easy as a carriage stop on a long journey," Kara said. "How do you propose we actually *do* such a thing?"

"When Rygoth needed an elixir to take away Sordyr's powers, she created Niersook," Taff replied, shrugging his shoulders. "All you need to do is create an animal that can stop time. Easy!"

At first Kara had balked at the idea, but then she remembered how Minoth Dravania, sitting beneath his tree in the Well of Witches, had playfully scolded her for still using the word "impossible."

Is it crazier than anything else I've done? she thought.

"Remember when you created the Jabenhook to save my life?" Taff asked. "Just do that. Only instead of a big bird who heals people, make one that stops time."

"Two problems," Kara said. "That spell used a grimoire, which I don't have . . ."

"Or need," Taff said. "You're *wexari*, remember?"

". . . and the Jabenhook was easy to imagine into being because it was part of a story that I had been telling you for years."

Taff, who had just recently learned how to snap his

fingers, relished the chance to do so now.

"That's it!" he exclaimed. "We'll just come up with a story so that our creature feels like it could really exist. And then you can build a mind-bridge to it and pull it into the real world."

"You want me to build a mind-bridge to a figment of my imagination?" Kara asked.

Taff crossed his arms over his chest.

"Got any better ideas?"

Kara had not. Every night since then they had told their story, and Kara had tried to make a connection with their fictional creation. She hadn't expected it to work right away, and in truth revising and improving the story—in an attempt to make the creature seem even more realis-tic—had been fun.

Five tries later, however, they seemed no closer to suc-ceeding, and Kara was beginning to wonder if their plan had any possibility of working at all.

As usual, Taff did not share her doubts.

"Tonight's the night," he said, smudging a charcoal line with the tip of his finger. "It's going to work. I can feel it."

Kara pondered his latest rendering.

They had decided to use a real animal as a basis for their imaginary one—which they had been calling a yonstaff—thinking that it would be easier for Kara to picture it this way. After much debate they had compromised on a large dog with red fur and black spots. At first glance, Taff's latest rendition of the yonstaff didn't look much different from the dozens of other drawings that covered the floor, but upon closer inspection Kara saw that Taff had added meticulously detailed gears to the joints of the legs, giving the dog a half-mechanical appearance.

"Why the change?" Kara asked.

Taff got to his feet. There were black patches on his knees and his forehead was smudged with charcoal.

"I think the spell hasn't worked yet because the creature we've been trying to bring into the world doesn't make any sense."

Kara couldn't help but smile at this.

"We're trying to create an animal that can stop time, and you're worried about it *making sense*?"

"Exactly," Taff said. "The creature has to fit its purpose. Like, let's say bears didn't really exist, and you tried to imagine one, but without claws and fur. It wouldn't really be a bear, would it?"

"Please don't take this the wrong way," Kara said. "But how long has it been since you slept?"

"All I'm saying is that our little guy needs to be more than just a funny-looking dog. It has to *look* like it can control time. I made some changes to the story, too," he said, pointing toward the words scribbled across the opposite wall. "It's not a question of magic. It's a question of *imagination*. We can't just *say* a creature called a yonstaff can control time and expect that to be enough. Your imagination has to be convinced that he actually exists. That's the only way Topper will become real enough for you to build a—"

"Topper?" Kara asked.

Taff blushed. "I gave him a name."

"He had a name, didn't he? Yonstaff."

"That's just his species," Taff said, "which was part of the problem. Instead of thinking of any old yonstaff you should be trying to imagine a specific one. It will be easier to build a mind-bridge that way. Naming something always makes it more real."

"There's sense in that," Kara said, willing to give anything a try. Her previous attempts to cast the spell had been like cupping a handful of mist. "But *Topper*?"

"I combined *time* and *stopper*!" Taff exclaimed. "Get it?"

Kara laughed.

"Topper it is."

She walked across the room to read Taff's changes to the story. Grievous errors in spelling and grammar made Kara feel guilty that she had not stayed on top of his lessons, but overall the revisions were good ones. The story felt fuller now, as though the characters were not just imaginary figments but living people dressed in words.

"This could work," Kara admitted. "We'll try it your way tonight. Maybe we could even—"

"Kara," Taff said, his voice a strained gasp. "I think we have a problem here."

She turned around. Grace Stone was standing behind her brother, a dagger to his throat.

"For once the little whelp's right," Grace said, smiling brightly. "You *do* have a problem."

THREE

When Kara thought of Grace, she didn't picture the red-robed Whisperer from the Well of Witches but Fen'de Stone's daughter, the perfectly dressed angel who always wore a brightly colored ribbon in her hair and had found new ways to torment Kara each and every day.

That girl was gone.

Grace's white hair had been shorn clean, leaving bristly stubble. Her clothes hung off her emaciated body like rags. Dirt streaked her face and encrusted her fingernails. Even her eyes had changed. They were the same stunning shade of blue, but now they twitched from side to side with a mind of their own, as though looking for a way to escape their failing mistress altogether.

"Does it please you, seeing what I've become?" Grace asked. She leaned heavily on a wooden walking stick, keeping the weight off her bad leg. "I bet you always dreamed of this moment."

"Don't hurt him."

"I've no interest in harming the whelp. I only want to talk."

"That's all?"

"That's all," replied Grace, lifting the dagger from Taff's throat. "But I can't have you conjuring one of your little monsters and attacking me before I say my piece. There's not much time, and I need your immediate attention if we're all going to live through the night."

Darno, having registered Kara's need for help, slunk into the room. The wolf's eyes remained fastened on Grace as he paced back and forth.

"Our new visitor does not make me feel very safe," Grace said.

"Free my brother and no harm will come to you," Kara replied. "I give you my word."

"And what word is *yours*, Kara Westfall? Sunshine? Happiness? Butterflies? You are just *so good*, after all. How can I possibly doubt you?" Grace shoved Taff away. "Here, take him!"

Kara stepped in front of Taff protectively as Darno knocked Grace to the floor. The wolf pressed his teeth against the soft flesh of Grace's neck and awaited further orders.

"No harm would come to me!" Grace exclaimed, her eyes wide with terror. "You promised!"

"And you threatened my brother's life. I'm not the forgiving girl you knew back in De'Noran, Grace. Now tell me why you're here, and *maybe* I can convince Darno not to tear your throat out."

"As much as it might surprise you," Grace said, "I'm

actually here to save your lives."

Taff rubbed his neck.

"You have a strange way of showing it."

"I needed to get your attention. Quickly. That's all. Now get this thing off of me and stop wasting time."

"Release her, Darno," Kara said.

The wolf, with some reluctance, slid his teeth from Grace's throat.

Just a nibble? he asked. *Hunting has been so scarce. . . .*

"I'm sorry, my friend." Kara could feel the burning pangs of Darno's hunger and felt guilty for teasing him with a meal. "But it's not safe to dine on this one. There's something inside her that's rotten and foul."

Rising to a sitting position, Grace took in the attic with a bemused expression: the drawings on the floor, the words scrawled across the walls.

"Have you two gone mad?" she asked brightly.

"Just say what you want to say," Kara said.

"Fine," replied Grace. "You trust me, right?"

"There aren't enough *nos* in the world for me to answer that question."

"You will, though. After tonight you'll never doubt me again." Grace brushed back hair that was no longer there. "It wasn't wise to stay in the same spot for so long. The twins have learned of your location. They'll be here any minute."

"How do you know?"

"Because I've been following you and I saw their approach."

"Following me? Why?"

"You're focused on the wrong part of the story. We need to leave right now, otherwise we'll be trapped in this farmhouse."

"Too late," Taff said, looking out the window.

Kara joined him. Falling snow obscured her view, but she could still make out two figures sharing a grimoire. Behind them, at the bottom of the knoll, loomed an additional four witches. The twins were taking no chances.

"How do I know you didn't lead them here?" Kara asked, turning on Grace. "This could be some sort of trick."

"Then why would I warn you?"

Kara shrugged. "I don't know. To gain our trust, maybe?"

"That doesn't make any sense at all. I'm putting myself in danger just standing here talking to you. Why would I risk—"

"I'm sure you have your reasons," Kara snapped. "You always do."

"Things are different now," Grace said in an overly calm voice. "*I'm* different."

Kara scoffed.

"Maybe we should sort this out later," Taff said, peering nervously through the window. "Where's Rygoth? I don't see her."

"She's not there," said Grace, ushering them toward the door. "And why does it matter, anyway? Let's just hop on that flying caterpillar of yours and get out of here."

Taff, hands on hips, spun to face Kara.

"Great idea!" he exclaimed. "Why don't we do that?"

"Is there a problem?" Grace asked.

"I sent Rattle away," Kara said. "She wasn't exactly inconspicuous, and I thought that after all that time trapped in the Well of Witches she deserved her freedom."

"Who said that was a terrible plan?" Taff asked, pointing to himself. "Who said we should keep Rattle close by in case of an emergency?"

"Is now really the time?" Kara asked.

Outside, the black-cloaked witches had gathered in a tightly knit circle, an eclipse of bodies against the snow. They spoke words from their grimoires. Kara couldn't hear what they were saying, but she felt her muscles tense in anticipation just before a flash of violet light illuminated the nighttime sky. The entire house jerked upward, as though a giant had torn it from its foundation and lifted it into the air—and then dropped it. Attic windows shattered. Beams split. Columns of crates fell over like catapult-struck towers, spilling their contents across the floor.

After helping Taff to his feet, Kara held up her arm against the snow now swirling into the attic and looked out the broken window. A wall of violet light enclosed the farmhouse and the approaching witches.

"What's *that*?" Taff asked.

"Not sure," Kara said, "but I have a guess."

She quickly built a mind-bridge to a nearby pack of wolves and gave them an order: *Flank the witches and attack them from behind.* They were all too eager to comply, given the gnawing emptiness in their stomachs—but this bloodlust quickly changed to frustration as they crashed into the purple wall.

"It's a magical barrier," Kara said, her initial suspicion confirmed. "I'm cut off from the animals in the forest. They can't help us."

"What about the ones already inside the dome?" Taff asked.

Kara shrugged. "Sheep and chickens. And Shadow-dancer. Nothing that can do much harm."

"What about rats?" Taff asked. "There's always rats."

Kara nodded. "In the basement. I'll send them. Maybe that will buy us a few minutes."

Don't forget about me, Darno said.

"No," Kara started. "There're too many of—"

But Darno was already out the door. Kara could have forced him to come back, but such a breach of trust would have ruined things between them.

Besides, Darno can take care of himself.

"We need to try the time-freezing spell again," Taff said. "It's our only chance."

Kara shook her head.

"Too risky. There must be another way."

"How about you surrender and tell everyone I captured you so they go easy on me?" Grace asked. "This way *one* of us lives."

Kara and Taff ignored her.

"We can do this," Taff said, grabbing Kara's hands. "I'll

tell the story. You do your witch thing. The spell will work this time. I can feel it."

"But if it doesn't—"

"It will!" Taff exclaimed. "Don't you believe it?"

If Taff had asked her this question just a few months ago, Kara would have said no. But things were different now. She had braved the *queth'nondra* and regained her powers. She had faced Rygoth in battle and survived.

"Start reading the story," she said.

"What *story*?" Grace asked. "What are you two babbling about?"

"I need to concentrate," Kara said. "That means *you* need to hold the twins back for a few minutes. Think you can do that?"

Grace could barely restrain her laughter.

"Are you asking for my *help*?"

"If you want to survive," Kara said, "I don't see what choice you have. I'm sure Rygoth knows exactly who undid the curse on my father and helped her prisoner escape. Do you really think she'll let that go unpunished?"

"You haven't noticed yet, have you?" Grace asked with an asymmetric tilt of her lips. "Then again, you never were the most observant sort."

It took Kara another moment before she realized what was missing.

"Where's your grimoire?" she asked.

Another flash of light shook the house. Two floors beneath them, something fell over with a giant thud. Grace nearly lost her balance, but Kara caught her before she fell.

"I tossed the evil thing to the bottom of an old well," Grace said. "I'm done with magic. *Done!*" She sighed with displeasure. "I will, however, do what I can to make a barricade. See how helpful I am!"

Grace limped away, her staff *tap-tap-tapping* against the wooden floor, and began stacking crates against the attic door.

What was that all about? Kara wondered.

There was no time to think about it now; Taff was starting the story. Kara sat on the floor—trying to ignore the worrisome zigzags now splitting the boards—and kept her gaze focused on Taff's most recent drawing of the yonstaff.

Not just any yonstaff, she corrected herself. *Topper. If it has a name it must be real.*

"Long before the remembrance of the oldest man on earth," Taff said, reciting the words from the wall, "Time was still a fresh-faced babe that hadn't yet learned to control its domain. Day and night fought for supremacy, hours would forget their order, and the minutes would sleep through their shifts. Needless to say, this caused all sorts of trouble for the humans, and so in order to help young Time until it mastered its duties, the gods created creatures called yonstaffs. They were hard workers who quickly settled the debate between day and night and taught the hours some good tricks to remember who came first. The real problem, however, was the minutes.

They were ridiculously lazy. Every day the yonstaffs had to nudge them all awake so they would be ready when their turn came. This was a lot of work, as you could imagine, and sometimes the yonstaffs fell behind and would have to stop the gears of time altogether while they caught up on their minute-waking duties. And this task of stopping time, when it arose, fell to the youngest yonstaff, whose name was Topper."

Kara closed her eyes, translating Taff's words to images. It wasn't enough to hear the story. If the spell was going to work, she had to *live* it.

"Now yonstaffs," Taff continued, "could not be seen by humans, of course—though those touched with magic might sense them as a warm breeze or a tingling at the ends of their fingertips—but the reverse was not true. Yonstaffs could see people just fine, and spent what little free time they had mocking the two-legs' odd habits and routines. All except Topper. The little yonstaff found the creatures delightful, particularly a poor boy named

Ruzen. The son of a tanner, Ruzen was eight years old and not particularly handsome or smart. He laughed often and easily, however, and was kind to animals. Every evening Ruzen would gather the dogs of the village and play a game with a leather ball he had made with his own two hands. Topper would watch them for hours, basking in their carefree happiness like a turtle in the sun. More than anything else in the world, he longed to play with the boy, to catch the ball between his jaws and feel Ruzen's hand pat the space between his ears. He wanted to hear the boy's laugh, not muffled by the barrier between their worlds as all sounds were, but joyously close."

As Taff talked, Kara tried to picture the individual elements of the story in as much detail as possible. The cowlick in Ruzen's hair that would never stay down. The leather ball, slightly lopsided and with the stitches already falling out, the handiwork of a child who had not yet mastered his father's craft. Most importantly, Kara focused the image of Topper in her head until it was as clear as a recent memory. *His tongue lolls to the left when he's out of breath. The pattern of dots on his chest looks like a constellation in the north sky. His breath smells like early morning dew.*

"Finally Topper's longing grew so great that he went to the gods and begged them for permission to slip between the cracks of time and walk in the world of mortals. The gods were reluctant at first, but the faithful yonstaff's longing was so great that eventually they agreed. They warned him, however, that he must keep his powers a secret, for the world was not yet ready for magic, and the consequences would be dire. Topper agreed. Within days he had found a place among the other dogs of the village, and days after that he had become Ruzen's favorite. The yonstaff could not speak—for his magic was so power-ful that even the slightest sound would release it—but it did not matter. The boy loved him, and this was all he needed."

Something was happening outside. Snarls, raised voices, a yelp of pain. The wind grew into a cyclone that tossed loose items around the room. Kara felt something made of glass strike her back and shatter. She ignored it and shut her eyes even tighter, driving the palms of her hands into her eyelids.

The story. Stay focused on the story.

"One day," Taff exclaimed, now shouting the words in order to be heard over the screaming wind, "Ruzen was climbing a tree, as he was wont to do, and at its highest point a branch broke and sent him falling through the air. Ignoring the gods' advice, Topper made a single sound and time stopped just before Ruzen hit the ground. The moment the yonstaff touched Ruzen, the boy could see how everything in the world had paused in its motions, and though he was astonished at this turn of events, he loved Topper more than ever for saving his life. For a time, everything went back to the way it was. These were the happiest days of Topper's life."

Kara felt a new presence enter the world.

It wasn't Topper yet—just a hazy jumble of thoughts

and ideas. She needed it to take a more concrete form before she could make it reality.

"Keep going, Taff!" Kara shouted.

"For a few years, Ruzen kept Topper's talent a secret," Taff said, talking faster. "However, as he grew older, his family's poverty began to seem like an unfair anchor keeping him from the good things in life. Ruzen wanted to know what it was like to go to bed with a full stomach, to wear silk clothes that hadn't been mended a dozen times. He saw in his pet's ability a way to make his mark on the world. And so Ruzen, using skills that he had learned but never grown to love, crafted a man and woman from patches of leather and placed them in the center of the village. When a crowd had gathered, he announced that his poor creations were embarrassed to be out in the open without any clothes on and needed their help. The crowd laughed, sensing some kind of jest, and Ruzen nodded toward Topper. The yonstaff knew it was a mistake, but his love for the boy clouded his judgment and he could not refuse. He made a sound. And while time was stopped, Ruzen went through the crowd and gathered various items—hats, gloves, boots, jewelry—and used these things to dress the leather man and woman. When time was set in motion again, it seemed to the audience that these items had flown to their new places in the blink of an eye. Their applause was ecstatic. They asked him to do the trick again. And again. Ruzen left a hat of his own near the feet of the leather man, and by the end of the day it was filled with coin."

Kara could hear voices on the stairwell and pounding on the attic door. *Focus. The story, the story, the story.* Topper was so close. She could hear him, a faint whisper in her mind different from any animal she had ever heard. Kara constructed a mind-bridge from memories of companionship—*Safi and Taff kicking their feet in the water, rolling dough with Aunt Abby*—but no matter how many memories she added, the bridge never seemed to be long enough to span between the shores of reality and her imagination.

Come into my world, Topper, Kara thought. *Let's be friends, you and I.*

Taff continued. Kara tried not to notice the fear in his voice as he competed with the pounding at the door.

"That night the boy, who was not really a boy any-more, slept with a full stomach, and in the morning he purchased three new sets of clothes. Topper hoped this would be the end of it. It wasn't. For the next year, Ruzen and the yonstaff traveled through the local villages, doing their show. Soon Ruzen's stomach hung over his belt and he had purchased so many sets of clothes that they needed a wagon just to cart them around. He shouted more. He laughed less. When Ruzen announced that they were going to the city where people had *real* coin, Topper knew it was a bad idea. He had noticed, in the past few villages, expressions of fear and revulsion mixed in with those of delight. Talk of Ruzen's 'trick' had spread, but there were those who wondered if it was a trick at all and not some kind of dark magic. The city would be dangerous and

Topper, thinking only of the boy's safety, tried to refuse. Ruzen locked him in a cage."

Kara rose into the air.

She opened her eyes. The attic floor was far below her. Wooden rafters pressed against her head. The twins stared up at her in triumph, flakes of snow melting in their hair. Other witches had positioned themselves around the room. A hollow-cheeked crone grasped Taff's face in two hands like an unloved aunt about to bestow a kiss. Grace lay on the floor, her eyes open but dazed. Blood ran freely from a gash in her head.

"We were so close to the end of the story," Taff said, his fists clenched in frustration. "So *close*."

The twins approached Kara in perfect unison, an open grimoire held between them. The remnants of the attic door crunched beneath their boots. They spoke in the guttural language that only they understood, and the words scratched at Kara's earlobes like a woolen hat.

"Put my sister down!" Taff screamed, struggling

against the old witch restraining him.

The twins smiled and flipped to the next page in the spellbook. They spit out a stream of strange words, never speaking in unison, braiding the spell together seamlessly. The roof bucked and rattled like the cage of a feral beast.

"What's happening?" Grace asked groggily as wooden shards and metal screws rained down around her. She turned toward the twins. *"What are you doing?"*

Kara felt the ceiling grow warm against her back and then vanish altogether as the top of the house shot high into the sky. Turning her head into the falling snow, she saw the roof hovering above her, flapping its bone-like rafters like a draconic marionette and peering down from a single, stalklike eye where its chimney used to stand. Despite her terror, Kara was awed by the grace of the newborn creature; it was as though the roof had been frozen in an inanimate form and was only now returning to its natural state. After trying to build a mind-bridge without success, Kara braced herself, certain that the roof-dragon was going to swoop down and attack her, but instead it flew just beyond the house and shattered into a gust of splinters.

The twins can't create true life, she thought. *Only destroy it.*

With her ascent unimpeded, Kara rose out of the house.

She heard Taff screaming her name, but soon this was lost to the swirling storm. Kara twisted and turned, but like an untethered balloon, she could do nothing to halt her ascension. The house grew smaller beneath her. In the dim lamplight far below she saw the twins clap their hands in unison.

She fell.

Kara's heart thundered in her chest as she plummeted through the sky. She kicked desperately, searching for a foothold that was nowhere to be found, and managed to twist her body around just in time to see the attic floor approach at sickening speed. Kara held her hands out in front of her . . . and jerked to a stop mere inches above the floor.

Gasping for breath, she turned her head to see the twins clapping their hands with glee and making short sputtering noises that sounded like giggles with all the joy clawed out.

"Stop it," Taff pleaded with them, tears in his eyes. "Let her go."

The twins raised their hands into the air.

Kara jerked upward, higher and faster than before. She used magic to call out to anything with wings, and droves of nearby birds flocked against the purple barrier enclosing the farmhouse, wanting to help but unable to reach her.

She fell. Rose again.

They're playing with me, Kara thought, trying to calm herself. *That's all. They won't really hurt me. They can't. Rygoth wants me alive.*

When she fell again, however—her nose almost grazing the wooden floor this time—Kara saw the twins exchange a tiny, rebellious nod that seemed to indicate the culmination of some prearranged plan: *Yes, we have our orders, but we can't allow this girl to live.*

It didn't matter that Rygoth wanted her alive. The twins, consumed by jealousy, were going to kill her anyway.

She rose slowly this time, as though the sisters wanted to draw this moment of triumph out as long as possible. Kara scanned the attic—searching for something, anything, that could help her—when she noticed a new arrival staring up at her: a medium-size dog with red fur and black dots. He had cogs instead of joints and was watching her with a look of pleasant expectation, as though she had a ball in her hand and was just waiting for the right moment to throw it. His tail, as it rocked back and forth in a steady rhythm, resembled the upside-down pendulum of a clock.

"Topper?" Kara asked.

The twins clapped their hands, and the magic holding Kara suspended in the air evaporated. She shot downward, faster this time, as though pulled by an invisible cord. The twins crossed their arms, confirming what she had already suspected: this time, they would not be halting her descent.

"*Topper!*" Kara screamed. "*Speak!*"

The yonstaff reared back on his haunches and opened his mouth wide, releasing a sound that was nothing like a bark at all but rather like a giant bell tolling a forgotten hour.

The world stopped.

FOUR

During the weeks that they had spent crafting Topper's story, Kara and Taff had engaged in many debates about what might happen if time actually stopped. Taff, who believed that magic had its limitations, thought that nature would go about her business as usual: the wind would blow, snow would continue to fall. Only people, and perhaps animals, would stand as still as statues. Kara, on the other hand, believed that everything would freeze in place like a painting, with only those who had cast the spell retaining their ability to move.

They were both wrong.

Looking around the attic from where she hovered several yards in the air, Kara saw that the current moment was not completely frozen but caught in a kind of net that permitted the slightest of movements but no escape. A fly dangled in midair, but its wings kept twitching. A snowflake vibrated like a recently struck tuning fork. Taff's body was frozen, but the lips of his wide-open mouth trembled in a silent scream. The air itself thrummed with sounds looped over and over again, becoming indistinguishable from one another as they merged into a high, insect-like drone.

Panting gently, Topper watched Kara with his head canted to one side. His pendulum tail, perhaps a register of time's movement, had stopped ticking back and forth.

"Good boy," Kara said.

Topper's chest puffed up with pride. Kara heard a whisper in her mind, as though the yonstaff were trying to communicate with her, but she couldn't make out the words. The mind-bridge had been strong enough to bring Topper into the world, but there was, in this way, an unspannable distance between them.

"Now how do I get out of here?" she mumbled to herself.

Kara kicked her feet and swung her arms, trying to swim through the air, but although she was able to turn her body all the way around, she could not get any closer to the ground.

Topper watched her struggle, a look of amusement on his canine face.

Thinking that this invisible tether might break if enough force were applied, Kara grabbed onto a column that had once supported the attic roof, drew herself close—and then pushed away with all her strength. She spun through the air and jerked to a sudden stop like a dog at the end of its leash. After repeating this a few more times, Kara found that she was able to travel a farther distance, as though the magic holding her in place was beginning to fray. Finally, on her sixth attempt, something snapped and Kara crashed to the wooden floor with a bone-rattling thud.

She rolled over on her back, cradling her left elbow, and found herself staring straight into Topper's muddy eyes.

"Hello," Kara said.

The yonstaff watched her, eager to see what the amusing human would do next.

Taff, she thought.

He had been frozen in the midst of a long stride, having managed, just before time stopped, to finally escape the old crone holding him in her grasp. His captor was reaching out for him, deep scratches and several bite marks lining her veined arms.

"Taff," Kara said, shaking him by the shoulders. "Wake up!"

But Taff's expression remained frozen in the same unsettling midscream—until Topper licked his hand.

Instantly, his eyes opened and he tumbled to the floor.

"Ow," he said, sitting up quickly and rubbing the back of his head. "What the *heck*?"

"The spell worked!" she exclaimed. "We *froze time*!"

She pointed at Topper to prove her point.

Taff's mouth fell open. "Is this . . . ?"

Kara nodded. "Topper, Taff. Taff, Topper."

Taff burst into a radiant smile and threw his arms around the yonstaff. "You saved my life!" he exclaimed.

Kara saw the pendulum tail tremble, as though Topper was struggling against some implacable force to wag it. *The tail can't move again until time does.* This had not been part of the story they created, but as Kara had learned when she conjured the Jabenhook, small details often changed during the magical transition from imagination to reality.

Taff rose to his feet, taking in his surroundings.

"This is *amazing*!" he exclaimed. Given his enthusiastic gesticulations, Kara suspected that Taff might have shouted the words, but his voice was strangely muffled in this suspended world, as though he were speaking through a closed door. "I mean, you've done some pretty incredible things before, but you actually *stopped time!*" He stood eye to eye with one of the twins, her face hardened into a permanent scowl. "Do you think she can see me?" he asked.

"I doubt it."

Taff stuck out his tongue anyway.

"Don't play with the frozen people," Kara said. "And it wasn't just me who did this. We created the spell together."

"I guess." Taff shrugged. "But it would have just been a story without your magic. I didn't really do anything at all."

It wasn't the first time that Taff had put himself down like this. Despite her brother's invaluable help, he never felt like he did enough.

I'll talk to him about it later, she thought. *Who knows how long this spell is going to last.* When Kara built a mind-bridge it was usually a permanent fixture that she could return to time and time again, but the one linking Topper and herself felt as insubstantial as a half-remembered dream. At any moment it might dissipate altogether, allowing time to continue its forward march.

"Let's go," Kara said, spinning around and nearly colliding with an auburn-haired witch whose nose twitched slightly, as though she had been frozen just before a sneeze. Kara stepped around her and navigated past the other figures spaced throughout the attic floor. Topper padded softly behind her. "Hopefully we can get past the barrier," she said, thinking out loud. "And we have to wake up Darno and Shadowdancer. And retrieve our supplies, too. We won't get far without—"

"Kara? Aren't you forgetting something?"

Taff stood over Grace. Her eyes were closed. It was the first time that Kara had ever seen her look truly at peace.

"We can't just leave her here," Taff said. "They'll kill her as soon as time starts again."

"What happens to Grace is not our problem."

"But it kind of is," said Taff. "Listen, no one hates Grace more than me——"

Kara stared at him with arms akimbo: *Really?*

"Okay, *almost* no one. But she really has helped us! She restored Father, just like she said she would, and if Grace hadn't warned us that the twins were coming you never would have had enough time to cast the spell."

"So . . . what then?" Kara asked. "We just bring her with us? You don't honestly think we can trust her, do you?"

Taff shook his head.

"We bring her somewhere safe," he said. "And then we part ways."

Kara exhaled through her teeth. If she left Grace here, it would be the same as murdering her outright. On the other hand, traveling with Grace, even temporarily, created a whole new set of unnecessary risks.

It's never easy, is it? she thought.

"Besides," Taff continued, "you heard what she said. She doesn't even use magic anymore. How dangerous can she be?"

After Kara was done laughing at *that* one, she called Topper over and held Grace's cold hand to his mouth. He licked her palm. Grace jerked suddenly awake as though woken from a nightmare.

Her first response was to wipe her hand on her shirt.

"Eww," she said, pushing Topper away. "Where did this ugly dog come from?" Then she noticed the change in their surroundings and her blue eyes widened with wonder. She turned to Kara, her mouth agape. "*You* did this?"

Kara shrugged. "Mostly it was Topper."

"Right," Grace said, giving the yonstaff a wry look. "Topper. How long will time stay frozen like this?"

"I don't know."

"Then let's make use of it while we can."

Reaching down, she removed a dagger from a sheath inside her boot and approached the nearest twin.

"What are you doing?" Kara asked.

"What needs to be done," Grace said, raising the dagger into the air.

Kara grabbed her wrist.

"You can't kill them," Kara said.

"Why not?"

"They're defenseless."

"Which is, literally, the best time to kill them. Haven't you learned *anything*? They'll keep coming for you if you don't stop them now. This makes sense and you know it."

"No killing," Kara said.

"Do you think these witches would show us any mercy if the situations were reversed?"

"Of course not. But that's what makes us different. So you have to ask yourself, Grace—what kind of witch are you? Are you more like them—or me?"

Grace turned from Kara to the twins, from the twins

to Kara. She sighed despondently.

"Are those really the only two choices?" she asked.

"You helped us," Taff said. "You wouldn't have done that unless there was good in you. Somewhere deep." He considered his own words. "Really, really, really deep."

With a groan of exasperation, Grace slid the dagger into her sheath.

"Being good isn't very practical, is it?" she asked.

They found Darno just outside the farmhouse. His jaws were locked in a fearsome snarl as he faced down a trio of witches. From the fingertip of the center witch sparked a bolt of black lightening frozen in midair. Topper awoke the wolf, and Darno—thinking he was still in the midst of battle—snapped fiercely at the unsuspecting yonstaff before Kara calmed him.

"It's okay," she said, holding his head in place so she could look directly into his eyes. "I've got you. You're safe."

A patch of blood matted his fur. After checking for a wound, Kara was relieved to see that the blood wasn't his own, though a scorch mark had burned through to the skin of his left flank. The hook-shaped stinger at the end of his scorpion tail was still wet from recent use.

Kara saw several witches lying motionless in the snow. When time was restored, Kara had the feeling that they would still be motionless.

"Thank you for protecting me," Kara said.

Darno stared at her strangely as he licked a minor wound on his paw.

Why thank you? Wind blows. Sun rises. Thank them too?

"It's different," Kara said. "You could have run, but you risked your life for me."

Not different. Sun gives light and heat. I protect Witch Girl. All we are.

Ignoring Grace's snide comment to Taff—"Does she always talk to herself like that?"—Kara crossed the front yard. Snowflakes slid off her body and then returned to their original position after she passed, like a curtained doorway. Kara paused before the barrier surrounding the farmhouse, which was even more imposing up close: a purple, semitranslucent wall that seemed to touch the stars. It provided surprisingly little hindrance, however, stretching like taffy as they passed through it and then snapping back into place. They gathered Shadowdancer from the stable and set off down the main road, Kara and Grace on the mare, Taff riding Darno's back.

"What happened to your hair?" Taff asked Grace.

"Lice," she said, running a hand over the stubble. "Had to shear it off. What happened to your nose?"

Taff, with a suddenly self-conscious expression, felt his face.

"Nothing!"

"My mistake," said Grace. "So what's the plan here? Keep walking until we collapse of exhaustion?"

Taff beamed, eager to share: "There's a man who's frozen in time and we're going to ask him about——"

"You don't need to know our plan," Kara interjected,

placing a hand on her brother's back. "Once time starts again we'll go our separate ways."

"We could do that," Grace said. "The Clen knows I've little desire to remain in your company. But I'm not convinced that's the wisest decision."

"And why's that?" Kara asked.

"Because we could help each other," Grace said.

"We don't need your help."

"And yet you've already taken it. Twice. I reversed the curse on your father, just like I promised I would. And then there's tonight."

"That hardly balances the scales between us, Grace."

"I know that, Kara. I can't undo the things I've done. It's just"—and here her voice softened to an uncertain whisper—"the World is a strange and unsettling place. There are so many things here that I don't understand. And it's so *huge*. It feels as though I could walk forever and never reach its end."

Kara felt an unwelcome sense of empathy for the frail-looking girl before her. Despite their differences, the two were tied together by a common birthplace, which meant that Kara understood Grace's feelings perfectly.

"People here don't call it the World," Kara mumbled softly. "They call it Sentium."

"Sentium?" Grace asked.

"It was strange to us at first too," Taff added. "You get used to it."

"I miss De'Noran," Grace said. "Things were simpler there."

"Because you were Fen'de Stone's daughter and could do whatever you pleased," muttered Kara.

"Well, yes," said Grace, as though this were obvious. "But it's more than that. De'Noran is my home." She crossed her arms and raised her chin, looking for just a moment like her old self. "I will return there one day. Now that Timoth Clen has left, the people of De'Noran will be ecstatic to see their rightful leader return."

Kara shook her head in disbelief. *Doesn't Grace remember how she terrorized the entire village? They'll never forgive her!* But, of course, Grace would never think about things from that perspective. She was incapable of considering anyone else's feelings but her own.

"I have bad news for you," Kara snapped. "Timoth Clen destroyed your precious village before he left the island. There *isn't* any more De'Noran to go back to."

Grace didn't say anything. When Kara glanced back over her shoulder, the girl's eyes were shiny with tears.

"I guess you two are all I have left then," she said with a sad smile. "Isn't life strange?"

Taff's face softened and he started to stay something comforting, but Kara glared at him and shook her head: *Don't you dare!* Back on De'Noran, Grace had consistently invoked the villagers' compassion through downtrodden expressions and pitiable sighs. It was how she had hidden her true nature, and Kara was not about to fall for those old tricks.

She's up to something, Kara thought. *The quicker we get rid of her the better.*

And yet she couldn't help but notice how small and broken the girl looked.

What if she really is trying to change? What kind of person would I be if I just abandoned her?

Don't be a fool! The minute you trust her is the minute she betrays you.

"What's that?" Taff asked.

Kara squinted her eyes, trying to make out the shape in the darkness, but all she could see was a dark blur. Whatever it was, it looked tall.

"I think it's a tower," said Grace. "Strange-looking, too. Like an hourglass."

Kara and Taff exchanged a knowing glance.

"We traveled along this road when we came to the farmhouse," Kara said. "I don't recall passing any tower, strange-looking or otherwise."

"Because it only appears when time stops," Taff said, beaming. "'A heathen frozen in time.' It has to be him!"

"Him *who*?" asked Grace.

Ignoring her question, Kara spurred Shadowdancer onward.

FIVE

The lonely road provided minimal evidence that time no longer ticked in its normal fashion: a tree limb caught in midfall, birds that hung from the sky like taxidermy models, a solitary traveler entombed inside a black coach. Were it not for the presence of the Hourglass Tower, now clearly visible on the horizon, it might have seemed like nothing more than a particularly peaceful night.

"Maybe we should take a break," Taff suggested, yawning his hands into the air. "This Querin guy could be good. But he might be the other thing, too."

"I could do with a little rest," Kara admitted.

In truth, she was exhausted. Maintaining her hold on Topper had been far more draining than expected, the mind-bridge between them constantly on the verge of collapsing. Kara had needed to sacrifice four additional memories just to stabilize the connection—something she had never had to do before.

The rules are different when you create an animal from nothing, she thought. *Topper doesn't belong in the real world—that's why it's so difficult to keep him here.*

The fact that Rygoth could control Niersook with seemingly no effort at all made the thought of battling her more disheartening than ever.

It's to be expected, thought Kara. *Rygoth is a two-thousand-year-old* wexari *who studied magic at Sablethorn. I'm a thirteen-year-old girl who has no idea what she's doing.*

They built a fire by the side of the road, and though the time-frozen flames did not snap and crackle like a regular campfire, the warmth they provided was comforting enough. Taff cradled his head against Topper's flank and soon both boy and yonstaff were snoring pleasantly. Kara, however, remained awake. She was pretty sure that Topper's spell would continue functioning while she was asleep, but she wasn't positive, and it made her too nervous to sleep.

Her other concern was Grace.

What is she up to?

As though hearing Kara's thoughts, Grace looked in her direction. Her blue eyes shone like otherworldly crystals.

"Is the whelp going to snore all night?" she asked.

"I'm surprised he fell asleep at all," Kara said. "He still has nightmares about you."

"That's sweet."

"It wasn't a compliment."

"I realize that. But still—it's nice to be remembered."

Kara couldn't tell if she was kidding or not. Grace enunciated every word carefully, as though speaking to an unseen audience—and yet Kara seldom knew what she *meant*.

"Are you going to tell me why we're going to this Hourglass Tower?" Grace asked.

"No."

"How about this Querin person you and Taff keep talking about? Can you at least tell me—"

"No."

Kara had accepted her responsibility to get Grace to safety, but she still didn't trust her. Their plans needed to remain a secret.

"Why did you get rid of your grimoire?" Kara asked.

"So you don't have to answer my questions," Grace said, "but I have to answer yours. Is that how this works?"

"Yes," replied Kara. "Why did you get rid of it?"

"I told you. It's evil."

"That never stopped you before."

"Things are different now. I know what it's like in the Well of Witches. I know what will happen to me if I go back."

"The Faceless?" Kara asked, remembering the guardians of the Well, their paper bodies and hideous masks.

"They'll be waiting," Grace said, her blue eyes popping with fear. "And this time, you won't be there to help me escape. They'll make me one of them." She touched her face as though to make sure it was still her own. "A monster."

Kara had witnessed Grace's terror of the Faceless firsthand, and she had to admit that there was a certain logic to her story. Grace would do anything to avoid being changed into one of them.

Anything? Even give up magic?

"You're afraid," Kara said. "That's why you got rid of your grimoire. You know that once you start casting spells you won't be able to stop, and it's only a matter of time before you end up as one of the Faceless."

"Well done, Kara," Grace sneered, clapping her fingertips together. "If Master Blackwood were here, I'm sure he'd let you wear the gold star. Yes, I'm too frightened to use magic anymore. Does that please you?"

"Nothing about you pleases me."

Grace shifted in her blankets until she was facing Kara. Without her hair she looked like a completely different person, yet the dismissive crook of her smile had not changed at all.

"Has it ever occurred to you that it was the grimoire that made me do the things I did?" she asked.

"I knew you before you became a witch, Grace. You were always bad."

"Why? Because I *picked* on you?"

"It was more than—"

"I wasn't the nicest girl in De'Noran. I'll grant you that. But if it wasn't for the grimoire I never would have *hurt* anyone. It's not my fault magic is evil."

"Magic isn't evil," Kara said. "It's sick."

"What do you mean by that?"

Kara wasn't sure herself. It was Minoth Dravania, the headmaster of Sablethorn, who had told her that something was wrong with magic. Since then she had often lain awake at night, pondering his final words to her before she entered the *queth'nondra.*

Magic is sick. And I suspect you're the one meant to heal it.

"I've met people who struggled against the grimoire's influence," Kara said, ignoring Grace's question. "They tried to stay good. But not you. You *embraced* it."

"What exactly do you want me to say?" Grace asked. She clasped her hands together in a mocking benediction. "I'm sorry I killed people. I still see their faces when I go to sleep at night, and I feel so gosh darn awful? What would that accomplish?"

"It would show that you're human."

"I don't have anything to prove! Especially to you!"

Grace turned away and faced the flickerless flames. Kara rubbed her temples, her thoughts as scattered as the cinders suspended in the air. She didn't trust her old enemy, that was for certain, and were it not for Darno's protective presence Kara would not have been able to sleep; Grace might be unwilling to cast spells, but there was always the dagger in her boot. On the other hand, Grace had now helped them on two occasions, and a nagging part of Kara's mind wondered if she was being unfair by not giving her a second chance. *After all, Mary Kettle and Sordyr had done terrible things but redeemed themselves.* And who was Kara to judge another's actions while under the influence of the grimoire? She herself had killed a boy named Simon Loder. . . .

Her eyes were drifting shut when Grace spoke again.

"How did the story end?" she asked.

"What?"

"With Topper and Ruzen. The twins interrupted you before you could finish the story, remember? Topper refused to go to the city with Ruzen, because he was afraid the boy would come to harm, so Ruzen locked him in a cage. What happened next?"

Kara had no idea why Grace was asking about this, but she decided that it would be faster to just answer the question than argue about it.

"We couldn't decide. Taff wanted Ruzen to learn the error of his ways and apologize to Topper. He wasn't sure how that would happen, but he had a last line: 'From that day on, Ruzen treasured the yonstaff's friendship and never asked him to use his powers again.'"

"And you?"

"I didn't think that was realistic. Ruzen is selfish and greedy. There's no changing some people."

"He grew up poor. It makes sense that he wanted money."

"It makes sense, sure—but there comes a point where you have to forge your own path." Kara closed her eyes, sleep almost taking her now. "How about you?" she mumbled groggily. "Which ending do you prefer?"

"I'm not sure," Grace said. "I haven't decided yet."

As soon as Kara opened her eyes she knew something was wrong. Her mind felt raw and exposed, as though someone had been tunneling through her brain. She reached out to Topper to check the connection between them and gasped in surprise.

The mind-bridge was cracked in nearly a dozen places. It should have crumbled apart by now, but black, leech-like creatures had inserted themselves between the gaps to hold the bridge together. Kara supposed she should have been grateful—after all, if the spell had failed and time started again while she slept, perhaps the twins might have found them—but all she could think about was the word *infection*.

What are you? Kara thought.

One of the leeches opened its mouth—like the tiny, sucking aperture of a snail—and Kara jerked in pain as moments and images were involuntarily pried from her memory and swallowed whole.

Father holds my tiny hands on the saw's handle and together we cut the wood for the birdhouse. Lucas looks over at me while plucking a pear from a branch and I forget what I am going to say next. Mother—

Gone, gone, gone.

Kara clamped her temples between her hands. It felt like someone was scraping the inside of her mind with a serrated spoon, bringing to mind an afternoon of carving jack-o'-lanterns with her mother.

As soon as the memory rose to the forefront of her mind it was stolen.

The leech's mouth closed, its appetite sated. For now.

"Kara?" Taff asked, his voice trembling with concern. "Are you okay? What happened?"

Kara realized that her head was cradled in his lap. She had no idea when that had happened.

"I'm all right now," Kara said. "I just need to rest for a minute."

"Too much magic, just like I thought," said Grace. "I *knew* you weren't powerful enough to cast a spell like that."

Grace beamed proudly, like a student who gives a correct answer to a particularly difficult question. She scanned the campsite, perhaps for someone to appreciate this imagined victory.

"Is she right?" Taff asked. "Did you use too much magic?"

Kara nodded. "More or less. The mind-bridge with Topper is different than the regular kind. It's . . . *hungrier.* And it takes memories whether I want it to or not."

Taff gasped audibly.

"That sounds dangerous."

"*Really* dangerous," Grace added, with more curiosity than concern.

"You should stop the spell now," Taff said. "We'll figure out another way to—"

"I'll be fine," Kara said.

"You can't do everything by yourself!"

"I don't have to," Kara said, reaching up to touch his cheek. "I have you."

"Oh yes," Grace said. "The whelp was *so* useful just now. I mean, without him—"

Even in her weakened state, Kara's glare was enough to stop Grace from continuing.

"She's right," Taff said, eyes downcast. "What can I really do?"

"You're the smartest boy in the world," Kara said. "And without you, we never would have gotten this far. Now help me up, little man. We have to get to that tower. Fast."

The mare and the girl had been through a lot together, and Shadowdancer sensed Kara's urgency without the need for magic. As soon as the two girls had mounted her back, the horse shot off through the silence of the evernight, galloping past ramrod-still nut sedge and rivers frozen without ice, her hooves pounding clods of dust into the air. The two other animals struggled to keep pace. Darno, his scorpion tail just long enough to curl around Taff like a belt, wore his usual determined expression, but the smile had vanished from Topper's face. He lagged behind the others, his tongue lolling from side to side. Kara was trying to figure out if the mind-bridge was somehow affecting him as well when she was struck by a spate of dizziness and almost fell off Shadowdancer's back.

"Thanks," she said, feeling Grace's hands around her waist, propping her up.

"If something happens to you," Grace said, "I think there's at least the possibility that I'll be stuck in this moment forever. So if you're going to die, do it later."

"Your concern is touching."

During the journey she lost several more memories, mostly of her first friend, a girl who had refused to play with Kara anymore after Mother's execution. *Good riddance*, she thought, trying to remember what the girl had looked like, or what games they had played together, or even her name. She knew the memory was there, but she didn't know where to find it. It was like searching for a chip of obsidian in a pitch-black room.

By the time they reached the Hourglass Tower, Kara no longer remembered that her friend had ever existed at all.

"Big place," Taff said, dismounting Darno and stretching his legs. "What do you think's inside?"

Kara checked to make sure that Grace wasn't listening.

"Answers about the *Vulkera*," she whispered.

"Got it," Taff whispered back. He paused. "What's the *Vulkera*?"

"Sorry—I forgot to tell you. Bethany said that's what the princess's grimoire is called."

"Swell," Taff said, considering this. "It gets its own special name. Like it's not scary enough already."

The tower was neck-crackingly tall. Stairs wound from the ground to a center point between the upper and lower halves, where a wooden door had been set into the stone. The tower was crumbling in several areas, and thousands of gouges marred the surface, as though some beast had tried to scratch its way inside.

"Stay here, girl," Kara told Shadowdancer, patting her flank. "You too," she said to Darno.

The wolf ignored Kara completely and started up the stairs. His job was to protect her, whether she liked it or not.

"Look at Topper!" Taff exclaimed.

The yonstaff was leaping from side to side with renewed energy. That wasn't the thing that caught Kara's attention, however.

Topper's pendulum tail was ticking back and forth.

"I don't get it," Taff said. "I thought his tail only moved when time did."

The air around the tower was still static, their voices still oddly muffled. But back along the road, time's resurrection was revealed in rustling leaves and quaking branches. An owl swooped down from the treetops to snatch an unsuspecting rodent.

"Time is already frozen inside the Hourglass Tower," Kara said, "and we're probably standing close enough to fall under that spell. Topper doesn't need to use his powers here."

The mind-bridge between them still remained, however, and while Kara had grown fond of the friendly creature, she knew it was dangerous to keep him any longer than necessary.

"Hey there," Kara said. "Time to say good-bye."

She bent down so Topper could lick her face. His breath smelled of morning dew, exactly how she imagined it. While Taff stroked behind Topper's ears, Kara shook the mind-bridge until the leeches fell away and the entire thing crumbled into dust.

Topper vanished.

"I wish we could have kept that little guy," Taff said. "I really liked him."

"Me too," Kara said.

They had barely started up the stairs when there was a loud rattle, like someone shaking the bars of a massive gate, and trees, field, and sky were replaced with a starless night in all directions.

"Where are we?" Grace asked.

"Not where," Taff said. "When."

"Fine. *When* are we?"

"No idea."

Despite the darkness the steps were easy enough to see, as though the tower itself provided some sort of interior light. A patch of ground still remained at its foundation, allowing a very nervous-looking Shadowdancer room to prance back and forth.

Be brave, Kara told the mare. *I'll be back soon.*

She hoped that was the truth.

SIX

The stairs winding around the tower had seen better days, and on several occasions the children had to leap across a span of crumbling steps or creep along a ledge. By the time they finally reached the entrance they were all exhausted. Kara's legs felt weak and wobbly, but she knew that her discomfort must pale in comparison to Grace's, whose cane had tapped each and every step.

The tower door was open.

Inside, the air was cool and humid, like a cave. Torches lit the circular room, their unflickering flames providing just enough light to illuminate the clocks packing the shelves. There were hundreds of them—maybe thousands—in every size and shape imaginable. Most featured an hour and minute hand along with the standard face, though some clocks—especially those along the top shelves—barely resembled traditional timepieces at all: a golden ring spinning upon the second of five wooden spindles; a tri-chambered hourglass partially filled with brackish liquid; a pair of ochre boxes labeled *TIME WASTED* and *TIME SAVED*.

"This place is amazing!" Taff exclaimed. He skipped from wonder to wonder—running his fingers along a shimmering pendulum, plunging his hand wrist-deep into a chest overflowing with silver cogs. It was too much to take in all at once.

Grace looked far less impressed.

"Well," she said, a sardonic tilt to her lips. "I guess whoever lives here always knows what time it is."

A door squeaked opened and a small figure entered the chamber.

He was no taller than Taff but had the broad shoulders

and weathered face of an adult. Beneath a checkered vest he wore a crisp white shirt, and his neat beard was freshly oiled and redolent of ginger. A long nose hooked downward beneath eyes as dark as charred wood.

"We're sorry for the intrusion," Kara said. "But the door was open and we thought it would be all right if—"

Holding up a finger, the man withdrew a watch resting in the outside pocket of his vest. It looked old but very well maintained, and was attached to a lower button of his vest by an expensive gold chain. He flicked its lid open with a practiced movement and nodded with approval, as though Kara had arrived on time for a previously scheduled appointment.

"No need to apologize," the man said, his voice as smooth as warm honey. "I'm glad you're here. It's a large tower for a small man, and occasionally I like to hear a voice that's not my own."

"Are you Querin Fyndrake?" Kara asked.

The man bowed with an elaborate flourish.

"At your service, my lady," he said.

Querin kissed the back of her hand, one arm folded carefully behind his back. He started to reach out for Grace's hand as well but reconsidered upon seeing her disgusted expression.

"It must have taken some crafty magic to get here," Querin said. He made no eye contact when he talked; instead, his eyes flicked from side to side, as though watching the progress of some unseen pendulum. "I'm impressed. Still, stopping the flow of time is not something you want to mess around with at your age, even a *wexari* as powerful as you, Kara."

"How do you know my name?"

"I'm in the business of knowing things." He pointed to each of them in turn. "Your brother, Taff, and your . . . traveling companion, Grace Stone." His eyes fell on Darno with just a hint of apprehension. "I'm not sure . . . what . . . exactly . . ."

"His name's Darno," Kara said. "Don't worry. He won't hurt you."

Unless you want me to, Darno told her.

Be nice.

"Are you a wizard?" Taff asked.

Querin smiled, revealing gold incisors along his lower row of teeth.

"Depends on your definition," he said. "As you must know—because you found me—I've been alive a good deal longer than your average man. So yes, I do have some knowledge of magic—but mostly I think of myself as an honest craftsman."

Kara nodded politely, though she couldn't help thinking of one of Mother's favorite sayings: *A man who claims to be honest is usually anything but.*

"Enough about me," Querin said, waving them along. "You look famished. Join me in the Slanting Hall. Let's continue this discussion over dinner."

"Yes!" exclaimed Taff, who had been complaining of an empty stomach their entire climb up the tower.

"I appreciate the offer," Kara said, "but time is of the essence, and I think you might be able to help us. My father said—"

"Hush, child, hush," Querin said. "Time does not pass inside the Hourglass Tower. There is no hurry at all. You will return to the real world at the exact moment you left it."

Kara looked at Taff, who made a begging motion with his hands, and Grace, who shrugged indifferently.

"In that case, dinner sounds lovely," Kara said. "Thank you for your hospitality."

"It is my pleasure," Querin said, guiding her deeper into the tower. "I have visitors so infrequently. I do like to make the most of them."

The Slanting Hall lived up to its name. Walking from one end to the other was like navigating a particularly steep hill. At either end loomed tall wooden doors. Upon first glance Kara thought that they were just heavily scratched, but while Querin prepared their meal she examined the lower door and saw that it was not scratches that marred its surface after all.

It was names.

The letters varied in size and shape, from careful etchings (*ALEXANDRA, JULIAN*) to less-practiced work (*TULA* in block letters, *JAMES* with the *s* reversed). In most cases only the first name had been carved into the wood, but occasionally a surname made an appearance as well. Some were written in alphabets that Kara did not recognize.

"I don't like the look of this," Grace said.

Kara nodded. "For once I agree with you."

"People carve their names in trees for fun," Taff said. "Could it be like that?"

"I doubt it's that simple," Kara said.

"Why not?"

"Because it never is."

Kara pressed all her weight against the door. It didn't budge. There was no knocker, no handle. She felt something when she touched its surface, however, a thrumming that passed through her skin and rattled her bones. Grace, her palm pressed against the wood, met Kara's eyes, and unspoken words passed between them: *There's powerful magic behind this door.*

By the time Querin had returned, carrying a tray piled high with food, the trio had retreated to the center table. Its legs had been cut shorter on one end in order to compensate for the tilted floor.

"What's with all the names on those doors?" Grace asked before Querin had even placed the tray on the table. "Even for a man who lives alone in a tower—that's pretty strange."

"Grace," Kara said pointedly. "Let's not offend our host."

"I'm just asking a question. It's not my fault if he gets offended. Besides, if they're the names of his victims or something, the sooner we know the—"

"Grace!"

She crossed her arms in a huff. "Like you weren't thinking it."

"The doors lead to the upper and lower portions of the tower," Querin said, ladling out stew with thick crusts of bread.

"And the names?" Kara asked.

"Eat first," Querin said, offering Kara a steaming bowl. "You must be famished."

Kara didn't like the way Querin avoided the question, but she took the stew anyway.

"Thank you," she said. "I know this is strange manners, but could I give a bowl to my wolf as well?"

Querin held his palms up and smiled.

"The last thing I want under my roof is a hungry wolf."

Kara placed the bowl of stew at Darno's feet. The scorpion-wolf sniffed it carefully and then began to lap it up. If it were poisoned or magically altered, Darno would have sensed it and warned her.

"Cautious one, aren't you?" Querin asked, smiling at Kara appraisingly. He shoved a heaping spoonful of stew into his mouth. "See. Perfectly safe."

"I'm sorry," Kara said, embarrassed that Querin knew the real reason she had fed Darno first. "We tend to find ourselves among people who mean us harm."

"I understand your caution," Querin said. "But you can relax. You're safe here. I only want to help you."

Kara started on her stew, which was oddly sweet but otherwise flavorful enough. She worked around the chunks of meat, having lost her appetite for dead animal about the time she came into her powers.

Querin put his spoon down and rested his chin on his folded hands.

"You see this magnificent tower, tucked away in time, and I'm sure you're dying of curiosity about the man who could make such wonders possible," he said. "Would you like the short or the long version?"

"I'm partial to the truth," Kara said.

"The short version, then," replied Querin. "Less embellishment. Do you know the story of how the four regions of Sentium were formed?"

Kara remembered what Lucas's grandfather had taught them during their journey from Nye's Landing to the Swoop station, and responded:

"King Penta, after defeating the witches two thousand years ago, wanted the world to start all over again. He destroyed any mention of magic from the history books and buried Sablethorn, a school for *wexari*. Then he broke the kingdom into four regions, each specializing in a different field of study: Ilma, Kutt, Lux, and Auren."

Grace looked completely lost, and Kara couldn't help feeling a tiny thrill of satisfaction. Back in De'Noran, the fen'de's daughter had always been quick to impress Master Blackwood with the correct answer, whereas Kara had been afraid to even raise her hand.

"You know your history," acknowledged Querin. "Or, at least, the history that the people of Sentium have chosen to remember. But there was almost a fifth region. Kronia. My people. We had been studying the mysteries of time for centuries, and we offered the king a golden opportunity: turn back the clock, undo the damage the witches had done." Querin's thick eyebrows sloped downward in anger. "The fool spurned us. He claimed that what we were doing was too dangerous, too much like magic for his liking."

"That was thousands of years ago," Grace said, "but you talk about it like you were there."

"I was," Querin said in surprise, as though this were obvious. "Time no longer moves forward for me. Actually, that's not exactly true. When I leave the Hourglass Tower, as I do when need warrants, the minutes of my life tick along as always. But as long as I remain within these hallowed walls, I am essentially immortal."

Since following a one-eyed bird into the Thickety, Kara had learned many things about magic, but the single overriding principal was that the more powerful the spell, the higher the cost. A feat as mighty as everlasting life would require a fearsome price.

The names on the doors. What do they mean?

She looked at Querin and for a moment glimpsed the sly, calculating stare of a cold-blooded reptile. The look was gone as quickly as it came, however, and Querin smiled broadly.

"As the king's head scientist," he continued, "I knew it was crucial to prove to King Penta that he was wrong, that Kronia needed to be at the forefront of this new world he was shaping. I pushed my experiments to the extreme in order to bend time to my will. I did things that not even Minoth Dravania and his precious *wexari* had ever dreamed possible!"

"What went wrong?" Grace asked, her eyes blazing with interest.

"How do you know anything—"

Grace held out a hand, stopping him.

"You live in a tower. Hidden in time. Alone."

She leaned back in her chair, awaiting his response.

"There were consequences," Querin finally replied, studying his stew. "My forays into time attracted the attention of a type of . . . entity, I guess you'd call it, though some might go as far as to call them gods. In any case, they did not take kindly to my experiments. These Khr'nouls—their name in the old tongue of my people— have rigid beliefs about time and its boundaries and see it as their duty to maintain some sort of order. One of them escaped through a tear I had made. There were some . . . casualties."

Except Kara could see by the haunted look in Querin's eyes that it had not been *some* at all. It had been more like *many*, or even *all*.

That's the real reason why no one speaks of Kronia anymore. It no longer exists.

"By the time the other regions sent their armies I had been painted as this insane zealot, too dangerous to live. But I'm a survivor. I was not about to let them execute me for one little mistake. So I found a nice little patch of time to hide in and continue my experiments." He spread his short arms wide. "And here we are."

Kara glanced across the table at her companions, hoping to gauge their reaction to Querin's tale. Taff shook his head slightly—*I don't trust him*—while Grace stubbornly regarded Kara with a mystifying half smile that could have meant anything. For her part, Kara was fairly certain that some of Querin's story had been truthful, but not all of it. He reminded her of the men her father used to barter with when they went to market, stretching the truth thin as taffy if it helped them make a sale.

"So," Querin said, "you now have me at an advantage. You know my story, but I don't know yours. What brings you to the Hourglass Tower?"

"Yes," Grace chimed in, crossing her arms and beaming at Kara. "What brings us to the Hourglass Tower?"

Kara paused, wondering if she should send Grace out of the room for this part, and then decided that it didn't really matter. *She's bound to learn the truth of why we're here sooner or later.*

"I'm looking for a special spellbook," Kara said. "It's

been split into four sections, and—"

"Ahh," Querin said, shifting forward in his seat. "The First Grimoire. The *Vulkera*."

From the corner of her eye she saw Grace sit straighter, listening closely.

"So you've heard of it?" Kara asked.

"Of course. Its power is legendary. You hope to wield it, *wexari*?"

"No," Kara said. The thought of ever using a grimoire again, especially one with such a history of evil, made her ill. "I want to keep it out of the hands of a very bad witch. She already has one grim. I need to find where the last three are located so I can get to them first."

Querin pulled at the end of his beard. His fingers glistened with oil.

"Such a thing is possible here," he said. "I must ask, though. Would it not be better to just leave them be? The pieces of the *Vulkera* have been hidden for millennia. Surely they are safe from this 'bad witch' you speak of."

"She's already found the first grim," Kara said. "There's no reason to think she won't find the others."

"I see your point. Very well. Count on my full support in your noble quest. The knowledge you seek can be found within the tower."

"You'll help us?" Taff asked. "Just like that?"

"Why wouldn't I?"

An uncomfortable silence settled over the group. Kara remembered her father's description of Querin as a dangerous man. She knew very little about him, but she could tell that he wasn't the type to give something for nothing.

"What do you want in return?" she asked.

Querin pulled out his watch. Checked the time. Slipped it back inside his pocket.

"Now that you mention it, there is *one* thing," he said. "A technicality, if you will. To enter the bowels of the tower, you must carve your name into the door—the Lower Door, since your question is about the past. That's the only way it will open."

"Why?" Kara asked.

"Is it so important to know? After all, you're trying to save the world. Surely your noble nature won't allow any minor impediment to stand in your way."

"Tell me anyway," Kara said.

"Let's just say that by inscribing your name in the door you are agreeing to a certain obligation——to be performed at a later date, of course. You'll have plenty of time to play hero before we reach that point."

Taff rose to his feet, his hand hovering over the slingshot at his belt.

"What obligation?" he asked.

"Oh no," Grace said, throwing up her hands in mock fear. "You've angered the whelp. Better tell us quick or face his wrath."

Querin sighed.

"Very well. Carving your name into the door constitutes a binding, mystical pact. I told you about the Khr'nouls, right——how they have these antiquated ideas that humans should be slaves to the forward march of time? Well, they're not too happy about my tower here. I have to keep moving it around, hiding in different pockets of time. Quite tiresome—and they always find me in the end."

Kara thought about the long scratches along the side of the tower, the rubble strewn along the stairs.

"But that's where you come in," Querin said brightly. "I can placate the Khr'nouls, at least for a little while, by offering them someone else in my place. They're angry that I'm using years well beyond what I'm entitled to, but if I replace those years with someone else's—it's all the same to them."

Kara rose to her feet. Darno stood with her, baring his teeth.

"The names in the door?" Kara asked. "Those are . . . sacrifices?"

"I don't particularly care for that word," Querin said. "The visitors who *chose* to carve their names in my doors required a certain piece of information, which I supplied in exchange for a later obligation on their part."

"You killed them," Kara said.

"Not *me*," Querin said, aghast. "The Khr'nouls."

"That doesn't make sense," Grace said. "You said those things were like gods. Surely one little life wouldn't be enough to fill them up."

"It wouldn't be," Querin said, "if it were only one little life. But when the Khr'nouls feast on someone, they don't just eat their present—they eat their future as well, their *unlived* time. Children who will now never be born, and their children's children, and so on and so forth—timeline after timeline erased from existence and swallowed whole. You understand? To the Khr'nouls, a human is far more than just a single meal. It's a banquet of infinite possibilities." Querin flicked the back of his hand through the air as though he were discussing an easily negligible detail. "But all that comes much later. Carve your name in my door today, and nothing will happen. The Khr'nouls aren't hungry yet, and you are not the first person on my list. And then one day—perhaps a year from now, or ten years, or maybe not until you're old and wrinkled—you'll hear a knocking at your door, and it will be your friend Querin Fyndrake. I'll take you back here to the Hourglass Tower and your debt shall be repaid."

The Slanting Hall was suddenly as silent as a tomb.

Grace turned to Kara.

"You should definitely do it," she said.

"No!" exclaimed Taff. "You can't! We'll find another way—*any* other way."

Querin held up his hand.

"Don't decide now," he said, consulting his watch again. "You need rest. Enjoy the hospitality of my tower and give me your decision in the morning. Or the next day, or the day after that." He looked up at Kara and smiled. "I have all the time in the world."

SEVEN

Kara's chambers were luxurious. Cedarwood incense burned in several ornate censers placed throughout the room. A pitcher of ice-cold water and a bowl of caramels sat on her nightstand. The bed was canopied with lace curtains and the mattress held her body like a warm embrace.

Nevertheless, she couldn't sleep.

Taff had gone to bed angry with her. He didn't understand why she was even considering Querin's proposal. "Do you have any other ideas?" Kara had finally snapped. "Because if so, I'd really love to hear them!" Taff had run into his room and bolted the door behind him, tears in his eyes.

He doesn't understand, Kara thought.

She wished she could gather those she loved and live her days in some obscure corner of the world, but it could never be. Precious few memories remained of her mother—most lost to the passage of years or sacrificed to magic—but the lessons imparted by Helena Westfall had become an incontrovertible part of Kara herself. The greatest of these was the importance of taking responsibility for your own actions.

I'm the one who freed Rygoth. I'm the one who needs to stop her.

This wasn't a conversation that she would bother having with her brother. Taff would just tell her that she was being too hard on herself. *He can't possibly understand. Safi saw the darkness that consumes the world after Rygoth gathers the pieces of the* Vulkera, *and if that happens it won't be Taff's fault. It will be mine.*

Safi.

Kara bolted upright.

Maybe there *was* another way.

She stumbled out of bed, nearly tripping over the bunched sheets in her excitement. On the other side of the room was a dressing table covered with vials of makeup and perfumed oil, an altar for princesses and pampered little girls. Kara didn't care about any of that.

All she wanted was the mirror.

Safi has been leading Rygoth astray intentionally, but I bet she can use her powers to locate the other three grims if she really wants to. We could rescue her. Or, if that's impossible, get the location of the grims by some other means: a message through Bethany, or maybe one of my flying friends. It's risky, sure—but a lot better than putting my trust in Querin Fyndrake.

She needed to talk to Bethany. Immediately.

"How do I do this again?" Kara asked herself, trying to recall her conversation with the witch. Since casting the spell that brought them here Kara's mind had been sluggish. *I just need sleep. That's all.* Finally, she remembered the information she needed. "Picture Bethany's face. Two fingers to the mirror. Not the thumb, though. The thumb breaks the spell."

Kara lit a candle and her reflection shimmered in the darkness. She placed her fingers against the cold surface of the glass.

Almost immediately, a plume of mist collided with the other side of the mirror and parted like a curtain.

"Bethany!" Kara began. "We need to talk. I have an idea—"

The mist cleared.

"Hello, Kara," Rygoth said. Her fragmented eyes sparkled with a dozen colors. "What a pleasant surprise."

The Spider Queen was wearing a garnet-red gown with long gloves to match. On her lustrous blond hair rested a webbed crown twisted from iron spires. She was clearly amused by Kara's shocked reaction, and yet the resultant smile actually diminished her beauty. Full lips and perfect teeth couldn't hide the truth: her interpretation of happiness was hopelessly broken, and only pain would ever bring her joy.

"Where's Bethany?" Kara asked. "If you've hurt her—"

"I don't hurt people, *wexari*. I kill them." Rygoth shook her head. "When are you going to realize that we're not playing a child's game here?"

Kara felt her hands tremble, but she managed to hold back her tears.

"Bethany's dead?" she asked.

Rygoth held her gaze, drinking in Kara's sorrow.

"Not yet," she finally said. "I was angry, of course, when I learned that she had betrayed me. But the witch still serves a purpose. Her powers, limited as they are, can allow us to communicate with each other from now on. That could prove useful."

Kara nodded blankly, though she could think of nothing she might ever want to say to the Spider Queen.

I can't tell her that, though, because then she has no reason to keep Bethany alive.

"I was impressed by your escape at the farmhouse," Rygoth said.

"I'm surprised you didn't come yourself."

Rygoth shrugged.

"I sent my twins because I have more important things to do. Killing you is an errand, nothing more. I'll get to it eventually. Right now I want to show you something."

Rygoth peeled off her glove, revealing a hand that had swollen to two times its normal size. Raw tunnels split the overstretched skin, which was unable to contain the expanding flesh beneath it. Kara could see a star-shaped welt near the base of the palm where Darno had stung her.

"I underestimated you. I freely admit that." Rygoth turned her misshapen hand in the air, regarding it from every angle. "Next time I won't be so careless. Knowing that, do you really think you can pit your magic against mine? And I don't mean a contest over the will of one insignificant creature. I mean a true battle."

"Maybe I'll surprise you."

Rygoth shook her head as though Kara had disappointed her.

"You already *had* your moment. Don't you understand? I have an army of witches. I can create monsters with the snap of my fingers. I control the minds of men and beasts."

"Then why do you need the *Vulkera*?"

"I don't *need* it," Rygoth said, stepping forward. "I *want* it. They've given me a crown, call me queen, but I have no desire to rule. All I want is the *magic*. Imagine what it must feel like to snuff out the light of the sun like a candle flame, or lift an entire city into the sky and flip it upside down. I'm bored of being *wexari*. I want to be a god."

Rygoth's hair had come loose and fallen over her fractured eyes. Plumes of breath fogged her side of the mirror.

Kara took a step back.

"What about all the people you'll hurt?" she asked quietly. "Don't you care at all?"

Rygoth smiled and began to tuck her hair back beneath her crown.

"I've enjoyed our conversation," she said. "You know what to do if you want to contact me again. There will come a time where even you realize that there is no point resisting anymore. I'll be waiting."

Kara picked up a censer and smashed it against the mirror. Glass shattered. A sliver found its way into her forearm. Kara absentmindedly picked it out and stared at the drop of blood welling at its end.

I can't let that monster get ahold of the Vulkera. *I need to get to the grims first and hide them where she'll never find them.*

And to do that, I have to carve my name into Querin's door.

Now that Kara had made her decision, it seemed point-less to wait any longer. She left her room and retraced her steps. As she grew closer to the Slanting Hall she heard a sawing sound. At first she thought it was just Querin doing some kind of late-night work, but then she realized what else the sound could be and quickened her pace.

The moment that Kara entered the hall she saw the

small figure standing in front of the Lower Door. She ran to him.

"Don't be mad," Taff said.

With rising horror she saw the knife in his hand, and then, looking past him, four letters, freshly carved:

Taff

"No!" Kara wailed, tracing one finger along the letters, praying her eyes were deceiving her. "You didn't!"

"I had to do something," Taff said.

"What have you done?" Kara screamed, shaking him by the shoulders. *"What have you done?"*

"You can't do this alone! I wanted to help!"

Kara took him in her arms and held him tight.

"I can't lose you," she said. "Not you. Anyone but you."

Kara's violent sobs reverberated throughout the Slanted Hall, muffling the creak of the wooden door as it yawned open.

EIGHT

Kara burst into Querin's bedchambers and demanded that he remove Taff's name from the door, but the little man, groggy with sleep, just smiled and shrugged his shoulders. "Couldn't even if I wanted to," he said. "Magical pact. What's done is done."

He made little attempt to hide his pleasure. The Khr'nouls would now have their sacrifice, affording him more stolen time to live in his tower.

He's like Rygoth. He doesn't care who gets hurt, as long as he gets what he wants.

"I'll take his place," Kara said.

"You are more than welcome to add your name. Plenty of room to be found on the Lower Door. Most visitors are interested in its twin on the opposite end, which leads to the upper half of the tower—a glimpse into the future, not the past. But sacrificing yourself won't change a thing as far as young Taff's fate. I told you: magical pact. The lad is an impressive negotiator, though. Before he carved his name he made me swear that you could both pass through the door and not just him." Querin took her hand and patted it gently. "Your brother sacrificed himself for you. That's true love. Can't you just enjoy it?"

Kara shook him away and called out for Darno. The wolf crept into the room, scorpion tail raised high.

"How about if—"

"—your beast kills me? I'll die, just like any mortal man. But you should know that if any harm befalls me, there are certain defenses that will be activated through-out the tower. You'll never make it out alive. And, just in case you were thinking you might chance it anyway, you should know that even if I die the Khr'nouls will *still* come for your brother."

"This isn't something you can fix, Kara," Taff said. "I wanted to do this. This is how I help you. It's okay."

"It's *not* okay."

"We can learn about the *Vulkera* now," Taff said. "That's why we came here. Everything else can wait."

"Listen to your brother," Querin said. "He's clearly the voice of reason in the family."

Taff's right, Kara thought. *We have to stay focused on the Vulkera right now. If what Querin said is true, the Khr'nouls won't come for a year, maybe even more. Plenty of time to figure out a way to stop them.*

"The door opened," Kara said through clenched teeth. "What's next? Do we just walk through it, or is there something special we have to do?"

Querin's arrogant smile stoked the flames of Kara's anger.

"Traveling to the lower half of the tower is far more complicated than just walking through a door," he said. "There are rules. Leave me so I can get dressed, and I will explain them to you."

They waited for him in the Slanted Hall, not bothering to wake Grace—Kara was in no mood for her smirks and amused comments. Finally, after far longer than it should have taken, Querin appeared. He was wearing a purple silk shirt and gleaming boots. The tail of his beard had been freshly oiled.

"So," he said, clapping his hands together. "Just give me a few moments to prepare a hearty breakfast, and—"

"No more delays," Kara said, shaking her head.

"As you wish," Querin said. "I can enjoy a quiet breakfast with your strange friend. A charmer, that one."

He hurried past them, leaving behind a whiff of flowered water, and together they passed through the Lower Door. The room beyond was circular and small. There were no doors or windows, just a hole large enough to fit a man and a thick rope dangling from the ceiling. Looking up, Kara saw that the rope led to a gigantic winch with coils layered fifteen feet deep around its bobbin. There was enough rope there to lead them from the top reaches of the tower to the ground below.

"First rule," Querin said. "You can't change anything. You can witness events unfold before you, but you will be like ghosts, unseen by anyone."

"Fine by me," Taff said. "We don't want to be seen anyway."

"Where are we going?" Kara asked.

"The tower will know where to send you," Querin said. "As you descend, it will read your needs, so keep them foremost in your minds. You want to know where the grims are hidden? It will send you to the moment in time best suited to give you that information. Just don't get distracted on your way down! Normally I only permit one traveler at a time, because if you're thinking different things it confuses the tower." He held a hand to his heart.

"But I'll make an exception this time, because I've always had a soft spot for children."

Right, Kara thought. *That's why you allowed Taff to trade his life so easily.*

"The second rule," Querin said, "and the most important one, is to never, under any circumstances, let go of the rope."

He handed it to Kara. It felt strange, and she saw that her hands were instantly coated in a powdery substance like the dust from crushed stones.

"I told you the Khr'nouls don't like it when people mess around with time, right?" Querin asked. "Well, they have scouts out there, making sure that everyone stays on the proper timeline. I call them *cogs*. Now this rope keeps you anchored to the tower, and as long as you're holding it, you're safe. They can't see you. But let go of the rope, even for an instant, and the cogs will sense that something is amiss. They might not come right away, but think of a shark in the ocean. You can only kick your feet so many times before it realizes what's going on and attacks.

There'll be signs first—time will start to do some truly strange things—and after that you're done for."

"What sort of strange things?" Taff asked.

"It doesn't matter," Querin said, "because you're not going to let go of the rope, are you? Which brings us to the third rule. The tower shows you what the tower shows you. If you run out of rope, there's a reason. Knowledge is a sacred privilege, children. Don't be tempted to take more than you're offered."

Kara peered through the hole in the wall, which led to a tunnel sloping into the darkness at a steep angle. She handed the rope to Taff.

"Remember," she said. "Stay focused on why we're here. The *Vulkera*. We need to know where it's hidden. The tower is going to read your mind." *Like the* queth'nondra, Kara thought, wondering if she would have to endure a walk through the same disgusting, jellylike substance.

"Got it," Taff said over one shoulder, already starting down.

Kara climbed into the hole. A not unpleasant smell

filled her nostrils, damp air after a summer storm. She yanked on the rope and it glided with ease from the winch.

"Any more rules?" she asked Querin.

"Just one," he said. "Keep your brother safe. His life belongs to me now."

He walked away before Kara could respond.

The tunnel seemed to descend forever, a surprisingly uniform spiral with bone-smooth features. Occasionally Kara would hear muffled sounds through the walls. Clash of swords. Pounding rain. Voices raised in anger. It was as though the tunnel were an underground passage that led beneath past events, bringing them further and further back in time.

Kara heard a low grumble. She thought that it might have been the sound of some great beast of lore before realizing that it was just Taff's stomach.

"Querin was right," he said. "We should have eaten breakfast first."

At long last the winding tunnel came to a square of light, and the two Westfalls tumbled out of the darkness and into the blaring sun. They were in the middle of a desert. Behind them stood the Hourglass Tower, but in every other direction dunes of featureless sand stretched as far as the eye could see. Kara kept one hand on the rope as she shaded her eyes, scanning the horizon for a reason why they might have been brought to such a desolate place.

"Querin tricked us!" Kara exclaimed. "There's nothing here!"

Taff held a finger to his lips.

"Listen," he said.

The desert was empty, but it wasn't silent. Behind the tower, Kara could hear sounds that indicated a distinctly human presence. The creak and groan of wagon wheels. Soft conversations. A steady tapping noise, like a pickax against a rock.

"Let's see what it is!" Taff said, yanking on the rope with excitement. Despite all the turns they had made on their downward journey, the rope slid with surprising ease from the exit and offered little resistance as they tugged it around the stone perimeter of the tower. Since Taff was in the lead, he saw the sight that awaited them on the other side first.

The rope fell from his hands.

"What are you doing?" Kara asked, shoving it back into his grip. "Don't you remember what Querin said? We can't let go, no matter—"

Then she saw what Taff was staring at and nearly dropped the rope herself.

Before them stretched a red surface as alien as that of a distant star. It had the smooth, shimmery quality of ice, but beneath it Kara could still see grains of sand, like lacquer that had been brushed over the original ground. In the center of this red shell, which extended many miles like a frozen lake, sat a massive castle that looked as though it had been frozen in the process of collapsing into ruins. Towers leaned over at impossible angles. The roof had fallen inward and then stopped. Above it all hung the tattered remains of what might have been, at one time, a great banner.

"The castle is covered with the same stuff on the ground," Taff said. "That's the only thing keeping it together. Like magical paste."

Kara nodded.

"I think this is Dolrose Castle," she said. "Princess Evangeline destroyed it with magic, remember?" Despite the heat she suddenly felt cold. "Seeing it in person is a lot different than reading about it in a letter."

"I feel bad for the people who were inside," Taff said. "This princess sounds even worse than Grace. Maybe even Rygoth. I'm glad she's dead."

"Don't say that."

"Why not?"

"Because death isn't something to ever be glad about."

Armored guards had been posted around the perimeter of the red shell. Though Kara and Taff were clearly in their line of vision, they could neither see nor hear the children. The Hourglass Tower was equally invisible.

"This must be what it feels like to be a ghost," Taff said as they made their way closer to the castle. He waved at the nearest guard. "Hey! Look at me! I'm from the *future!*"

The man didn't even blink.

"Taff," Kara said. "Let's not . . ."

". . . play with people from the past who can't see you." He sighed and shook his head. "I love you, Kara, but you've got rules about *everything*."

About a quarter of the way around the red shell they could see a large caravan of wagons sitting in the sun. They made their way toward it, dragging the rope with them. It was slow going, and Kara knew that her hands would be covered with calluses by the end of the day. She wished she had thought of wearing gloves.

Finally, they reached the wagons and found a small

group of people that had gathered on the edge of the red shell. They were having an important-looking discussion. Five of them sat on small stools. The final man stood before a table on which five red chests had been arranged in a perfect line. Four chests were the same size, big enough to hold a dozen apples. The last one was considerably smaller. Back on De'Noran it might have been used for a promise ring, given from one beloved to the other.

The standing man turned. Kara recognized him instantly.

"That's Minoth Dravania!" she told Taff, gripping his arm. The headmaster of Sablethorn did not look much different than when Kara had met him in the Well of Witches: bald head, dark birthmark across his face, kind eyes. Only his clothes had changed. Instead of green robes he wore a formal-looking white cloak embroidered with silver runes.

That's why the tower brought us here, Kara thought, running toward the headmaster as fast as the rope would allow. *A powerful* wexari *like Minoth will be able to see me for sure! He can answer all the questions I have, all the ones that I didn't have time to ask in the Well.*

But even when she stood before him the *wexari* paid her no heed. Apparently not even Minoth Dravania could see through the mists of time.

The tower brought us here for a reason, Kara thought, biting back her disappointment. *Even though I can't talk to Minoth directly, I'm sure there's much to learn by simply listening.*

The initial conversation, however, was surprisingly dull. It was clear that the five men and one woman had not seen one another in many years, and etiquette demanded that they spend time catching up before jumping into the matter at hand. The only benefit to this talk of weather and family was that it gave Kara a chance to learn the identity of all the participants, so that by the time they finally got down to the true purpose of their meeting she knew who was who.

"Enough," King Penta said, puffing on a pipe. He

looked young for a king, no older than forty, and the iron crown on his head was simple and bereft of gems. "I have nothing but affection for the lot of you, but I'm a busy man and I've traveled a long way. Now tell me, Minoth, why have you called us all to this ghastly place?"

"My question exactly," said the only woman, Kenetta, who had a habit of echoing the king's sentiments. She wore a glass cloak that shimmered in the sun. "We could be at my palace in Lux right now, sharing a bottle of the finest wine in Sentium."

The man to her left, Landris Ilma, grumbled something in disagreement, and Kenetta rolled her eyes. "You can't *possibly* think that swill you call wine in Ilma is superior to a Luxian vintage," she said. Kara had already grown used to these little squabbles. With the exception of Minoth and the king, each of the participants represented a different region of Sentium: Ilma, Kutt, Auren, and Lux. They were quick to bicker about the most insignificant matters.

"I am sorry for the inconvenience, revered guests," Minoth said. He spoke softly, yet Landris and Kenetta instantly stopped their childish debate and gave him their full attention. "But Dolrose Castle seemed a fitting place to tell you this news. As you know, we've been studying the *Vulkera* at Sablethorn for many years now, and while our attempts to destroy it have been unsuccessful, we have at last managed to divide it into four sections." He turned to King Penta. "Your Highness, I know how concerned you are about the princess's grimoire falling into the wrong hands. I suggest that we send these grims, as I call them, as far from one another as possible, so they may never be rejoined."

King Penta chewed on the stem of his pipe.

"You have a plan for this, I assume."

"You know me well," Minoth said, smiling. He lifted one of the larger chests off the table and handed it to Kenetta. "The first grim, the cover of the *Vulkera*, should go to Lux. The last time we met you spoke of a stronghold that your people had recently built using the most modern of your crafts."

"Ta'men Keep," Kenetta said with obvious pride. "No place safer in all of Sentium." She turned the chest in her hands. "How do you open this thing?"

"You don't," said Minoth.

He handed the second chest to an unsmiling old man wearing an iron visor that covered his eyes. His name was Mazkus, and he had spent the entire conversation with his head bowed, listening carefully.

"The back cover of the *Vulkera* I place in the hands of our neighbors to the east, the great region of Auren, where I am sure they will guard it with all the austerity that—"

"Keep the cursed thing," Mazkus grumbled. "I don't want such evil within our borders. Give it to Ilma."

Landris bristled.

"Why should *we* take it? Ilma is far too important to Sentium. We create new sources of power. All you

Aurians do is hide behind your mountains and—"

"The grimoire is harmless as long as it's kept asunder," Minoth interjected patiently. "And Ilma is too close to Lux. The idea is to keep the grims as spread out as possible."

"Give it to Kutt, then," said Mazkus.

"Yes!" exclaimed the final man, rocking back and forth on his stool. A shock of mauve hair sprouted from the top of his head, and his clothes were stained and torn. Kara had seen him, on numerous occasions, reach down to take an interesting-looking pebble or piece of debris and slip it into his bag. "Give it to me!" he exclaimed. "Kutt has nothing like a grim. It would be an honor to add it to our museum!"

He stretched his hands out eagerly and Kenetta recoiled in disgust; the man's fingertips were peeling, his skin stained by some sort of blue chemical.

"I had already planned to give you one," said Minoth, handing the man, whose name was Delvin, the third chest. "The spine of the *Vulkera*. I thought that fitting, given your people's interest in the workings of the human body."

"The spine!" exclaimed Delvin. "I get it!" He laughed fiendishly.

"That one's mad," Taff whispered—though there was, of course, no need to lower his voice at all.

"What about Timoth Clen?" asked Mazkus. "A fine warrior, that one. I think he'd covet the opportunity to guard such an evil artifact."

Minoth's face darkened with rare anger.

"Timoth Clen is a zealot and a murderer."

"It's true," added Ilma. "His methods have grown increasingly erratic of late. And his followers have begun to treat him like some sort of god. The Children of the Fold, they call themselves. Worrisome, don't you think?"

"I am well aware of the situation," King Penta said. "We are grateful for Timoth Clen's services against the witches, but his time has passed. Measures will be taken."

The council nodded with approval.

"Now if you truly do not want the grim in Auren," Minoth said, "I suppose I can bring it back to Sablethorn for further study—"

"No," said King Penta. "Sablethorn has already been involved enough in this matter. The grim goes to Auren, as planned."

Mazkus bowed and took the chest. Minoth looked displeased at this, though he quickly hid his consternation from the king. Kara thought she understood: *Minoth needed to offer the grim to Auren, for form's sake, but he wanted to take it back to Sablethorn. Penta stopped that from happening. Why?*

"And the fourth grim?" Kenetta asked.

"That will remain here, in Dolrose Castle," Minoth said.

This was met by a storm of disapproval (except from Delvin, who had found some interesting-looking weeds growing from an outcropping of rocks and was pinching them into glass vials). Eventually Mazkus's voice, as gruff as winter wind, rose over the others.

"I cannot speak for my honorable peers," said Mazkus, "but in Auren the grim shall be placed in the Silent Vault and guarded by Sentium's finest warriors, day in and day out. Who will perform such a duty in this desolate place?"

"And it's the actual pages in that chest, isn't it?" asked Kenetta. "I'm no expert in these matters, but I'm pretty sure that's the most important part. Couldn't a witch just get by with those alone?"

"No," said Minoth. "All four sections of the grimoire need to be joined together in order for it to regain its power. And as for your other concern, the nearest village is six days by horseback. Do you know what they call these ruins? Heathen's Valley. No one will come here. Fear and superstition will guard the grim even better than Aurian swords."

Ilma cleared his throat. "I appreciate the sentiment, Minoth, but a witch capable of using the grimoire is not going to be dissuaded so easily."

"That's *if* they discover the grim is hidden here," Minoth said. He reached for the final, and smallest, chest. "And on the off chance that someone discovers the truth, I assure you that the final grim will be well guarded indeed."

Unlike the other chests, this one had a latch. Minoth opened it now, revealing a tiny black egg freckled with red.

"What's that?" King Penta asked.

"Horror," Minoth said, snapping the lid shut. It was the first time that Kara had seen fear in his eyes. "Damnation. Ruin. Otherwise known as a faenix."

"Is it a guardian?" Penta asked suspiciously. "Or a monster?"

"Both."

"Monsters don't live forever," Ilma said, shifting uneasily on his stool. "What happens when this creature of yours dies?"

"That's the point," Minoth said. "The faenix cannot die. It cannot be defeated. Any unfortunate who wanders into Dolrose Castle will meet a truly terrible demise, from now until the end of time. As soon as we've finished our meeting here, I'll place it in the ruins myself and start the hatching process."

Taff looked nervously at Kara and a thought too terrifying to speak aloud passed between them: *If we want the grim, we're going to have to face that thing, aren't we?*

After this, King Penta demanded a formal vow of silence from all the participants, and the conversation, having run its course, ended in a series of awkward farewells. Mazkus, still angry about the chest in his hands, was the first to leave, and though the iron helm blinded him he moved with the grace of the sure-sighted. Ilma whispered something in Kenetta's ear and the two left together. Delvin proceeded slowly to the awaiting carriages, his eyes scanning the ground for any treasures he might have missed.

"We know where to find the grims now!" Taff exclaimed. He enumerated what they had learned with his fingers. "The first one doesn't matter so much since Rygoth already has it, but the second one is in the Silent Vault in Auren, the third one's in some kind of museum in Kutt, and the fourth one . . ." Taff looked nervously at the small chest. "What do you think is in that egg?" he asked.

"Shh," Kara said, placing a hand on his wrist.

Minoth and King Penta had remained behind, and the two men stared at each other uncomfortably, as though unsure how to begin. The sun blazed in the western sky. Beads of sweat ran down their faces.

Finally, Minoth broke the silence.

"After the egg hatches even I won't be able to re-enter the castle, so I'm going to request—"

"Not this again."

"—that I be allowed to bring the pages of the *Vulkera* back to Sablethorn in order to study them. We believe that Princess Evangeline's spirit still resides within the grims. If you just give us a little more time, we might be able to figure out what happened."

King Penta waved his arm, signifying the destruction around them.

"*This* is what happened. What else do you need to know?"

"It could be nothing, your highness. Then again, it could be *everything*."

With a sigh of resignation, Penta overturned his pipe bowl, dumping tobacco onto the ground, and rose to his feet. He wore two swords, a long one and a short one. They looked well used.

"Come, old friend. My bottom aches from this blasted stool. Walk with me."

Minoth folded his hands within the large sleeves of his cloak and joined the taller man. At first, as a sign of deference, Minoth walked slightly behind the king, but Penta slowed down and guided him forward, indicating that they should proceed as equals.

Kara started to follow them, but after only a few steps

the rope pulled taut in her hand.

"Guess that's the end of it," Taff said. "No matter. We've gotten what we came for. Let's head back."

Gripping the rope with two hands, Kara yanked it as hard as she could. It didn't budge.

She let it fall to the ground.

"What are you doing?" Taff asked, horrified.

"Minoth mentioned Princess Evangeline in the Well of Witches," she said, already backing toward the two men. They were walking at a steady clip, their backs growing smaller in the distance. "I have to hear what he says about her. This is important. I feel it!"

"But remember what Querin said? If you let go of the rope the cogs will be able to sense you!"

"I'll be back before they even know I'm here," Kara said. "Stay put."

She started after the two men. Ignoring her instructions completely, Taff dropped the rope and followed her.

NINE

It was even more difficult to move without the rope in their hands, like running on sand. Kara quickly developed a theory about this, and would have shared it with Taff had she not been so out of breath: *Now that we're no longer connected to the tower, Time can feel our presence. This is a warning that we're not welcome here, an opportunity to leave while we still have the chance.*

Before the cogs come.

You know where the sections of the Vulkera are now—just go! Can this really be worth risking your life over?

Her instincts screamed *YES!*

She had first read about Princess Evangeline in Sordyr's letter, and even then she had thought that there was something a little off about what had happened at Dolrose Castle. Her suspicions had later been confirmed by Minoth in the *queth'nondra: I've always found it hard to believe that one little girl could have been responsible for transforming a magnificent place like Phadeen into the Well of Witches. You might want to think on that at some point.* Kara had followed this advice on countless nights, tossing and turning while she tried to assemble a puzzle for which she lacked all the pieces.

The grimoires. The Well of Witches. A new way of doing magic that corrupted the caster.

The whole world had changed in a heartbeat. And it had all started with Princess Evangeline.

I need to know the truth.

Kara and Taff caught up to the two men. The conversation between them had grown heated; both their faces were flushed with anger.

". . . the devastation that magic has wreaked!" King Penta exclaimed. His hand rested on the pommel of the longer sword. "We can't take any chances. We have to wipe all record of it from our histories, start anew." His voice softened. "You know what that means for Sablethorn, of course."

It was clear from the devastated look on Minoth's face that he knew exactly what the king was talking about— as did Kara. *Penta intends to destroy Sablethorn so no trace of magic remains.* It gave Kara some degree of satisfaction knowing that the king would only be half successful at this. Minoth's magic would protect the school from harm, and it would lie buried beneath the Forked Library, completely abandoned until Kara entered it in two millennia.

"For countless generations the *wexari* of Sablethorn have been a force of good in the world," Minoth said.

"The world has changed. The witches—"

"Are *victims*, your highness."

"Because grimoires *force* them to do all these evil things, right?" Penta shook his head. "You've never been able to prove that."

Minoth and King Penta fell into an awkward silence as each of them took a few moments to leash their tempers. They continued to walk at a steady pace, however, leading Kara and Taff farther from the safety of the rope.

"Did you ever meet Princess Evangeline?" Minoth asked.

"Once," King Penta said. "Lord Gareth invited me to celebrate the completion of Dolrose Castle. I stayed here for a fortnight."

"Strange that he built a castle so far away from civilization, isn't it? And construction began——when was it again? Two years after Evangeline's birth?"

"What are you getting at?"

"I think she exhibited signs of being *wexari*. And I think Lord Gareth wanted to hide her away."

"Why?" King Penta asked.

"Lord Gareth was a good man, but he had no love for Sablethorn. He would have hated the idea of his daughter growing up among our kind—as would have been required by law, once she was identified. What was your opinion of the girl when you met her?"

Penta smiled in remembrance.

"Cute little thing. Always wanting to climb on my lap and hear tell of different lands. It didn't matter to her that I was the king. She just liked my stories."

"The apple of her parents' eye, no?"

"They loved her something fierce," Penta admitted. "Where is this all leading?"

"How does an adorable ten-year-old girl become a monster who wiped out her entire castle and transformed Phadeen into the Well of Witches?"

"You're the one who said that grimoires turn their users evil," Penta said, cracking his neck from side to side. "What happened to Evangeline only proves your point."

"Kara," Taff whispered.

She shushed him, not wanting to miss a word of the conversation, but he turned her head until she faced a purple flower that had suddenly sprouted from the barren ground. The flower wilted before their eyes, petals falling.

Sprouted again. Wilted.

"Time," Taff said, "doing strange things. Querin warned us. The cogs are close. We need to get back to the rope."

"Just another minute," Kara said. She wasn't exactly sure what she was waiting for, only that it hadn't happened yet. Kara didn't have visions like Safi, but she had strong instincts, and she had learned to trust them.

She turned her attention back toward Minoth.

". . . perfectly happy child doesn't change completely. Something was wrong with Evangeline *before* she received the grimoire. Lord Gareth—no doubt with some reluctance—requested Sablethorn's assistance months before the catastrophe, claiming that his daughter had become a different person, as though some-one had 'sucked all the love from her heart.' His words, not mine. I still have the letter. I sent two of my *wexari*, who reported that Evangeline was just a spoiled child with a penchant for cruelty—certainly not unheard of among royalty." Minoth sighed bitterly. "If only I had attended to the matter personally, perhaps things could have been different. We know now that an expelled student of Sablethorn named Rygoth was in the castle at the time, and I cannot help but think that she was somehow involved in—"

"I don't see how any of this matters," Penta said. "It's too late to change what happened."

"But maybe we can use what happened to shed some light on our current problems. See, all grimoires are connected, but the *Vulkera* is special. It has the ability to control all the others, almost like a brain. No, that's not right. More like a *soul*, a conscience. And although the *Vulkera* is currently a source of great evil whose darkness infects all other grimoires, I don't believe that it started that way."

Kara felt her heartbeat quicken. *Yes! This is what I need to know!*

"My student Sordyr created the first grimoire as a gift for Princess Evangeline, a bit of sunshine to lift her spirits. I had watched him experiment with such books at Sablethorn, and their effects were completely harmless. Say a few words, make a top spin on its own or a flash of fireworks light up the night sky. An innocent bauble for children, nothing more. But there was something about Princess Evangeline that transformed the grimoire completely." The sky flashed and for a moment Kara saw the castle standing there in its majestic splendor, courtyard teeming with people now dead. *Time acting strange again,* she thought. Taff spoke another word of warning, but Kara ignored him and remained focused on Minoth. ". . . that's why I believe that Evangeline was actually a *wexari* whose talents had escaped our notice, which explains how she had the power to push the grimoire beyond its limits. What it doesn't explain is the darkness eating away at her soul, or why she used her Last Spell to create the Well of Witches. Or, for that matter, why only females can——"

King Penta held a single hand in the air. Kara could see, in the set of the king's face, that he remained unconvinced by the *wexari's* rambling arguments.

"Again—and for the last time—what will any of this *change?*"

Minoth replied with measured tones, trying to hold his temper.

"There's so much we don't understand, and Evangeline is the key. Her spirit still resides in the *Vulkera*, trapped forever. Let my *wexari* study its pages. Perhaps we can figure out the origin of this unexplained darkness. And once we know that, maybe we can undo the——"

"Kara!" Taff screamed.

The sky grew dark as a black cloud darted in their direction like a swarm of bees. Instead of buzzing, however, the tiny creatures made a sound like the inner workings of a clock. A thousand ticks and tocks assaulted Kara's ears.

"Cogs," Taff whispered.

He yanked on her hand, meaning to pull her away, but there was no need. Kara knew that the time had come to run.

They sprinted toward the rope, which looked as small as a length of yarn in the distance. As Kara ran, she reached out with her *wexari* senses, hoping to build a mind-bridge to the cogs, but she couldn't feel their presence. Perhaps it was because Kara was in the wrong time period. Or maybe the cogs weren't animals at all but a natural force more akin to wind or sunlight. Either way, magic wasn't going to help them.

The swarm grew closer.

Kara felt something swipe across her neck with the sickening speed of a scythe cutting grain. Blood trickled. *Doesn't matter. Keep moving.* The world around them flickered again and again, time out of joint. Day. Night. The road packed with wagons. Starlit emptiness millions of years from now. They lost the location of the rope and found themselves going in the wrong direction, circled back. *The rope? Where's the rope?* Taff swatted at the back of his hand and Kara saw a bloom of red there. The swarm hovered just above their heads, the ticktocking deafening now. It was like being trapped inside a clock itself, lost in a labyrinth of gears. Kara, gasping for breath and completely disoriented, was suddenly pushed to the ground. Taff mouthed words she couldn't hear and shoved something into her hands.

The rope.

Her fingers wound about its powdery surface just as the swarm descended. A single cog hovered before her eyes. Up close, it looked more mechanical than insectile. There were no eyes or face, just a kidney-shaped torso spattered with rust, attached to two gears spinning with blurring speed. Kara shielded her face with one hand, certain that the cog was going to attack, but instead it rejoined the swarm. As one they zipped out of sight.

They were safe.

Kara and Taff walked back to the tower in silence. They didn't let go of the rope once.

When they reentered the Slanting Hall, Querin and Grace were sitting at the center table, playing cards like old friends. Querin seemed only mildly curious about her journey, but Grace asked all sorts of questions. Kara kept her answers as vague as possible. Although Grace claimed to have sworn off magic, Kara still didn't like sharing information about an all-powerful grimoire with her.

"There's one thing I don't understand," Grace said, turning to Taff. "Why did you carve your name into the door? Don't you know what's going to happen to you now?"

"I knew that if I didn't do it then Kara would," Taff said.

Grace nodded vigorously. "Precisely! And then Kara would be the one getting eaten by the Khr'nouls, not you. Isn't that better?"

"Nothing could be worse," said Taff.

Grace stared at him, blue eyes wide.

"You're a very strange boy," she said.

Now that Querin had gotten what he wanted—a new sacrifice to appease the Khr'nouls—he dropped the facade of helpful host and ushered them quickly toward the exit. They stepped through the door and onto the exterior landing that jutted out between the two halves of the tower. Far below them, Shadowdancer whinnied happily. They were back in the original field where they had first found the tower. In the distance, Kara could see the farmhouse where they had encountered the twins.

"Don't worry," Querin said, reading the concern on her face. "Your enemies are long gone. After some consideration, I allowed four days to pass in your time. I thought that would be safest for you." He noticed a thin red line on the back of Kara's neck. "I see you had a run-in with the cogs."

"It's just a scratch."

"It's more than that. The touch of a cog shortens your timeline. That little scratch cost you a week of your life."

Kara shrugged.

"Then I ought to make the best of it." She crouched down and met his eyes. "As far as my brother is concerned, stay away. I don't care about any 'magical pacts.' You can't have him. Ever."

Querin looked at her very seriously for a moment, trying to hold a straight face, and then burst into laughter.

"Oh, Kara. You really don't get it, do you? The moment Taff carved his name into the door, he died. In fact, from the Khr'nouls perspective, I'm sure it's happened already! They don't live time going forward, you see, but in a circle of sorts—which means they have already devoured brave little Taff, probably more than once." All traces of humor left his face. "You need to learn your place in the world, witch. At some point your brother will hear a knocking at his door, and it will be me, come to take what's mine. And there won't be anything you can do to stop me."

Querin closed the door and bolted it shut.

BOOK TWO

THE MUSEUM OF IMPOSSIBLE THINGS

*"A soul stained with magic
can never be cleansed."*

— *The Path*

Leaf 38, Vein 12

TEN

Two days later, Lucas found them.

They were settling in for the night, having set up camp in the crook of a rocky stream, when he slipped through the trees. Lucas wore the same gray cloak as the last time Kara had seen him and a glorb-bow on his back. He pushed back the hair that hung over his forehead and smiled.

"*There* you are," he said.

Kara dropped the bowl she was about to eat from and mushroom stew splattered her boots. She didn't care. She ran into Lucas's arms and held him tight, breathing in the smell of him until she was certain that he was real.

"How?"

"I'll tell you everything," he said. Catching sight of Taff, Lucas picked him up and spun him around in a circle. Kara's heart rejoiced at the increasingly rare sound of Taff's giggles.

"Look at the size of you!" Lucas exclaimed. "You're going to be bigger than me soon!"

Lucas's eyes settled on Grace and his smiled faded. He lowered Taff to the ground.

"Grace," he said.

"Evening, Lucas. No hug for me?"

He sent a questioning glance in Kara's direction—*What is* she *doing here?*—but said no more, joining them around the campfire. Taff handed him a tin cup filled with water, which Lucas downed gratefully.

"Do you have news of Father?" Taff asked anxiously.

"He's well," Lucas said. "Doing a masterful job

pretending to be Timoth Clen. The other graycloaks have no idea. He's completely changed the way the Children of the Fold go about their business. They've stopped hunting girls just because they have magical talent." He swiveled toward Taff, who was gape-mouthed in ardent fascination. "The graycloaks are fighting the witches who try to hurt people, nothing more. They're a force for good now. All because of your father."

Taff didn't say anything. He didn't need to. His smile spoke volumes.

Kara slung an arm around her brother's shoulder and kissed him on the cheek. She was so proud of the good her father had done, but her concern for him had not diminished; he was taking a great risk impersonating the famous witch hunter. The graycloaks would kill him instantly if he were discovered.

"I'm surprised he told you that his soul had been restored," Kara said. "That wasn't his intent, last time we spoke."

"He didn't tell me," Lucas said. "I figured it out on my own. He could fool the others with ease, but he wasn't as surefooted around me. I think he felt a little guilty about hiding the truth—and for locking me in a cell for six weeks, though he really didn't have a choice. I had to be punished for helping you."

"Sorry," Kara said.

"The other graycloaks clamored for my head on a block, and no doubt if the real Timoth Clen had still been in charge—" Lucas rubbed his neck with a grim expression. "The fact that I was allowed to live was another clue that something had changed. After I was released I cornered your father and he told me the truth of what happened. He set you free—covering his tracks by blaming magic—and sent you to find the pieces of an ancient grimoire before Rygoth could get to them."

"It's called the *Vulkera*," Grace added, annoyed that she was being excluded from the conversation.

"I snuck out of camp the next morning to find

you," Lucas said, scratching his forearm. "Looked for Shadowdancer's tracks—rode her close to a year, so I know them well—but too much time had passed. Your father told me you headed west, though, and there's only one main road going in that direction, so I followed it, asking guarded questions in the towns I passed. Occasionally I heard tell of a tall girl traveling with her brother. And then a few days ago an old farmer told me about a flash of purple light in the sky."

Kara and Taff exchanged a knowing look: *the twins' barrier.*

"Figured it was something magical," Lucas said, "so I decided to take a look. Picked up Shadowdancer's tracks near an old farmhouse that looked like some kind of battle had been fought inside it. Followed the tracks . . . and found you."

"Scintillating tale," Grace said. "Why are you *here*?"

Lucas had grown taller and broader-shouldered, yet the changes in him went beyond the physical; he now spoke with a directness that had not been present back on De'Noran, where he spent long hours of servitude burning Fringe weeds. Upon hearing Grace's question, however, Lucas folded his hands together and the features of his face softened into an uncertain expression. He looked, for that one moment, exactly as Kara remembered him before they left the island, and she smiled. While she liked Lucas's newfound confidence, Kara was relieved that her best friend had not changed *too* much.

"This *Vulkera* thing sounds pretty dangerous," he started, refusing to meet her eyes. "I thought I should find you, lend a hand. Plus . . . I needed to know that you were all right, Kara. I couldn't bear the thought that something bad might have . . . I couldn't do anything else but worry all the time. . . ."

He looked up. Their eyes met. Even by the light of the dim campfire Kara could see his cheeks redden.

"And Taff!" Lucas added, throwing his arm around the boy. "I really missed Taff."

Grace pointed to herself and grinned.

"You not so much," Lucas said.

Kara told him everything that had happened since the last time they had spoken at length, including their journey into the Well of Witches and their more recent expedition into the past. As always, Lucas listened with complete attention. Sometimes, looking into his eyes— the soft brown of sun-baked soil—Kara forgot her place in the narrative or what part she had told already.

I've missed him so much.

By the time Kara had finished Taff was snoring gently.

"We have an important decision to make," she said. "Which grim do we go after first?"

"Not the one in Auren," Lucas said. "The graycloaks were already marching in that direction when I left. Your father planned to speak to the king there, and after that continue onto Lux and Ilma. He was going to try and convince them to join their forces together in the fight against Rygoth." Lucas threw his head back in frustration.

"I should have brought a carrier pigeon with me! We could have sent him a message, let him know what you've learned."

Kara couldn't help but smile.

"Um, Lucas."

"What?"

"I'm sort of good with animals. Remember?"

"Right," he said, smiling at his own foolishness. "Magic. Let's send your father a message tonight. Maybe he can track down the grim while he's in Auren. Where did you say it was hidden? The silent room?"

"Silent Vault."

"Excellent plan," Grace said, clapping her hands together in a slow, mocking cadence. "And a good thing Rygoth can't read the minds of animals, because then sending our most important secrets via a bird would be a really horrible idea."

Kara bit her lower lip, mad at herself for being so careless. For a few pleasant moments she and Lucas had seemed lost in their own private world, and she had foolishly forgotten that Grace was listening as well. As a result, Kara had revealed more information than she ever intended. Judging from the smirk on Grace's face, she knew exactly what had happened, which was why she had kept so uncharacteristically quiet during the conversation.

"Grace has a valid point," Lucas admitted. "Maybe using animals isn't the best plan."

"Rygoth can't listen to all animals at all times," Kara replied with more confidence than she felt. "It will work."

"So that leaves Dolrose Castle and Kutt as possible destinations," Lucas said. "I think I've learned enough about Sentium geography over the past year that I can lead us to either place. We would have to cross the Plague Barrier to get to Kutt, and its inhabitants, if rumors are to be believed, have some truly strange customs. On the other hand, Dolrose Castle is farther, and has a literal monster waiting in its depths. . . ."

"The castle first," Kara said. "I need to learn more about Evangeline."

"The dead princess?" Grace asked. "What in the world for?"

"Because whatever went wrong with magic started with her. Maybe if we understood what happened, we could . . ."

Kara hesitated, Minoth's words echoing through her head: *Magic is sick. And I suspect you're the one meant to heal it.*

"What?" Grace asked.

"I'm not sure yet," Kara replied. "You'll just have to trust me."

"Whatever you think is best," Lucas said.

Grace rolled her eyes.

"I called out to Rattle," Kara said. "She should be here by morning." The rustle-foot had been a long way off, lazing in warm winds with no direction in mind, embracing her newfound freedom. Kara felt guilty calling her back, but they needed to go airborne if they wanted to stay in front of Rygoth.

"Ugh," said Grace. "The caterpillar again?"

"You don't have to worry about that," Kara replied. "You're not coming with us."

Kara expected Grace to lose her temper. She was ready for that. What she wasn't ready for was the hurt look in her eyes, as though Kara were a dear friend who had betrayed her.

"Have I done something wrong?" Grace asked.

"It's not that," Kara said, stunned. *It's that I can't trust you and I have enough to worry about as it is.* "Listen, why would you want to come with us in the first place? Don't you know how dangerous it's going to be? You're not even a witch anymore!"

"I can still help."

"How?"

"I'm clever. And I . . . I think how a witch thinks. I can figure out what Rygoth is going to—"

"There's a town a short walk north of here," Lucas suggested. "Scemed nice enough. If you're sincere about mending your ways, might not be a bad place to start over again."

Grace gave Lucas a pointed look—*This doesn't concern you*—and turned back toward Kara.

"You can't do this," she insisted. "You can't leave me all alone."

"I think it's for the best," Kara replied.

There wasn't much to say after that, so they all found a spot to sleep for the night. Lucas passed out fast, but Kara remained awake, staring up at the stars.

What if I'm wrong about Grace? she thought. *What if she really is trying to change? How can I just abandon her?*

Kara heard movement to her right and turned her head. Grace was sitting up beneath her blankets. She held her walking stick across her lap and traced its simple wooden grains with her index finger.

"Can't sleep?" Kara asked.

Grace shrugged. "Nothing new. I haven't been able to sleep for a while now."

Kara nodded in understanding.

"The Faceless have plagued my dreams as well."

"That's not the reason I can't sleep," Grace said, shaking her head. "Not tonight, at least. I was thinking about my father."

Kara didn't say anything. Fen'de Stone, the leader of De'Noran, had been a particularly cruel man. She did not mourn his death.

Grace shifted beneath her blanket until she was facing Kara.

"I was thinking about a bedtime ritual we had," she said. "Not drinking a warm glass of milk or singing a lullaby, of course. No, my father, the great Fen'de Stone, would stand behind me at the mirror and say the same words each night. 'Behold the face of evil, child. White hair. Withered leg. You're the reason your mother died. You're sick with the taint of magic, and you poisoned her from inside.' And then, while he scrubbed my face clean with hot water, I would recite a passage of his choice from the Path—from memory, of course—and he would chant, 'Water to scrub the skin clean, words to scrub the soul.' And if I misread the passage, he . . ."

Grace grew suddenly silent.

"Why are you telling me this?" Kara asked.

"Because I think maybe you're right to send me away," she said. "My own father thought I was evil. How could there possibly be any good in me?"

"There's good in everyone," Kara said. "It's just a matter of bringing it out."

"Then *help* me," Grace pleaded.

Her blue eyes swelled with desperation and need. It was hard to believe that this was the same girl who had tormented Kara and tried to kill her brother.

But it was.

"Go to sleep," Kara said, turning away. "It'll be morning soon."

ELEVEN

Kara awoke to the sound of fluttering wings.

It was Rattle, who passed above them and then landed softly just outside their campsite. Kara ran to greet her. She stroked the rustle-foot's leathery ears and her blue wings, gold at the tips, shook with pleasure. While Rattle drank her fill at the stream, Lucas tottered over to join them, his face still groggy with sleep. He had always been slow to rise, and it was a comfort knowing that some things hadn't changed.

"Morning," Kara said.

"Morning."

Kara kept waiting for them to fall into the familiar rhythms of their friendship, but there was something inexplicably awkward between them now. *Have we both changed so much?* Lucas was still quick to smile around Taff, more like his old self. When he was around Kara, however, he seemed to spend an inordinate amount of time staring down at his shoes.

"You want me to bring Grace to that village I was talking about before we leave for the castle?" Lucas asked.

"Grace is coming with us," Kara said.

Lucas nodded, as though he was expecting this.

"Because you feel bad for her?"

"Of course not," Kara snapped. "I truly think she can help."

"How? You said it yourself—she's not a witch anymore."

"She has good ideas."

"We already have Taff for that."

"It's different. Taff is smart. Grace is . . . crafty."

"Which makes her dangerous."

"If she was going to do something bad she would have done it by now," Kara said.

"Maybe that's what she wants you to believe," Lucas replied. "Maybe she's just biding her time, waiting for the right moment."

"To do what?"

"We're searching for an all-powerful grimoire. Grace might be playing nice so she can steal it for herself."

"Grace said she's done with magic . . ."

"And we just believe what Grace says now?"

". . . and," Kara added, "she didn't even know the *Vulkera* existed until *after* she joined us."

Lucas ran his good hand—the one with all its fingers— through his hair.

"There's much I haven't told you about the past year," he said. "Things I wish I never saw." His voice grew soft, as though he were reluctant to speak these thoughts aloud. "But the very worst horrors, the acts that made me wonder if the Fold had been right about magic all along—they all had one thing in common. Once a grimoire has a witch in its clutches, she'll do anything to keep its power. *Anything.*" He met Kara's eyes. Perhaps it was just her imagination, but in that moment they seemed a hue darker, as though stained by what they had seen. "Do you truly believe that Grace, of all people, has given up magic completely?"

"I think it's possible," Kara said, crossing her arms.

Lucas looked up at the morning sun.

"Maybe you're right. Maybe she has changed. I've never pretended to understand how that girl's mind works. But cutting her hair off, claiming how homesick she is, it all feels a little—"

"Pitiable?"

"Calculated," Lucas said. "She knows you, Kara. The more helpless someone is, the more you'll want to help them. Grace might be taking advantage of that."

"I could be making a mistake," Kara said. "I fully acknowledge that. But when I woke up this morning, one of my mother's favorite sayings was knocking around my head. 'If you're going to err, err on the side of compassion.'"

"I believe that's true," Lucas said. "For the most part. But you can't save everyone, Kara."

"Why not?" she asked.

"Because not everyone wants to be saved."

They walked back to the camp in silence. Taff was still deeply asleep, but Grace had begun to gather her belongings. She paused and looked at Kara expectantly, waiting for her decision.

"Hurry up," Kara said. "We haven't got all day."

Ignoring the disapproving look on Lucas's face, Kara set to filling their canteens. She wasn't sure how much Dolrose Castle had changed in two thousand years, but a desert was a desert and she doubted that they would find much in the way of fresh water. After she had packed away the canteens, she called forth a sleek falcon and slipped a message to her father into its talon. She made sure that the falcon understood to deliver the message only when her father was alone; being seen with an enchanted bird would hardly help his standing as a witch hunter who hated magic.

A more difficult problem was what to do with Shadowdancer and Darno.

Kara supposed that they might be able to secure the scorpion-wolf to Rattle's back with enough rope, but it was risky and Darno would hate every minute of it. Shadowdancer, on the other hand, would be impossible to transport without some sort of harness. Taff had half a dozen ideas about how to accomplish this, but Kara was worried about not only the time it would take to gather the materials and construct the contraption, but also how Shadowdancer would react to her legs dangling through the air.

It was Grace who came up with the best solution.

"Shadowdancer rode with the graycloaks for quite some time, right? Do you think she could find them again on her own?"

"She's a runner, not a tracker," Kara said. "But if Darno were there to help her—yes, I think it's possible."

Grace glided her hand over the silver patch that ran along Shadowdancer's chest, not quite touching it.

"This is distinctive-looking. I'm sure the graycloaks would recognize her. Shadowdancer would be safe with them until you met up again. And Darno could just follow them at a distance."

Kara ran the idea past the animals. Darno was confident that he could find the graycloaks with ease, but he felt that his place was with Kara, where he could protect her.

By the time you find my father, Kara thought, *he may have a grim. If that's the case, he will be in far more danger than me. And Shadowdancer requires your protection as well. She's special to me and must not come to harm.*

If this is your wish, Darno thought, bowing his head. *I will obey.*

Not obey, Kara said, lifting his head up so she could look into his eyes. *I am not your master. We are friends, you and I. And we shall meet again soon.*

She kissed the scorpion-wolf on the nose and he set off, scouting ahead for the safest path. Kara turned to Shadowdancer and ran her fingers through the mare's mane. "Be safe," Kara whispered. Shadowdancer whinnied and galloped away—happiest, as always, when running free.

By consulting a scrolled map and compass that he had "borrowed" from the graycloaks, Lucas piloted the rustlefoot in the direction of Dolrose Castle. The land beneath them grew increasingly barren, dirt and trees changing to desert sand. They wet rags and tied them around their heads, yet still grew sunburned and windburned and developed sores on their legs from riding so long. At night their sleep was deep and dreamless.

Just when it seemed as though they had left civilization behind and come to the very tip of the world, they arrived at their destination.

The changes that had taken place since Kara's previous visit brought a smile to her face: *Even in the harshest of climes, life still finds a way.* The red shell that covered the area around the castle had cracked in countless places, freeing desert flowers with spiky fronds and narrow geysers of pressurized water. Armored creatures violently slurped from the resultant puddles, while tiny birds with diamond-hard beaks pecked at the shell, digging for food.

They all scattered at Rattle's approach. The rustle-foot landed carefully, not wanting to slip, and Kara slid off her back.

Dolrose Castle loomed before her.

It was still standing, but just barely—the magic that had kept it from crumbling into pieces was finally beginning to fade. The northernmost tower had collapsed into the sand, and errant sandstone clung to dangling strips in the red shell like scabs in need of removal.

Kara started toward the castle and Rattle nudged her gently back.

Don't.

"What is it?"

Inside big red house. Smell foul like death.

"There was a great tragedy here," Kara said. "Many died. It's to be expected."

No. Not dead death. Living death.

"The faenix," Kara muttered.

She reached out with her *wexari* senses, listening to the sounds of the hidden world just as Mary Kettle had taught her. At first she caught the thoughts of the armored creatures, bored of water and eager to taste the liquid gushing through the veins of these new arrivals. After building a quick mind-bridge and putting these ambitions to rest, Kara focused on the ruins. Inside the castle she sensed only a single presence, but nestled inside this one mind, like spiders in an egg sac, were thousands of voices, each a slightly different variation on the original. They all shared the same thought, a magically implanted command that was even more important than eating or breathing.

Protect the chest. Protect the chest. Protect the chest.

"What do you hear?" Lucas asked, noticing Kara's bone-white face.

"There's only one creature inside the castle, but there's also enough of it to fill the entire world."

"Have you lost your mind?" Grace asked. "I'm not judging. Just curious."

"I don't really understand what I'm hearing, to be honest."

"It's a monster," Grace said, stifling a yawn. "Isn't that your area of expertise? Just order it to come out here and drop the chest at your feet. Maybe you can give it a treat and a little pat on the head."

Taff burst out laughing.

"What?" he asked in reaction to Kara's displeased expression. "That was funny."

"I can't just control any creature I want," Kara told

Grace. "Unlike using a grimoire, it requires a certain amount of skill and craft. And whatever is inside that castle might be too powerful for me. I'm not sure how we should proceed."

"Distract it," Grace said. "You use magic. Lucas uses his bow. And while the faenix is busy with you two, the whelp steals the grim."

"That's actually a pretty good plan," Taff said.

Grace curtsied.

Kara didn't savor the idea of sending Taff anywhere near the faenix, but she didn't like the idea of being apart from him, either. Since Taff had carved his name into the Lower Door, Kara hadn't let him out of her sight. For all she knew, Querin could be watching them right now, waiting for her to leave Taff alone.

If Querin comes for Taff while I'm inside the castle I won't be able to protect him. At least if we go with Grace's plan we'll stay together.

As was often the case, Kara's decision came down to

figuring out which was the lesser of two evils.

"All right," Kara said. "Let's try it."

"What about you, Grace?" Lucas asked. "What's your contribution to this brilliant plan?"

"I'm going to stay behind and watch Rattle," Grace said. "Imagine if something *terrible* happened to her! We'd be stuck in the middle of nowhere, with no way to get home!"

The logic seemed reasonable enough, but the words sounded vaguely threatening coming from Grace's mouth, as though she were the one planning to hurt Rattle. *That wouldn't make any sense, though*, Kara thought. *Then she'd be stuck here too.* Still, Grace's motives were as difficult to discern as a black cat at night, and Kara was suddenly nervous leaving the rustle-foot alone.

Lucas was right. It would have been safer to leave Grace behind.

Safer, yes—but could Kara have really done it? *She has no one else in the world. If I abandon her, what kind of person does that make me?* On the other hand, was the distant possibility of bringing her enemy back into the light worth endangering the lives of Lucas and her brother? *Not everyone wants to be saved*, Lucas had said. If that was true—and Kara wasn't convinced it was—then cutting ties with Grace was the obvious decision, the *easy* decision.

That didn't make it right.

Allowing Grace to come with us might turn out to be a terrible mistake, Kara thought, *but it was still the right choice.*

Nevertheless, she told the sharp-beaked birds to keep an eye on Rattle and make sure that the blue-eyed girl behaved herself. A little caution had never hurt anyone.

TWELVE

In its prime, Dolrose Castle must have been truly amazing. The arches leading from one massive hall to the next were filigreed with gold. Marble fountains stood in the center of each room. Bejeweled walls refracted the sun's rays into dazzling mosaics of color on the floor. Now, though, arches and fountains were covered with the same hard shell as the exterior walls, and the sunlight that made its way into the castle was filtered red. It was like seeing the world through the prism of a ruby.

The shell covering the stone floor had been broken

into shards that crunched beneath their feet like crushed ice. Kara's hopes of taking the faenix by surprise quickly faded.

"What is this stuff anyway?" Taff asked, picking up a shard. Though it was as thin as a sheet of paper he was unable to break it between his hands. "Tougher than it looks. Like ice, only it's not cold."

"Must have been one of Evangeline's spells," Kara said.

"Guess she didn't like being a princess," said Lucas. "Doesn't make sense to me. If I grew up in a place like this, I'd be pretty happy."

"You can't know that for sure," said Kara. "You *didn't* grow up in a place like this."

"You're right," he said. "I grew up a slave risking his life every day burning poisonous plants." Smiling slightly, he indicated their once lavish surroundings. "This seems better."

Kara, ready to debate the point, couldn't help but smile in return. Lucas had a sneaky sense of humor, peeking out at the most serious of moments. She had missed it.

"No one answered my question," Taff said, still brandishing the red shard. "What is this made of? Why this specific spell? Evangeline could have just burned the castle down to the ground if she hated it that much."

"I don't know if it was even Evangeline's choice," Kara said. "The grimoire must have been controlling her completely at the end."

"How could it, though?" Lucas asked. "If what Sordyr said was the truth, and the grimoire was just a harmless plaything—"

"Sordyr wouldn't lie," Kara said, surprised at how defensive she felt on his behalf. "He never meant for any of this to happen."

"Fine," Lucas said. "But there's no denying that grimoires exert an evil influence. If Sordyr didn't make them that way, it must have been the princess. Which means she was in control until the very end."

"I guess," Kara said, though she still had trouble

believing that it was true. How had Minoth and King Penta described the girl? *Cute little thing? The apple of her parents' eye?* She looked around at the ruins of the castle.

Could she have really done all this?

"What about Rygoth?" Taff asked. "She was the king's adviser at the time. I'm sure she was involved somehow."

"Maybe she's the one who destroyed the castle," Lucas said.

"Rygoth hated Minoth," said Taff, nodding his head in agreement. "And the Last Spell transformed Phadeen, his pride and joy, into the Well of Witches. Plus Rygoth is a lot more powerful than some princess. It makes sense."

"No," said Kara. "This was definitely the work of the princess and the *Vulkera*—Minoth Dravania said as much. Plus Rygoth is vain beyond all measure. If this was her doing she would've bragged about it by now."

That doesn't mean she's not involved, though. Could she have taken over the princess's mind and forced her to do all these things?

"Where are all the people?" Taff asked. "The bodies, I mean—or the bones, at this point."

"Lord Gareth probably sent them to safety once he knew how dangerous his daughter had become," Kara said.

She didn't think Taff believed her, but it was a nice story.

They entered the throne room.

It was surprisingly simple. The thrones, if indeed they could be called that, were little more than fancy wooden chairs. Stools had been set out so that those who requested an audience with Lord Gareth could sit comfortably. Kara was left with the impression of a leader who exerted his authority by the quality of his rule, not force or wealth.

"Where are these scratches from?" Lucas asked, running his finger along deep grooves in the stone floor. "I saw a bunch of them outside too."

"It looks like someone was dragging something," Taff said.

On the far side of the room, a large shape darted between two wooden posts and vanished into the shadows.

Kara didn't ask if the two boys had seen it. Lucas already had an arrow notched to his bow. Taff's slingshot was pulled back.

They had seen it.

"Hello," Kara said, reaching out with her powers. To build a mind-bridge, she first needed to learn what the creature wanted; she could then build a link with it using corresponding memories from her own experience. All of the faenix's thoughts, however, were buried beneath the one command magically grafted into its mind: *Protect the chest.*

"We don't want to hurt you," Kara said, slowly making her way closer to the shadowy corner where the faenix had vanished.

Deep with the darkness, something moved.

"Kara," Lucas whispered.

She put one finger to her lips while indicating, with her other hand, that he and Taff should stay put. Kara sent the faenix images of water rippling along a peaceful pond, hoping to calm it.

I know your job is guarding the chest, she told the creature. *And you've done it faithfully for a long, long time now. But your responsibility was to keep what's inside the chest from bad people, not from us. We're here to*—

The faenix leaped out of the shadows.

Its entire body was covered with black-and-red scales save three chicken legs that ended in razor-sharp talons. Kara fell backward in surprise and enormous yellow eyes tracked her, blinking rapidly with two pairs of eyelids— from top to bottom, left to right.

Lucas whispered, "I don't think this one is listening to you."

"Just give me a little more—"

The faenix threw back its head and screeched. A sound like metal scraping against metal reverberated throughout the throne room as the creature rushed her, red claws extended.

Kara heard a *thwack* and Lucas's glorb-powered arrow passed through the creature's chest, clacking against the wall behind it.

The faenix fell to the ground and stopped moving.

"You hurt?" Lucas asked Kara, helping her to her feet.

She shook her head. "Nice shot."

"I've been practicing," Lucas replied. "Still, after everything you said I thought it would be harder than that."

"Me too," Kara admitted. "But I'm not complaining. Now all we have to do is find the grim. If this thing was guarding it, you figure it has to be close."

"Found it!" Taff exclaimed.

He pointed directly at the fallen faenix. For a moment Kara didn't understand what he meant. But then, looking closer, she saw the red corner of the chest, seemingly poking out of the creature itself.

"It has a pouch in its stomach," Taff said. "I've heard of animals who carry their young around like that so they can protect them. Only this one carries around a red chest. So weird!"

Lucas stepped closer to the faenix.

"Wait," Kara said. She still heard a chorus of thoughts emanating from the motionless body before her. But how could that be? The arrow had passed right through its heart.

"It's dead," Lucas said. "Right?"

"Yes," Kara said. "No. I'm not sure."

"Thanks for clearing that up," Lucas replied, smiling nervously. "Okay, then. I guess there's only one way to—"

The faenix shuddered violently.

"Not dead!" Taff shouted, pulling Lucas back. "Not dead!"

The beast's yellow eyes sank into its body with a sucking sound and its chicken legs shriveled into dust. The seams between its scales vanished as the separate plates joined together, covering every inch of the body. Within moments, the faenix had vanished completely, leaving behind a speckled red egg.

It hatched.

This wasn't a slow process—the steady pecking away of an unsure beak trying to find its mother—but an eruption of life, shell fragments exploding everywhere as a new, fully grown creature sprang forth into the world. It was twice the size of its predecessor, with the same black and red scales but a fiercer demeanor.

Lucas fired an arrow. It bounced ineffectually off the faenix's chest.

Its scales have changed, Kara thought. *They're as hard as armor now.*

The faenix opened its beak, revealing rows of new fangs, and charged. Kara dove out of the way as it swung its talon at her. Taff screamed "Over here!" while firing with his slingshot. *Ping, ping, ping!* The invisible projectiles didn't seem to hurt the faenix, but they got its attention. Leaving Kara behind for now, it galloped in a lurching quickstep toward Taff.

Lucas took careful aim and shot an arrow through its eye. The faenix collapsed.

Kara wondered how long its death would last this time.

"Get the chest!" she shouted. "Quick!"

Lucas was closest, but by the time he reached the faenix its shell had begun to harden into an egg again. He tried to pierce it with arrows but the shell was impenetrable.

It hatched even quicker than the first one.

The faenix that emerged took some time to unfold itself. This version towered over the children—though it retained the same chicken legs, looking somewhat ridiculous supporting its now-monstrous frame—and had grown steel plates for eyes. The creature tottered unsteadily, still groggy with birth, and the children used this opportunity to sprint out of the throne room and into the main hall.

"This way!" Taff exclaimed, leading them through a smaller archway on their right. "It's too big to fit through here."

There were no windows in this part of the castle. Although a little light slipped through the cracks in the edifice, the passageway that stretched before them vanished into darkness. She could hear the faenix in the main hall, shards cracking beneath its newfound weight. It was looking for them. From this angle, Kara could see only its disproportionately thin legs and the curl of a new, snake-like tail.

The children backed away, keeping their eyes on the beast. They spoke in whispers.

"I saw some pretty strange monsters when I was a Clearer," Lucas said, inadvertently touching the stumps of his two fingers. "But I've never seen anything like that before. Can someone explain—"

"Each time it dies, it's born again as a better version," Kara said. "It learns from its mistakes. Adapts. You can't kill it the same way twice."

"That's hardly fair," Taff said.

"Then how do you kill it?" Lucas asked.

Kara shrugged. "I don't know if you can."

An undefeatable foe, the perfect guardian for the grim, Kara thought. *That's why I heard so many voices when I tried to build a mind-bridge. Within this strange creature are thousands of possible lives, ready to be called into existence when needed.*

The corridor crooked to the right into even deeper darkness. They followed it, holding their hands outward to protect themselves from walking face-first into an unseen obstacle.

It was colder in this area of the castle. Kara's teeth began to chatter involuntarily.

"Hold on," said Lucas, digging in his rucksack as they backed cautiously away from the doorway. He pulled out a glass lantern filled with water, unscrewed a tiny knob in its lid, and dropped what looked like a tiny tapioca pearl through the hole. As the glorb dissolved the water began to swirl light, casting the corridor in an eerie blue glow that revealed hundreds of deep gouges in the floor, identical to the ones that Lucas had found in the throne room.

"I think I liked it better when we couldn't see," Taff said.

As Kara bent down to examine the gouges more closely she heard a mad hiss of frustration and the crash of a large body against the stone archway. Again. And again. The walls of the corridor shook with each impact.

"We need to keep moving," Lucas said. "We're trapped if that thing finds a way through."

They ran down the corridor, the sounds growing more distant and then suddenly stopping altogether, plunging the castle into an eerie silence. The floor sloped downward and emptied into a ballroom with a domed glass ceiling. The sand that had collected on the exterior of the glass blocked much of the sunlight, but the ballroom was still bright enough to reveal hundreds of red blocks standing upright on the floor like giant dominoes.

"What are they?" Taff asked nervously.

The blocks varied in height. Some were shorter than Taff, others rose taller than Kara. All were semitransparent, with shadowy shapes within them.

"Stay here," Kara told Taff. "Let me see what this is first."

She approached the nearest block for a closer look and jumped back in surprise.

A man had been entombed inside like a fly stuck in amber. He retained the general appearance of a living person, but his preserved face was doughy, as though the bones beneath his skin had dissolved long ago. Kara imagined that the block was the only thing keeping him together, and that if she cracked it open the corpse would pour to the ground in a puddle of decayed flesh and muscle.

"What is it?" Taff asked.

"Don't get any closer," Lucas said, waving him away.

He had taken a glimpse inside a different block and was bent over on his knees, his face ashen. "You don't need to see this."

Kara glimpsed inside a few more blocks and saw much of the same. The final moments of these people had not been peaceful. A soldier with his shield raised. A little boy covering his face with two hands. A young woman, either mad or oblivious, caught in midlaugh.

It was while Kara was looking at this last one that Taff, his curiosity finally getting the best of him, snuck up behind her and took a peek. He immediately turned away and buried his face in Kara's cloak. It wasn't often that he reacted so strongly to the horrors they faced on an all-too-frequent basis, and this need for comfort caught her by surprise.

"Sorry," he said. "Monsters are one thing, but these people—that's what death really looks like. Faces blank and everything gone inside. It just hit me that some-day . . . someday soon . . ."

He's thinking about what's going to happen when Querin returns for him.

She rubbed his back gently.

"I won't let him take you," Kara said. "Not now. Not ever."

"I know," he said, straightening. He drew the magic slingshot from his belt. "I'm fine now."

Lucas, understanding that the two siblings needed a private moment, had strayed to another corner of the room. He called back to them now.

"The gouges on the floor end in this room," he said. "These people were all over the castle when Evangeline cast the spell that encased them in these blocks. It wasn't until afterward that something dragged them all here."

"It must have been the faenix," Kara said. "But why?"

Taff gasped.

"Look!" he said, clutching Kara's arm. "Those two girls over there have been angled together so that one looks like she's whispering in the other's ear. And those soldiers—the one with the sword and the one with the shield—could be having a fight! These people haven't just been dragged here. They've been *arranged*. Like toys."

Now that this pattern had been pointed out to her, Kara could see that it was true. The blocks had been placed together in groups of two or more, giving the impression that people whose paths might have barely crossed in real life were eternally arguing or walking together or sitting down for a meal. Those who did not conveniently fit into any of these forced groups waited along the walls like lonely souls at a dance.

"These poor people," Taff said. "Why would it treat them like this?"

"It's a monster," Lucas said. "It doesn't know what compassion is. Otherwise why would it have made this"—he struggled to find the appropriate word—"graveyard?"

"You're wrong," Kara said. "A true monster only cares about feeding and killing. It wouldn't go through all the trouble of moving these blocks at all. That requires a certain degree of thought. We're missing something here."

Kara felt like she had all the pieces to a puzzle but didn't know how to configure them in a way that made sense. *One creature with countless voices. Bodies arranged like toys. Guard the chest. Remain in the castle.* The answer was so close. If she could just sit down and think about it for a few minutes she knew she could figure it out.

The faenix stumbled into the room.

No time, Kara thought.

It was a new version: much smaller, with yellow eyes that glowed in their sockets and skin the color of a plucked turkey. The faenix took a few tottering steps toward them and then stopped, hacking pathetically until it spit out a glob of green phlegm.

"How did it change again?" Lucas asked. "We didn't kill it."

"It kept hitting itself against the wall until it died," Taff said. "That's why it got quiet so suddenly."

"Why would it do that?" Lucas asked.

"Because it needed to hatch again into a version small enough to fit through the archway," Taff said.

"And the glowing eyes are so it could see in the dark," Kara added. "That makes sense." She watched the faenix fall to the ground and struggle to rise again. "But why does it seem so sick?"

"Maybe it's getting weaker," Lucas suggested, raising his bow. "Maybe it can only resurrect itself so many times. Let's find out."

"No!" Taff shouted.

He was too late. Lucas's arrow hit its mark. The faenix fell.

"What?" Lucas asked.

"Now that it's here it needs a more powerful body!" Taff exclaimed as though it was the most obvious thing in the world. "That's why it made itself so weak—as soon as this version died, it could hatch into something stronger! You just gave it what it wanted! Look!"

Something was happening to the faenix's body. The scales rose to the surface and fused together, forming a new egg that quickly swelled in size, knocking down many of the red tombs and blocking off the only exit from the room.

The shell split apart, revealing a new version of the faenix curled into a tight ball.

It rose and seemed like it would never stop rising, unfolding itself until its head was nearly as high as the ceiling. Its scales had been replaced by brown skin with the half-melted appearance of dried mud, and there were no eyes on its face—these could be found only at the ends of the dozens of tentacles trained on the children. *It wants to make sure it doesn't lose us this time*, Kara thought. Reaching out with two long limbs, the faenix pressed its claws against the upper walls of the castle for balance and stared down at them. Past the tentacles, and well out of reach, Kara caught a tantalizing glimpse of the red chest in its pouch.

She felt Taff trembling next to her.

"What do we do?" he asked, frozen with fear.

"I'll distract it," Lucas said. "Look for a way out."

He fired two quick arrows. They hit the faenix in the chest with a disheartening lack of sound and sunk harmlessly into its body.

A tentacle whipped around Lucas's ankle and tossed him across the room like a child's toy.

"Lucas!" Kara screamed. She ran toward him, but the faenix shuffled over to block her way. A tentacle wrapped itself around her neck and squeezed tight. Kara gasped for breath and found none.

Please, she said, reaching out with her mind. *Don't do this. We mean you no harm.*

But it was like talking in a crowded street, her voice impossible to distinguish among the thousand others. There was no way for her to build the necessary connection to the faenix that her magic required.

The room began to grow hazy. Darkness tugged at her with greedy hands.

"Don't move," Taff exclaimed, placing his slingshot against the tentacle.

He pulled the sling back as far as it would go and released it.

Kara fell to the floor as the faenix wailed in pain, throwing all its tentacles high into the air and inadvertently punching through the ceiling. Glass and sand rained to the floor. Kara saw a man-size shard dropping toward her and rolled to her right just before it shattered against the stone. Broken slivers stung the back of her neck.

"Come on!" Taff shouted, pulling her up. The faenix, trying to escape this sudden onslaught of glass, had forgotten about them for a moment. *It's distracted*, Kara thought. *This is our chance.* Only there was nowhere to run. The walls were made of stone and the faenix was still blocking the only exit. *Maybe we can climb on its back and onto the roof?* Kara thought. *No, that won't work, especially if Lucas is hurt.*

She pulled Taff behind a pair of the red blocks: a man caught in a half yawn listening to another man yakking away.

What do we do? What do we do?

Kara heard a dragging sound. She risked a peek around the corner of their hiding spot and saw the faenix wrapping its tentacles around the red blocks, setting the ones that had fallen upright again.

"What's it doing?" Taff whispered.

"Oh!" Kara exclaimed, the fear leaving her body. "I understand now! Poor thing!"

I should have figured it out before, she thought. *But I was too busy thinking about the grim. What I wanted. Not this pitiable creature.*

Kara took a seat on the floor, her back pressed against the red block, and closed her eyes. She knew what the faenix wanted now. *So lonely in this castle for all these years. It didn't arrange those people to glorify death. It was lonely and wanted to feel like it was surrounded by talking, laughing, living. The dead were its only companions.*

Kara remembered a simple dinner when she was four years old. Sitting on Father's lap while Mother told a story to Aunt Abby and Constance Lamb. The laughter and candlelight and warmth. *They were so involved in their conversation that Aunt Abby burned the cake, but they ate it all anyway, every bite.* It was a memory that Kara treasured, but she reluctantly sacrificed it to build a mind-bridge and heard the faenix screech with surprise as she slipped inside its mind.

Tears came to Kara's eyes as she felt the depths of its loneliness.

It's not fair, she said. *Minoth was cruel to abandon you here for so long. Leave us the chest and go. Explore the world! I release you from your duty.*

Kara gifted other memories of friendship. At first the faenix seemed to be mollified, but gradually its anger rose. Kara's memories were just a tease of companionship, like looking upon a crowded city from a locked tower.

What do you want? Kara thought.

MY OWN, the faenix replied.

I can't do that. It's beyond my powers.

MY OWN. OR YOU WILL STAY HERE. FOREVER.

"Kara," Taff said, his voice strained. Her eyes were closed, so she couldn't see the tentacle around his neck, but she sensed its presence. "I dropped my slingshot. I can't—"

"Shh," Kara said. "I won't let it hurt you. Everything's going to be all right."

"I'm . . . glad," Taff choked, "you're so . . . confident."

Kara took a deep breath to steady her nerves and began to create the faenix a companion. It was different than it had been with Topper. She had molded the yonstaff from her own imagination, but here the building materials could only be found within the faenix itself, chosen from a thousand voices longing to be freed. Kara set out her strongest memories of companionship like a trail of breadcrumbs, trying to lure one of these half lives to fruition, but they remained in place.

A regular memory won't cut it, she thought. *It has to be something more powerful than that. Life-altering.*

She knew the perfect choice, but she hesitated, not wanting to sacrifice it.

Let it go. You have to.

Kara remembered what it had been like to hold her baby brother for the very first time: the warmth of his body, the trusting eyes looking up beneath the folds of the blanket, the joyous feeling that she would never be alone again. In some ways, it had been the day that she was born as well.

Kara released the memory.

One of the voices in the faenix leaped at it eagerly, and once the hook was bitten Kara pulled back with all her might, trying to reel the disembodied entity into the world. Just as it had with Topper, this great expenditure of magic attracted the mind leeches like bystanders to a blazing fire. They clung to the bridge between Kara and the faenix, sucking away at her past with voracious appetites. This time, however, Kara was ready.

Get off! she commanded, shaking the bridge.

The mind leeches dropped into the void, taking several irreplaceable moments of Kara's childhood with them.

Something materialized in her arms.

It was no bigger than a dog but looked very much like the original faenix, with black-and-red scales and chicken legs. Its glossy eyes were the color of finished pinewood.

"Welcome to the world, little one," Kara said.

The larger faenix, upon seeing the babe cradled in Kara's arms, instantly released its hold on Taff and screeched with desperate longing. Its voice rang through Kara's head: *MINE! MINE!*

Kara rose on aching limbs and faced the creature.

"I'll trade you the child for the red chest," Kara said. She held out the little creature, now nibbling playfully on her finger. "Besides, you're going to need room in that pouch of yours for this one. A fair exchange, don't you think?"

The faenix roared angrily, and a large pane of glass shook loose from the ceiling and shattered against the floor.

WE MUST PROTECT THE CHEST, a cloud of voices screamed at her.

"You long for the child in my arms more than anything," Kara said sympathetically. "But that command has woven itself into the very fabric of your being. You are incapable of disobeying it."

WE MUST PROTECT THE CHEST. And then, softer, with a hint of regret: WE CAN DO NOTHING ELSE.

"I understand," Kara said. She smiled as an idea formed in her mind. "But perhaps we can come to a compromise."

Kara told the faenix her plan, and the creature, after a long moment of indecision, agreed to it. After all, it would not technically be disobeying the order that Minoth had imprinted into its brain. That was all that mattered.

Reaching into its pouch, the faenix removed the chest and pounded it on the floor until the lid burst open. Sheaves of loose paper spilled across the floor. Taff set to gathering them.

The faenix slid the chest back in its pouch.

WE MUST PROTECT THE CHEST, it thought.

"You do that," said Kara, smiling. "Never let it out of your sight."

She placed the tiny creature on the floor and it crawled

toward the faenix, sniffing its leg with curiosity. As Taff finished gathering the papers Kara found Lucas, who rose shakily to his feet but was able to walk on his own. The three children made their way out of the ballroom. Kara looked back one last time and saw the faenix cradling the newborn and clicking softly in its ear.

She hoped it was a lullaby.

THIRTEEN

The children did not feel safe spending the night so close to the accursed castle, and so they flew Rattle south for an hour and then made camp. Though the sun had barely slipped beneath its covers, the two boys fell quickly asleep. Kara watched them, and the persistent worries that shadowed her thoughts slipped away.

The night is warm. We are together. All is well.

Kara wished that she could fall asleep beneath this unexpected blanket of contentment, but there was something that she needed to do first.

She shifted her attention from the sleeping boys to the pages of the *Vulkera*. Taff had bound them together with a rope crossed and tied at the center, and Kara used this knot to lift them now, careful not to touch the actual pages. She dropped the entire thing close to the campfire, so she could gaze upon them in the best possible light. It landed on the sand with a soft thud.

Grace took a seat just behind her. Kara studied the girl's face, wondering if she would revert to her old ways in the presence of such magical power. There was no possessiveness in the girl's eyes, however—only intense curiosity.

"There are fewer pages than in our grimoire," she said.

"Only sixteen," Kara said. "Taff counted. And it wasn't *our* grimoire. We don't share anything, you and I."

"If you say so," Grace said. "Are you going to cast a spell?"

"It won't work."

"Why not? You can tear pages out of a grimoire and

still use them. We've both done it."

"If it were that easy, then this is the only grim that Rygoth would care about. The *Vulkera* won't work again until it's restored completely." Kara studied Grace's face suspiciously. "Why? You thinking of trying to cast a spell when I'm not paying attention?"

"How many times do I have to tell you? I'm done being a witch!" Grace placed her hands on her hips. "Sometimes I feel like you just don't trust me! Really, Kara, what have I ever done to you?"

Kara was about to say something unladylike in response when the crack of a smile split Grace's lips.

"You're joking," said Kara. "That's funny."

"I thought so."

"Anyway, these pages are useless without the other three grims," Kara said.

"So then why won't you touch the pages?"

"Because I can *hear* them," Kara said.

Grace slid closer, her curiosity aroused.

"Is it a Whisperer?" she asked.

For a few moments, while discussing the strange inner workings of magic, Kara had almost felt a kinship with Grace, their previous history forgotten. But this current turn in the conversation forced Kara to recall Grace's job in the Well of Witches: to whisper in the ears of those caught in the thrall of the grimoire, tempting them to do harm.

Never forget who she is, Kara thought, on her guard again.

"It's not a Whisperer," Kara said. "It's not trying to get me to cast a spell."

"Then what do you hear?"

"I'm not really sure. Whatever it is, it sounds like it's really far away. Like I'm standing on a mountain listening to something happening on the ground.

"Maybe you could hear it clearer if you actually touched a page," Grace offered.

"This isn't a normal grimoire. I don't know what will happen."

"You're scared."

Kara turned to Grace. "You don't hear *anything*?"

"Nothing. Then again, I'm out of practice."

Even though Grace had gotten rid of her grimoire, Kara still had trouble believing that she had renounced magic forever. If they were going to continue to travel together, she needed to put her doubts to rest once and for all.

"Here," Kara said, picking up the bundle by the knot. "Maybe you'll hear it too if you get close enough."

She dropped the pages at Grace's feet.

The girl reacted as though Kara had tossed a rattle-snake in her direction, flinging herself backward and crawling away like a crab, her ruined leg dragging along the ground. "*Get it away from me!*" she screamed, slapping at the air. "If I feel the magic I'm going to want to cast a spell and then another one and then before I know it I'll be back there and then *the Faceless will make me one of them!*"

"I'm sorry," Kara said, her cheeks flushed with shame.

"I shouldn't have done that. I just needed to know for sure that you weren't lying to me."

Grace folded her knees to her chest and looked away. Her entire body shook with feverish convulsions.

"Who's the cruel one now?" she asked softly.

Kara didn't apologize again; she knew there were no words that could undo her action. Instead, she reached down, intending to pick up the grim by the knot and move it out of sight. Her hands were trembling, however, and she accidentally brushed the top page with her index finger.

Suddenly she was no longer herself.

This new mind in which she currently resided had only ever known bleakness and despair. Its oppressive weight pressed down on Kara, and she reached out desperately for a single recollection of love, a trickle of light to buoy her in the darkness. Kara had lost access to her own memories, however, and this mind was an alien landscape that had never experienced even the most workaday of kindnesses: a tucked blanket, a warm smile, a goodnight kiss.

No light. No hope. No love.

Kara opened her eyes.

A desperate need for human contact overwhelmed her, like a drowning girl who breaks free of the surface and gasps for air. She grabbed the first person she saw—Grace—and held her tight.

"What's . . . happening . . . right . . . now?" Grace asked. Her arms were ramrod still at her sides, her breath squeezed beneath Kara's embrace.

Lucas and Taff, awoken by all the commotion, stared at Kara with alarmed expressions. Grace tried to indicate with raised arms that she had no idea what was going on, but Kara was holding her so tightly that she could only manage to flap her hands.

"Evangeline!" Kara exclaimed, tears flowing from her eyes. "I felt what it was like to be her. It was terrible! She hadn't known a single moment of happiness her entire life. No one had ever . . . not one act of kindness, of compassion. All she knew was hate and disdain and . . . I couldn't take it a moment longer. It was like . . . suffocating in sorrow. It's no wonder she did the things she did."

Grace managed to free one arm and patted her on the back.

"There . . . there," she said. "This is all . . . very tragic. But I need . . . to breathe. . . ."

Kara jumped back, suddenly realizing who was in her arms.

"Sorry," she said, wiping the tears from her eyes with the back of one hand.

Grace waved Kara's apology away, too flustered to respond. She used her walking stick to rise to her feet, and leaned on it heavily.

"This means that Evangeline's spirit is trapped inside the *Vulkera*," Taff said. "Just like Minoth said."

"Yes," Kara said. "I'm sure of it." Noticing that there were no longer any sounds coming from the grim, she held her hand above the top page, like testing to see if a pan was hot, and then touched it with the pad of a finger.

Nothing happened.

"Is she gone?" Taff asked.

"Not exactly," Kara said. "But that's all she can show me right now. She's weak. It's because we only have a single grim."

"So you're saying that if we put the *Vulkera* back together, we'll restore Evangeline's spirit as well?" Lucas asked.

"We might," Kara said.

"And is that a good thing or a bad thing?"

Kara wasn't sure. She had never experienced such complete desolation in her life. *Even the deadliest creatures in the Thickety knew the joy of a good kill, or the satisfaction that comes from teaching their young to hunt.* Princess Evangeline, on the other hand, was just *empty*: closer to a shell than an actual human being.

And yet Minoth and King Penta had said she was such a

happy child. What happened?

"Rygoth," Kara said. "It can't just be a coincidence that she was at Dolrose Castle. What did she do to that poor girl?"

They set out for Kutt the next morning, leaving the desert behind and flying over a mountainous region sprinkled with tiny villages and encampments. The devastation that Rygoth had wrought was even more obvious from the sky: burning villages, caravans of people fleeing their old lives, houses toppled to the ground. The worst part, Lucas pointed out, was that Rygoth might not have even been to these areas at all. Her mere presence in Sentium was enough to create chaos.

"I saw a lot of that when I was with the graycloaks," Lucas said. "People hear stories about the great evil coming their way and they panic, lose track of who they are. They steal, hurt others—all in the name of survival." A somber expression settled over his features, making him look far older. "It wasn't always witches we fought in order to keep the peace," he said.

"That's terrible!" Taff exclaimed. "Why can't everyone just stick together?"

"They're scared," said Lucas, placing a comforting hand on Taff's back. "And it wasn't everyone. Some people rise to the occasion. And not always the people you'd expect."

"Like us!" Taff exclaimed.

Kara was certain that Grace was going to roll her eyes, but instead she simply looked away.

By the fourth day, they had passed beyond the mountains and there were no more villages. The land below them grew swampy. Sickly-looking trees lay half submerged in green water; pockets of gas belched noxious fumes into the sky. At the end of each day, Kara built mind-bridges to a few local creatures suitable for guarding them during the night. It wasn't as easy as it used to be. Her mind, once a well from which she could draw memories with ease, had begun to run dry.

Too many spells, Kara thought. *I have to slow down.*

At the very least, she couldn't risk conjuring another creature from nothing, as she had with Topper and the baby faenix. Spells of creation—and the mind leeches they drew like moths to a flame—drained her far more than any other magic. *How does Rygoth create animals so easily?* Kara wondered. Sometimes she felt as though she were doing magic completely wrong, like a carpenter trying to build a house with a garden hoe.

Then again, maybe Rygoth is so powerful that the rules don't apply to her.

It was a disheartening thought that put Kara in a foul mood for the rest of the journey, which went on a full four days longer. Finally, just after she decided that she might in fact exchange the grim in their possession for a hot bath, they saw a black mist in the distance.

"The Plague Barrier!" Lucas exclaimed. "We're finally here."

Rattle landed as close to the mist as possible. From the ground it was even more intimidating, a wall of swirling miasma that seemed to blot out the sun. The stench was unbearable. Kara, who had learned much about healing from her mother, recognized the smell of infection gone to rot.

"This is impossible," Taff said while holding his nose. "Mist doesn't just *stop*. It has to spread out. Unless—is there a glass wall or something we don't see?"

"I don't think so," said Lucas. "People call it the Clinging Mist. It never moves. It never leaves. No one can really explain why—though if Grandfather were here I'm sure he'd have all sorts of fascinating theories."

Lucas smiled sadly, and Kara could see how much he missed his only living relative, a kindly old Mistral of Nye's Landing named West. Her heart ached for her friend: *All those years longing to find his family, and after he finally does to have to leave so quickly . . .*

"You'll see him again soon," she said. "And just think

about the stories you can tell him! He'll be so proud of you."

Lucas grinned, comforted by the words.

"I can only tell you what I've heard about the Clinging Mist," he added with renewed energy, "which is mostly rumor and supposition. The most common story, especially by the more religious types, is that the mist is Kutt's divine punishment."

"For what?" Grace asked, with an oddly cheerful lilt.

"They're scientists," Lucas said. "And they specialize in the mysteries of the human body. But there are those who question how they've gone about their research. I won't get into all the grisly details."

"But that's the best part," said Grace.

Taff nodded enthusiastically.

"As far as the Clinging Mist goes," Lucas continued, ignoring them both, "the story is that they were trying to make a disease but things went horribly wrong."

"Why would anyone *try* to make a disease?" Taff asked.

"They were trying to figure out a way to use sickness as a weapon," Lucas said, "but instead they destroyed their entire region. If that mist touches your skin you'll be inflicted with an incurable plague. Death comes quickly."

"Then where do the people live?" Taff asked.

"In underground cities," Lucas said, stroking the area above his upper lip where a few hairs had sprouted. "Can't imagine what kind of life that's like, never seeing the sun."

"How do we get to them?" Kara asked. "Tunnels?"

Lucas shook his head and told them what they needed to find. For once, it was easier than Kara had thought it would be. They hadn't even walked ten minutes before Grace glimpsed the glint of something metallic.

"Swoop station," Lucas said.

His eyes met Kara's, and he instantly blushed and turned away. Kara felt her heart quicken.

Our almost-kiss. He remembers.

The windowless building stood on tall stanchions and was constructed from large plates of flattened steel that had turned black with corrosion. There was no way to determine the length of the station; it began outside the Plague Barrier and vanished into the mist.

They followed a set of rickety stairs into the station.

A long Swoop train dangled from a water-filled track that stretched into the darkness. The train had been corroded black by its many trips through the Clinging Mist, though faint veins of green provided a sad remnant of its original color. Their boot heels clicked against a platform lined with cracked benches and abandoned food stands.

A small booth stood against the wall, the word *TICKETS* glowing glorb blue on its awning. A woman sat behind the glass window.

They approached the booth, Kara in the lead.

"Good morning," Kara said. She found herself whispering, not wanting to disturb the silent station. "I was wondering if you could help us."

The ticket seller looked up.

Her skin was the red of fired clay. Enlarged veins

protruded from her forehead and neck. Kara could see the blood pulsing through them.

"What's wrong with her?" Taff whispered.

"Kuttians are forced to take special medicine from the day they're born," replied Lucas, too soft for the woman behind the window to hear. "It protects them from their proximity to the Clinging Mist . . . but it changes them, too."

"Been weeks since I've seen a visitor," the ticket seller said. "Where you from?"

Kara, caught off guard by the question and uncertain how much of the truth she should reveal, glanced back at the others with a quizzical expression.

"You're in charge," Lucas whispered in her ear, grinning. "You'll think of something."

He gave Kara a playful push toward the window. The woman's expression grew suspicious.

"Where you from?" she repeated slowly. "It's not a hard question."

Grace, smiling sweetly, slid in front of Kara.

"We hail from an island of no consequence, far, far away from here," she said, her hands clasped together. "We hope to bring news of true civilization back to our people."

The ticket seller nodded, apparently satisfied. Grace stepped back behind Kara.

"Good job," whispered Taff.

"Thanks," said Grace. "Lies always go down better with a spoonful of truth. Remember that."

Kara glanced over her shoulder.

"Could you not give my brother life lessons?" she asked.

"Destination?" the ticket seller snapped, tired of being ignored. To her left sat a countertop machine with all sorts of buttons, knobs, and levers. Something shifted behind the woman: a fat cat with spikes like a cactus. It looked up at Kara, quickly decided that she wasn't worth the trouble, and went back to sleep.

"We're not exactly sure," Kara said.

The woman sighed.

"I can't tell you where you're going," she said. "I can only send you there."

Kara remembered that in Ilma Station there had been a board listing possible stops, but there was nothing of the sort here. Apparently you were just expected to know your destination. She thought about what Delvin, that strange representative of Kutt, had told Minoth about the grim: *It will make an excellent addition to our museum.* That was over two thousand years ago, and it could have been moved since then, but she supposed it was worth a try.

"We're heading to the museum," she said.

The woman sighed again, as though this was exactly what she *didn't* need today.

"The great region of Kutt is home to over two hundred sixty-five museums, collections, and cabinets of curiosity. Please specify."

"We're interested in old books," Lucas tried.

"Kutt's largest library is in the city of Zu'norg. I will arrange transport there. If that is not to your liking you can always transfer to another library."

The woman's fingers flew over the machine next to her in a frantic blur: punching buttons, pulling dials.

"I don't know," Taff said. "That doesn't sound right. The weird guy said *museum*, not *library*."

"You're right," Kara said.

Taff tapped the glass with his knuckles, and the woman twisted in his direction, the blood in her veins pumping visibly faster.

"*Do not touch my window!*" she shrieked.

Even the spiked cat raised its head for a moment at that.

"Sorry, ma'am," Taff said. "But I think you're sending us to the wrong spot. We're looking for something that's really, really rare."

"Zu'norg Library has three entire buildings housing rare books."

"Fine," Taff said. "More than just rare. This book is . . . special." Ignoring the warning look in Kara's eyes, he added, "Some might even call it magic."

The ticket seller stopped punching buttons on the machine.

"Why didn't you say that from the start?" she asked.

She squeezed a bulbous lever, apparently erasing all she had done, and began to punch buttons at an even more furious rate. Finally she pulled the largest of the levers and a flat stone with tiny bumps shot upward through a glass tube that took it all the way to the first car of the train.

"The conductor has received your destination. You may board."

"How much is it?" Kara asked nervously. They were almost out of coin, and she was worried that they wouldn't have enough for all of them.

"Transit and admission are free," the woman responded. "The museum's wonders, all nine hundred eighty-six rooms of them, are Kutt's gift to the world." She smiled, revealing teeth that were disturbingly white against her red skin. "In fact, it's said that anyone who visits the Museum of Impossible Things will never look at the world in the same way again."

FOURTEEN

The doors of the train closed behind them with a sucking sound. It was warm inside the car, and stuffy, like a room whose windows have remained shut for an entire season. Lifting the lid off a trunk bolted into the wall, Kara found black jumpsuits and masks connected to metal canisters. According to the placard inside the lid, these were to be used only in the event of an emergency, in which case they would be forced to evacuate the train and traverse the Clinging Mist by foot.

Kara really hoped there wasn't an emergency.

Though it was a fair assumption that someone was driving the train, they were its only passengers. Before they even had time to sit, the Swoop began to pull away and then jerked to a sudden halt. A loud screeching noise filled the car. Pressing her face against a long, soot-cornered window, Kara saw a metal wall in the process of closing behind them, sealing off the station from the infectious air. Once this was done, a second partition opened in front of them, and they pulled out into the darkness.

The ride was smooth, and it was difficult to tell how fast the Swoop was going, though Kara suspected that they were moving very fast indeed. Through swirling mists she saw the shapes of buildings, some abandoned, some cast in the bluish light of the glorb lamps that surrounded them like tiny moons. The track headed off into many directions and glowed in the darkness like a phosphorescent web.

"Except for the threat of horrible death just beyond these windows," Lucas said, "this is actually kind of fun."

He slid into the seat next to her and their hands brushed together. Kara felt her cheeks grow warm. Grace, sitting on the opposite bench, looked from Kara to Lucas and back again.

"Why don't we go see what's in the other cars, Taff?" Grace asked, her eyes remaining on Kara. She grinned in a knowing way.

"Really?" Taff asked, his voice flush with excitement. "You want to *explore?*"

"Oh yes," Grace said in a perfect deadpan. "I live to explore. Make sure you ask a ton of questions, too. That will only make it better."

Taff scrambled to his feet. Kara could still hear him talking as they moved to the next car: "So I think what we should do is start from the very end and then make our way back again. Do you want to count the windows? Also I really want to look underneath all the benches. I find that hidden spots usually hide the most interesting——"

The door between cars slammed shut.

"Do you trust her with Taff alone?" Lucas asked.

"She won't hurt him," Kara said, surprised by how certain she felt. "She likes Taff, in her way."

"It just seems strange, after what you asked me to do," Lucas said, referring to a request that Kara had made several nights ago when everyone else had been asleep. "It made me think that you didn't trust her."

"That was just a precaution," Kara said. "I believe that she's changed, but . . ."

"She's still Grace," Lucas said.

"Can we not talk about her anymore?"

It was the first time that she had been truly alone with Lucas since their reunion. Such privacy should have afforded them the chance to talk about countless matters, but Kara suddenly couldn't think of a single thing to say. She stared down at his hand: three perfect fingers and two stumps. *Did he brush it against mine on purpose? Doesn't he know that if he wants to hold my hand I'll let him? Should I reach out and take his?*

"How are you, Kara?" Lucas asked.

She looked at him strangely. *Perhaps he can't think of anything to say either?*

"Fine," she said. "How . . . how are you?"

"Are you really fine?" he asked. "I can't tell. Back on De'Noran, I always knew what you were thinking. That was the best part of my day, meeting you on that hill at lunch. Except for when that squit almost drilled into my back," he added with a disgusted expression.

Kara smiled, though she had no recollection of the incident. *I must have used it to build a mind-bridge at some point.*

"Ever since you returned from the Well, you've been so focused on the task at hand that there's been this sort of armor around you. I just want to make sure that everything's okay."

"My feelings don't matter," Kara said. "If I don't stop Rygoth, a lot of people are going to get hurt and—"

"How about this?" Lucas asked, lacing his fingers

behind his head. "Let's pretend we're on the hill back on De'Noran. Tell me what's going on, just like it's any other day."

Kara pushed her hair back. It would have been more convenient to secure it in a bun, but she had spent the first twelve years of her life being forced to wear it that way, and she wasn't about to go back now.

"Mostly I feel overwhelmed," she said. "I beat Rygoth once, but that was only a trick. Magic is so hard for me, but it's not like that with her—she can destroy entire armies and not break a sweat. I have no right challenging her. I'm just a girl who grew up far away from this place and has no idea what she's doing. You want to know how I'm feeling? I'm scared, Lucas. All the time. Aren't you?"

"No."

"Why not?"

"I'll show you." Lucas reached into his pocket and pulled out a large seashell. "Recognize it?"

"Of course," Kara said, smiling. "It's one of Mary

Kettle's toys. I had the other one. We used it to communicate, until . . ."

"Until you stopped," he said.

Kara was shocked to see tears in Lucas's eyes.

"I'm sorry," she said. "We lost all the toys in Sablethorn. There was no way for me to—"

"I understand," Lucas said. "It's not your fault. And it wasn't your fault that time works so strangely in the Well of Witches. For you, it was only a few days. But for me, it was an entire year." He turned the shell in his hands. "Every day, I called your name into this shell. Every day, I listened for your voice. For the first few months—it was hard, but I believed that you were okay. I know how strong you are. How brave. But after that? After that, I didn't think I'd ever hear your voice again. So when you ask me if Rygoth scares me—sure, maybe a little—but nothing could ever be more frightening than those days talking into the seashell, thinking that I would never—"

Kara leaned forward and kissed him. Lucas was

surprised, but only for a moment.

"I was getting to that," he said when their lips parted.

"I know," replied Kara, resting her forehead against his. "I just got tired of waiting."

When the Swoop came to a stop some time later, a dozen men wearing crisp white uniforms were waiting for them on the platform. They had the same light-red skin and pulsing veins as the ticket seller, and stood with the practiced stillness of trained soldiers. Lucas had just started to reach for his bow when the soldiers parted and a tall woman wearing a lush green headscarf stepped forward.

"Welcome to the Museum of Impossible Things," she said, smiling wide. "My name is Xindra Ta-Fign."

She raised her hands, palms out, and stared at Kara expectantly. The silence grew awkward.

"I'm sorry," Kara said. "I don't know what you want me to do."

Xindra laughed.

"Hold out your hands. Close to my palms, but without making contact."

Kara did so, and Xindra nodded enthusiastically.

"Good! Now we're friends! This is the standard greeting here in Kutt. We do not shake hands as others do. Our lives are spent battling the contagion that surrounds us, so physical contact is avoided unless absolutely necessary."

Xindra spoke each word with precision, her accent short and clipped. She was even taller than Kara and her face was warm and open. Kara liked her instantly.

"Are you going to show us the museum?" Taff asked.

Xindra bent down so she could talk to him eye to eye.

"I could do that, Taff, if you'd like. But first your sister and I have some business to discuss."

Kara was instantly on guard.

"How do you know—"

"—who you are? We have been waiting for you, Kara Westfall, that's how! We received a letter from Timoth

Clen just two days ago. He told us about the Spider Queen, and how she was gathering the four grims in order to assemble a weapon of unspeakable power. He learned about the one we have here, and told me to give it to you for safekeeping before Rygoth arrives."

"Rygoth is coming here?" Grace asked.

"According to our reports," Xindra said. "She is still a few days off, but good to hurry anyway, no? I wish you the best of luck on your noble quest, of course, but the faster this grim is out of Kutt, the better. You are to take it and meet the Clen at Naysayer's Bay. You know this place?"

"I've heard of it," Lucas said. "But I wouldn't trust myself to find it."

"I will arrange a guide for you," Xindra said. "Food and water as well. The grim remains in the same place it has been for two thousand years, in the lowest floor of our museum. Let me take you to it now."

Kara wanted to trust the woman, but the idea that

someone would just hand her the grim was difficult to swallow. She looked at Lucas and saw similar reservations written upon his face.

This seems too easy.

"Could I see the letter?" Kara asked. "From my . . . from Timoth Clen?"

Xindra bowed deeply.

"It grieves me to say that I destroyed it, knowing that such information could be truly dangerous in the wrong hands."

"What about the guards?" Lucas asked. "If we're friends, as you say, are they really necessary?"

"It is because we are friends that they are necessary! Rygoth has spies even here in Kutt. I must keep you safe." Xindra bowed again. "I am so sorry that life has burdened you with suspicion at such a young age. Excuse me for saying that it is very sad."

"We're just being cautious," Kara said.

"Of course," Xindra said. "These are cautious times.

And Kutt has not always enjoyed the best reputation. We have had a dark history. Madmen and their experiments, not showing the workings of nature the proper respect. I know this to be true." She bowed again. "But this is the dawn of a new Kutt! Look at our museum! The white walls! The brightly lit exhibits! Soon thousands will flock here to bask in our wonders."

Kara did not think this was very likely as long as the Plague Barrier remained in place, but she did not want to douse the woman's enthusiasm. *Who knows?* she thought. *Stranger things have happened.*

Xindra clapped her hands together.

"Follow me! Rygoth is still a good distance away. The grim first. And then, on our return, perhaps I can show you some of our splendid museum."

Taff asked, "Are the things here really *impossible?*"

"Of course," Xindra said. "I am so honored to be the curator here. Within these walls you will find exceptions to the natural order that exist nowhere else in the world.

A fire freezing to the touch and a block of ice that scalds your skin. A pit that has no bottom. The embalmed corpse of a man who managed to live for one hundred fifty-two years without a heart or any other major organs."

"Those things sound like magic to me," said Taff.

"Use the word if it pleases you. But there are splendors to be found in nature that would put any wizard to shame."

As Xindra continued to dazzle Taff with the wonders of the museum, they followed her into a white corridor so narrow that they were forced to walk single file. The polished walls gleamed brightly, allowing Kara to see her reflection everywhere she turned. Strips that ran just below the ceiling emanated an artificial light that made her slightly dizzy, as though she were walking on a ship bobbing up and down. As they continued to descend she found herself breathing fast.

"Are you all right?" Lucas asked.

"I'll be fine," Kara said. "I just don't like going

underground. Rygoth's cave, Sablethorn—same thing. I start thinking about the dirt and rocks above us, and what would happen if they fell."

"People have been living here for a long, long time," Lucas said. "I'm sure it's safe."

"I don't know how they manage. I would lose my mind if I never saw the sun."

"Not if you were born here," Grace said behind her. "Then you'd never know the difference. People learn to live the life they're given."

Kara looked back over her shoulder.

"Everyone deserves to see the sun at least once."

Grace scoffed.

"And what happens after that?" she asked, her walking stick clicking against the clean white floor. "They scuttle back to the darkness with a full understanding of what they're missing? That sounds more like cruelty than anything else."

"I just wish things were better for these poor people,"

Kara said, her anger beginning to rise now. "That's all."

"'Poor people,'" Grace said in an exaggerated mockery of Kara's voice. "You do love to pass judgment, don't you? Has it ever occurred to you that this might be how they *want* to live? Why is your way always better?"

"Stop twisting my—"

"Besides, we're Children of the Fold, remember? Wishes are forbidden."

"De'Noran is gone, Grace!"

"De'Noran made us who we are!" Grace exclaimed, an uncharacteristic hint of desperation in her eyes. "Nothing can change that! Not even a glimpse of the sun."

Kara started to reply but Lucas touched her elbow and shook his head: *It's not worth it.* She exhaled through her nostrils, still steaming. In some ways Kara preferred the old Grace, whose wickedness was as reliable as the ticking of a clock. *Now there's no predicting how she'll act. You might be able to have something close to a civilized conversation with her one minute, but the next minute she'll bite your head off.* Kara glanced back, befuddled, but Grace's face betrayed no emotion. *She was so nice on the train, watching Taff so Lucas and I could be alone. That was something that a friend would do. I thought we might have turned a corner, but now . . .*

Reviewing their recent history, Kara noticed that Grace usually fell into her darkest moods just following these moments of kindness. *Like doing something nice to apologize for losing your temper, only in reverse. Grace needs to do something mean in order to make up for being nice.*

I'll never understand this girl.

Through long windows spaced periodically along the corridor Kara glimpsed the brightly lit exhibits of the museum itself: oddly shaped skulls in glass cases; a small Swoop with metal wings, hovering just off the ground; a zoo housing great apes with transparent skin that revealed the inner workings of their bodies. Kara had to keep pushing Taff onward, his face pressed against the glass as though it were the window to a toy maker's shop.

"Can't we just go inside for a little while?" he finally begged, gesturing to an inviting door that read *THE NATURE OF INVISIBILITY.*

"This way is much faster," Xindra said. "It's crowded in the museum today."

She was right. The patrons' skin varied in color from salmon pink to the angry red of a fresh welt, but other than that the Kuttians acted no differently than a group of villagers enjoying a town fair. An especially large number of children, all wearing white uniforms, were being shepherded by just a few adults. *School trip?* Kara wondered. She watched as a little boy stepped into a black box and instantly stepped out of an identical box across the room. The other children applauded quietly. Their excitement was subdued, and there was no casual shoulder wringing or shoving between them.

Since birth they're taught to avoid contact with others, Kara thought, remembering the odd way that Xindra had greeted her. *Being wary of disease is a constant way of life with them.*

They followed the corridor to an older tributary constructed from actual rock. For a little while Kara had managed to forget that they were beneath the ground, but now her original fears returned. She breathed deeply, trying to remain calm.

"This is part of the original museum," Xindra said with distaste. "I suppose it has historical value for how Kutt *used* to be, but we do not allow people to visit it these days. Too dark and gloomy. We haven't gotten around to modernizing it yet. But we will, we will!"

They came to an iron gate marked with strange symbols that Kara did not recognize. Xindra fitted a key into its lock and gestured for two guards to push it open; their difficulty in doing so, along with the squeaking hinges, told Kara that it had been a long time since the gate's last use. The guards shuffled ahead in order to light several braziers beyond the gate in the passageway, which Kara and the others followed to a large chamber with a single stone pedestal at its center.

On the pedestal was a familiar-looking red chest.

Words had been engraved into the rock in the same ancient language as the gate. Kara turned to Xindra, hoping to get a translation, and saw that the woman was no longer next to her. She remained with the guards just outside the chamber, looking nervous and out of sorts.

"It reads, 'Book fragment from the ruins of Dolrose Castle,'" Xindra said, anticipating her question.

Kara let a short laugh escape her lips.

"It's not wrong," she said.

She hesitantly touched the red chest, not sure if she'd be able to sense anything without holding the grim directly, and flinched as the familiar feeling of emptiness washed over her. *No light. No hope. No love.* It was even more overwhelming than the last time, as though having the two grims in such close vicinity was giving the *Vulkera* strength, and there was something new: the high-pitched voice of a little girl. For the most part her words were too muffled to understand, like a conversation in another room, but every so often a single word slipped through: *". . . punish . . . forever . . . alone . . ."*

And then, in a sudden rush of breath that tickled Kara's ear, the girl screamed: *"WHO ARE YOU?"*

With a shocked gasp, Kara jerked her hand from the chest.

The voice vanished.

"What happened?" Lucas asked.

"I heard her," Kara said, wrapping her arms around Lucas, once again craving the warmth of another person. "Evangeline. She talked to me."

She looked past Lucas and noticed that the guards had stationed themselves at each exit. They had drawn their weapons, curved blades glowing a faint green.

Xindra watched the dawning realization in Kara's eyes with an apologetic expression.

"I'm sorry," said Xindra. "I truly am."

She pulled a lever on the wall and panes of glass fell from above, perfectly cut to block each exit. The glass was the color of onyx but still translucent; Xindra and the guards looked like they were draped in gauzy black curtains.

"Let us out," Kara said.

"I wish I could."

Lucas pounded on the nearest gate, and when that proved ineffectual he drew his glorb-bow and fired. The arrow bounced off the glass and clattered to the floor, failing to leave the slightest scratch.

"Glass blown by the winds of a Starlit Tornado," Xindra said, her voice slightly muffled. "Imported from Lux. Incredibly rare and completely unbreakable." She smiled sheepishly. "Impossible things."

"Why are you doing this?" Kara asked.

Xindra's red skin flushed crimson. She bowed deeply.

"I must apologize again for deceiving you, but this seemed like the most efficient plan for capturing you safely. The guards might have been able to take you back at the Swoop station, of course, but I heard about what you did at the Battle of Clen's Grave. I know that you are powerful, and I did not want to risk any lives being lost. This is so much cleaner, don't you think?"

"You're helping Rygoth," Kara said.

"Oh *no*," said Xindra, honestly shocked at the suggestion. "I mean, I'll be giving Rygoth you and the grim, so from that perspective I suppose what you say has an inkling of truth. But I have no desire to *help* her. I've simply been put in a situation where the only viable solution is to do what Rygoth wants. Surely you understand."

Kara stepped closer and pressed her hand against the glass.

"I really don't."

"I'm so sorry," Xindra said, bowing again. "I will explain, and this time without duplicity! I received no letter from Timoth Clen. This was a ruse to gain your trust."

"Then how did you know we were coming?" asked Taff.

"There was indeed a letter," Xindra said. "So part of my story was true! See, not all lies!" She paused, as though waiting for some acknowledgment of her honesty. Looking rather disappointed at Kara's unaltered expression, Xindra continued. "The only difference was that this letter was from Rygoth and not Timoth Clen. She had recently learned that the grim was stored here. She also knew that you would arrive before her."

"That's impossible," Kara said. "Rygoth may be able to do a lot of things, but she can't see into the—"

Safi, she thought. *Who knows what Rygoth has done to her? Maybe she finally broke.*

"No," Taff said, reading the thought in Kara's eyes. "Safi would *never* lead Rygoth to us. No matter what."

"You're right."

She touched Taff's cheek and saw Xindra wince in disgust at the physical contact.

"I don't know who this Safi is," Xindra said. "Or how the Spider Queen knew your future whereabouts. The letter simply informed me that she expected both you and the grim to be waiting for her when she arrived. What choice did I have?"

"You could have said no," suggested Lucas.

"And then what? A repeat of the massacre at Ta'men Keep, only with Rygoth murdering families and children instead of soldiers? Why sacrifice those lives when in the end she'll take what she wants anyway?"

"But *our* lives can be sacrificed?" Kara asked. "Why is that okay? Because we're not from around here?"

"Excuse me kindly please, but you outsiders do not know what it's like to live under the cover of darkness for two thousand years. Only now are we climbing back into the light, and to lose all the progress we've made . . . if I do as Rygoth asks, she'll create a creature capable of swallowing the Clinging Mist. The Plague Barrier will lift forever. My people will walk in the warmth of the sun again. How can I refuse?"

"She's lying to you."

"Perhaps," Xindra admitted. "I am not a fool. I know what she is. But a chance at life is still a better choice than certain death, no?"

"It depends on the cost," Kara said. "You want to lead your people out of the darkness? Stand with me. We'll fight Rygoth together."

"Excuse me for this, but you are just a child."

"I am," Kara said. "And yet Rygoth seems awfully worried about me, doesn't she? One might even say afraid. Let me out of here and let's give her a surprise. This is your chance, Xindra. The people of Kutt can become Sentium's greatest heroes!"

The woman teetered, tasting honor on her lips. *Come on*, Kara thought, knowing that it was useless to say anything more. *Come on!*

Xindra bowed.

"I am so sorry," she said and started walking away.

Kara pounded her fists against the glass pane.

"Think about what I said!" she shouted. "There's still

time to change your mind. Rygoth won't be here for days yet."

Xindra turned around.

"About that. Another falsehood. So sorry. The Spider Queen is traveling through the Clinging Mist as we speak. She'll be here any minute."

FIFTEEN

After Xindra left, no doubt to prepare for Rygoth's arrival, the children stood in stunned silence. Kara had been tricked before—more times than she wanted to remember—but she thought she had been getting better at noticing the telltale signs of duplicity. She supposed that Xindra had fooled her so easily because there had truly been no evil in her heart. *In her mind she's doing the right thing—sacrificing strangers in order to save her own people.*

Knowing this didn't make Kara feel much better, nor

did it change their current predicament.

"What's the plan?" Lucas finally whispered.

He kept his voice low. There were still guards just out-side the chamber, their backs pressed against the glass.

Taff halfheartedly lifted his slingshot. He fired an invisible pellet that plinked off the glass so pathetically that the soldier stationed there didn't even turn around at the sound.

"Thought so," Taff said.

"Magic?" Lucas asked.

Kara shook her head.

"I reached out with my powers while I was still talking to Xindra," she said. "There are animals in the museum—so many that it's hard to sort through all their voices. They're all locked up in cages, though. No way they can get here."

"Rats?" Taff asked, with a hint of a grin. "Come on. There's *always* rats."

"Not even them," Kara said. "Knowing how the

Kuttians feel about disease, I'm guessing they figured out a way to eradicate all the vermin. I don't even sense any *insects*. And there's nothing alive in the Clinging Mist whatsoever."

They couldn't have picked a more perfect prison for me, Kara thought.

Chuckling to herself, Grace tottered over to the other side of the room and leaned against the wall. She tapped her walking stick against the floor in a steady rhythm.

"I'm sorry," Lucas said. "Are we boring you?"

"Why are we even talking about this when the solution is so obvious?" she asked.

"We're all ears," replied Lucas.

"And no brains," Grace said, "so I'll talk slow and keep it simple. Kara uses her powers to control the mind of one of those guards outside. He kills the other guards and opens the gate." Grace pointed her walking stick in their direction. "Then we kill the guard that helps us—or just knock him unconscious. I do think it's important to reward a job well done."

For a few moments, Kara was too furious to speak.

"How can you even suggest something like that?" she asked.

"Are you saying that my plan is not the best option?"

"I don't *kill* people."

Grace smiled.

"Sure you do," she said. "Or have you forgotten about my friend Simon?"

"That was different," Kara said. When she was close to losing her temper she got quieter, not louder; her voice was barely above a whisper now. "He was going to kill Taff."

"And what do you think Rygoth will do to the whelp when she gets here? Play a round of marbles?"

"Kara," Lucas said, stepping between the two girls. "Is it possible to—not kill anyone, of course—but just make the guard pull the lever for us . . ."

"So you're on *her* side now?" Kara asked, jabbing a finger in Grace's direction.

"Of course not," Lucas said in a calming voice. "I just

think we ought to consider all the possible—"

"I can't force another person to do my bidding."

"Can't?" Grace asked. "Or won't?"

Kara ignored her and kept her attention on Lucas.

"Controlling people's minds is *really* dark magic," she said. "I'd be no better than Rygoth."

"And so we all die," Grace said, "because Kara mustn't get her pure little hands dirty."

Kara spun in her direction.

"Even if I wanted to cast a spell like that, I couldn't. I don't have it in me. I'm not like you."

Grace sighed with relief, as though the conversation were finally heading in the right direction.

"I disagree," she said. "I've seen how much you enjoy bossing people around. Forcing them to do your bidding seems like the next natural step."

"Stop it!" Lucas exclaimed. "This is getting us nowhere!"

Grace grinned triumphantly, like a general who has just thought of a military maneuver that would guarantee victory, and turned on Lucas.

"Do you really think you're in a position to give orders, *Stench?*" she asked.

Lucas winced at the word, a particularly nasty name for a Clearer. Kara hadn't heard the insult since leaving De'Noran.

"Don't call me that," he said through gritted teeth.

"Why not?" Grace asked, leaning forward on her walking stick. "It's what you are. The lonely Stench who followed a pretty girl across the ocean. Pathetic. You're just Kara's shadow. Without her, you barely even exist. Do you really think someone like her could love a boy like you? Your own parents didn't even want you!"

Lucas took a step forward, eyes blazing. Kara blocked his path.

"Don't listen to her," she whispered, trying to control her own temper. "It's not true. None of it is true."

While Kara tried to calm her friend, Taff took a step forward. He looked sadly up at Grace.

"I thought you'd changed," he said. "Why are you being so mean all of a sudden?"

"Because this is who she really is," snapped Kara. "She could only hide it for so long."

"Yes!" Grace said, her expression oddly pleading. She gripped Kara by the arms and shook her madly. *Tell me! Tell me who I am! I need to hear it!"*

The dam broke, releasing Kara's anger in full force. She shoved Grace away.

"You're a foul, evil, hideous *witch*!"

Grace started to laugh, a barely human cackle dancing along waves of madness. Kara and Lucas froze in place. Taff clapped his hands over his ears.

"Thank you," Grace said. "That was exactly what I needed to hear. I'm foul. Evil. Hideous. I had almost forgotten. How fitting that you should be the one to set me on my proper path again."

Grace snapped the walking stick in half.

The two pieces of splintered wood seemed to come

alive in her hands, twisting like a snake, re-forming into something new. Grace was changing as well. Long white hair regrew from her scalp. Her leg healed itself with loud cracking sounds. The shoddy clothes she had been wearing for weeks transformed into a bright-yellow dress.

Kara knew that she should act, that each moment lost was a moment wasted, but all she could do was watch in astonishment as Grace rose to her feet, her former beauty completely restored.

I'm such a fool, she thought.

The walking stick, now just a swirling cyclone of splinters, exploded in a flash of blue light. In its place was a large book the color of sunflowers, which lingered in the air for just a moment before dropping into Grace's open hands.

A grimoire.

"The look on your face is even better than I imagined," she said.

Lucas reacted first, diving forward in an attempt to

knock the spellbook away. He wasn't fast enough. Grace read a few words from the grimoire and Lucas flew across the room, slamming against the wall. When he tried to charge her again the wall held him fast, stretching against his efforts like a web.

"Mmm," Grace purred. "Magic. It's been such a long time."

Taff reached for his slingshot and it froze in his hands. He dropped it in shock. The slingshot shattered into a hundred pieces.

"Yes," Grace said. "How could I ever question . . . this is what I am. This is right."

She looked up at Kara, her blue eyes suddenly calm and in control, and read from the grimoire. Kara winced at the flow of unrecognizable syllables.

This is the end, she thought, pulling Taff close. *This is the . . .*

A yellow ribbon materialized in the air and landed in Grace's open palm.

"Shall I tell you a story?" she asked.

Gasping with relief, Kara backed away as Grace began to weave the ribbon through her hair.

"You might not believe me," she said as her fingers worked nimbly, "but I really did get rid of my grimoire at the start. I was willing to give up magic forever if it meant I would remain safe from the Faceless. I slept in barns and begged for scraps of food. It didn't matter. I was just happy to be alive. An old carpenter and his wife even took me in for a while. They had lost their own daughter, and I had this misguided notion that maybe I could start over again. That lasted for about three weeks." Grace twisted the ribbon in her hair one final time and knotted it tight, creating a perfect bow. "Then Rygoth found me."

The Kuttian guards peered through the glass, watching the unexpected developments with interest. They looked uncertain about whether they should enter the chamber or remain safely outside. As she spoke, Grace strolled around the perimeter of the room, examining each man in turn.

"At first, I thought that she had come to kill me," Grace said. "After all, I had helped save your father. In her mind, I was your friend—and she *really* doesn't like you, Kara. But Rygoth wasn't angry with me at all. Just the opposite. She saw great potential that had been wasted, a 'gorgeous flower wilted by the world.' Those were her words exactly." Grace smiled with genuine joy. "She didn't want me to be anyone different. She *understood*."

Kara kept backing away, trying to keep as much distance between Taff and Grace as possible. She scanned the room for some sort of weapon, but there was only the red chest sitting on the pedestal.

Maybe I could throw it at her, she thought, her mind racing. *Knock her unconscious.* She reached out with her *wexari* powers but found nothing new; all her winged and clawed saviors were locked in cages, unable to help.

"Rygoth gave me this," Grace said, raising the yellow

book with reverence. "My true grimoire. One that spoke my name. And then she asked for my help. See, her seer, your friend Safi, had turned out to be a lot more stubborn than anticipated, and so Rygoth needed someone new to find the grims."

"Let me guess," Kara scoffed. "You."

"Actually, no," Grace said, savoring the moment. She pointed directly at Kara. "You."

"What are you talking about?"

"The Spider Queen's hatred for you knows no bounds, but you're the only person to ever face her twice and survive. There is a grudging respect there. She knew you'd search for the grims, and that there was even a possibility you might find them. Rygoth decided to let you do her work for her and then take them in the end. She couldn't keep an eye on you herself, obviously, so she sent someone you trusted instead."

"*You?*" Kara asked. "Odd choice."

"That's what I thought at first," Grace said. "But

Rygoth, in her infinite wisdom, anticipated that this would be the perfect way to flaunt your weakness."

"And what is my weakness?" Kara asked coldly.

"Compassion. You'd never be able to resist a lost soul in search of redemption. And so I cut my hair and dirtied my clothes, in order to play the part, and transformed my grimoire into a walking stick. My job was to stay close, help you on your quest. Endear myself. Whenever I had a chance—like when you left me alone at Dolrose Castle—I sent Rygoth messages. I told her that we had the pages from the *Vulkera*. I told her we were coming here. I even told her about the grim stored in Auren." Grace clasped her hand to her face in mock concern. "Oh no! That's where you told your father to go, wasn't it? That means you sent him right into a trap!"

Kara picked up the red chest and hurled it at Grace as hard as she could. Her aim was true, the chest spiraling right at Grace's face.

It stopped in midair.

"I'll be honest," Grace said. "I expected better from you."

Kara's satchel burst into flames. She tossed it away before the fire could spread across her body . . . only there was no fire, not anymore. It had been an illusion.

The unharmed satchel flew into Grace's hand.

"Half the *Vulkera*," she said, opening the drawstring in order to add the chest. "Rygoth will be pleased. But I am going to place these prizes in her hands myself. Why should I wait here and allow that foolish Kuttian to get the credit? I'm the one who did all the work. All she did was lock a door."

Grace turned to a new page in the grimoire, spoke several jarring words, and yanked an old rag out of the book. She wiped this across one of the glass gates, back and forth, as though cleaning the surface.

The glass vanished.

The guards, who had abandoned their positions and gathered in a tight circle, raised their weapons. This would have been far more intimidating were it not for their shaking knees and sweat-stained jumpsuits.

Grace raised the rag.

"This works on people, too," she said.

The guards ran off.

"What now?" Lucas asked, his hands still pinioned to the wall. "You kill us? Bring our bodies back to your *master?*"

Grace waved her hand and Lucas fell from the wall.

"You're all free to go," Grace said.

Lucas rose to his feet, rubbing his wrists. He exchanged a bewildered look with Kara.

"Is this another one of your tricks?" he asked.

"No trick," Grace said. "You freed me from the Well of Witches. I'm returning the favor. That's all."

Kara had never been more confused in her life.

"What about everything you just said? You're working for Rygoth! You can't just set us free!"

"Kara," Lucas said, leading her toward the door. "If she

wants to let us go, let's not argue with her."

"My job was to get the grims," Grace said, "which I now have. That's all Rygoth cares about."

"That's not true and you know it. She won't be happy when she learns you let us go."

"Oh, right," Grace said. "You think this is all about you. As always."

"Come on," Lucas said, pulling Kara away.

"It doesn't matter," Grace snapped. "You probably won't even escape this place alive. They'll be looking for you. Not just Rygoth. Everyone in Kutt."

The words were harsh, but Grace's eyes were fearful and confused. Even while sending them away she had taken a few inadvertent steps in their direction.

She doesn't know who she is right now.

Kara shook free of Lucas's grip.

"Come with us," she said.

"What?" asked Lucas and Taff in unison.

Kara pointed to Grace's grimoire. More than half the

pages had already been used.

"You're running out," Kara said. "Soon you'll be at your Last Spell. Then it's back to the Well of Witches. Don't make the same mistake again."

"That won't happen this time," Grace said. "After Rygoth has the *Vulkera*, she's promised to make me a grimoire with an unlimited number of pages. No Last Spell ever again. I'll be safe."

"You can't trust her."

"Like you care."

"I do," Kara said, stepping forward. "And I think you do too, more than you want to admit."

"Have you not heard a word I said? I was only *pretending* to care so that—"

"It might have started that way, but there came a point where we grew comfortable with each other. Not friends, exactly, but no longer enemies. We traveled across Sentium together. You ate with us every night. You shared the story about your father."

"That was just something I made up," Grace said weakly. "So you would feel bad for me . . . it was all a trick. . . ."

Kara walked slowly toward her, as she might approach a wild animal she didn't want to scare away.

"That's why you insulted me before," Kara said. "You wanted me to get mad. And when that didn't work, you were cruel to Lucas . . . you *wanted* me to say mean things and force you to do something that you no longer had the heart to do."

"That is the most *ridiculous*—"

"And that's why you're letting us go." Kara placed a hand on Grace's elbow. "There's a part of you that wants to be good, but you're afraid to let it out. Come with us. We'll find it together."

Grace features softened. It was like a mask peeling away, revealing a scared and confused thirteen-year-old girl who had been left alone for far too long.

It only lasted for a moment.

"People don't change," Grace snapped, yanking Kara's hand from her arm. "You're the good witch. I'm the bad one. That's just the way things are."

She clapped her grimoire shut and vanished.

SIXTEEN

The displays on this floor of the museum were completely different from the brightly lit exhibits above them. Kutt's obsession with the interior machinations of life was evident at every turn: eyeballs floating in a giant vat of clear liquid like fish in a tank; iron wires running between a decayed heart and a black box; a massive sandbox in which children could dig for human bones. Kara was glad that they were running, for these weren't the worst things they passed, and she was happy to reduce the truly gruesome exhibits to a nightmarish blur.

"We have to stop," Lucas said, out of breath. "Figure out where we're going before we get even more lost."

Kara nodded, trying to catch her breath as well. The air, sharp with the stench of some unidentifiable chemical, made her throat burn. At least they were alone. There were no crowds, no schoolchildren. Kutt's dark past had been buried here like a murdered corpse.

They'll be coming soon, Kara thought. *The guards will report what they've seen. They'll conduct a search.*

She listened and thought she heard sounds in the distance. Footsteps. Maybe even voices.

"We can't go back the way we came," Lucas said. "We'll run right into them."

"There must be another way to the surface," replied Kara.

They found it a few minutes later: a winding set of metal stairs that looked like they hadn't been used in centuries and wobbled beneath the children's weight. With Kara in the lead they dashed toward a glimmer of light overhead, at last reaching a hallway with white walls much like the corridor through which they had first entered, except with a complicated series of pipes running beneath its ceiling.

They were back in the newer part of the museum again. There were no visitors in this area, which seemed to be for workers only. Creeping forward, Kara peeked through a door with a small window and saw hundreds of people milling from exhibit to exhibit. There was a long line at a food cart; even through the door they could smell something sweet.

"What's that?" Taff asked, recklessly peeking his head out. "I'm starving."

Kara pulled him back.

"What now?" Lucas asked.

"I don't know," she replied. "I came up with the finding-the-stairs plan. Your turn."

Lucas stared out at the crowd of Kuttians, their heads bald and their faces various shades of red.

"Well," he said, "we can't exactly go out there and blend in, on account of we look completely different than every single person here."

"Fair point," Kara said. "But we have to somehow make it back to the Swoop station."

"No," Taff said. "We need to stop Grace! If Rygoth assembles the *Vulkera* then none of this will matter."

"She won't," Kara said. "I promise. Right now the most important thing is for us to get as far away from here as possible."

"But how can you be sure——"

"No time to explain," Kara said. "Just trust me."

"What about those animals over there?" whispered Lucas. "If we set them free we can use them as a distraction."

Kara couldn't see the encaged animals very clearly from her vantage point—a spiked tail, a wisp of golden fur—but she could hear the despair in their thoughts, their desire to run free and *TEAR CHEW PUNISH* those two-legs who had imprisoned them.

"Too dangerous," Kara said. "If we set them loose in a crowd, and my control slips for even a moment . . . innocent people will die."

"We have to do something," Lucas said, "and fast. I'm getting nervous standing here out in the open."

Kara felt the same way. The hallway was brightly lit, and with the door to the museum in front of them, the stairs to their left, and an intersecting hallway behind them, it seemed inevitable that someone would find them soon.

"Wait!" Taff exclaimed, bending his neck at an awkward angle so he could see as high as possible through the tiny window. "I've been wondering why we're still alive, and if I'm right, then . . . yes! There! There!"

Kara pressed her face to the window, trying to see what her brother was talking about, and in the process saw a small boy sucking on a candy stick point in their direction. Just as the child started to tug on his mother's sleeve, Kara ducked out of sight, pulling Lucas and Taff with her.

They sat on the floor with their backs against the door. Kara hoped it was locked.

"Explain," she said.

"The whole time we've been in Kutt I've been trying to figure out where all this air is coming from," Taff said. "We can't breathe the Clinging Mist. It isn't safe. But we're not dead, so the air must be coming from somewhere else. I could only think of one possible solution, and it turns out that I'm right." He pointed up at dozens of slits lining the highest point of the wall like fish gills. "Look. The good air comes through there, from somewhere past the Plague Barrier. That means there must be a tunnel that we can use to get back to Rattle."

Kara kissed him hard on the forehead.

"You," she said.

"One problem," Lucas said. "How do we get up there?"

The hallway ceiling was a normal height, but the one

beyond the door rose high overhead, allowing for larger exhibits such as steel columns that shot lightning between them and an aviary packed with reptilian birds.

"If anything goes wrong with those"—Taff paused a moment, thinking of the right words for the slits lining the upper wall—"air gills, then no one would be able to breathe. There has to be a way up there in case workers have to make repairs. The entrance would probably be around here somewhere, not out in the crowd. Otherwise you'd have children climbing up the ladder all day long." He grinned. "That's what I would do."

"Let's find it fast," Lucas said, looking around nervously. "I don't know how much longer our luck is going to hold out."

They dashed along brightly lit corridors that were eerie in their emptiness. Lucas led the way, peeking around corners before waving the other two along, but it was clear that this particular area of the museum had been completely evacuated. Kara didn't even hear talking behind any of the doors they passed.

When they finally came to a ladder—leading up to a small hatch in the ceiling—Taff paused a moment to peek through a small window to the museum.

"Where are they going?" he asked.

The crowd was being ushered out of the hall by museum workers. Though the people were packed tightly together, they moved in slow, evenly spaced lines, careful to never touch.

"I think they might be evacuating the museum so they can search for us easier," Lucas said.

"Why?" asked Taff. "It's not like we can hide among the visitors. We sort of stick out."

"It doesn't matter," Lucas said, climbing the ladder. "As long as it's keeping everyone busy."

He pushed open the hatch and a man's heavy boot crashed into his face, knocking him to the floor.

"Look at that!" the Kuttian said, landing with a thud. "A little outsider is trying to use my ladder."

He was a giant of a man, unable to stand at his full height without hitting his head on the ceiling pipes. His enflamed skin was the color of a fresh sunburn. Two bulbous veins crossed in the center of his forehead.

"Outsider girl," the man said, wincing with disgust at Kara's appearance. "Repulsive. Skin like a maggot. The others have gone to see the Spider Queen. I am sorry, but I must bring the three of you!" He slipped work gloves onto his gigantic hands. "Much reward for me and my family."

Kara tried to dash past him, but the man was faster than he looked. He grabbed her with his gloved hands and lifted her with ease, holding her at a distance like a caught python, his face turned away.

Taff reached for his slingshot before realizing that it was gone forever.

"What are you looking for, outsider boy?" the man asked. "No matter. Walk in front of me. There is no need to hurt you."

Shoulders slumped, Taff started to walk past the man, who shifted to one side in the narrow hallway, not wanting to risk accidental contact.

Taff paused and looked up at him. Kara had seen that look in his eyes before, wheels spinning as he formulated an idea.

"Keep walking," the man asked.

Taff jumped up and touched the man's neck.

"NO!" he shouted, releasing Kara and clapping a hand to his neck as though he had been scalded. "What did you . . . who knows what kind of horrible diseases you filthy outsiders are carrying?" A feral noise escaped his lips, and he bent forward, meaning to seize Taff. The crossed veins in his forehead popped dangerously.

Taff sneezed in his face.

The man's scream was long, hysterical, and surprisingly high-pitched. He tottered backward in stunned horror before spinning around and sprinting away from Taff at full speed, immediately banging his head on a low-hanging pipe and crashing to the floor, unconscious.

Kara and Taff stared at the motionless man.

"Bless you," Kara said.

Taff giggled.

They helped Lucas to his feet. His bloody nose was still recovering from its encounter with the Kuttian's boot, but Lucas had experienced worse injuries during his time with the graycloaks and waved away Kara's ministrations, content to just wipe his face clean with the back of his sleeve.

"First the faenix chucks me across the room, now this," Lucas said sheepishly. "My uselessness is getting embarrassing."

"None of that," Kara said. "Let's keep moving."

They hurried up the ladder and found themselves standing on a small platform. Before them, two rows of evenly spaced crystal stalactites hung from the ceiling like giant icicles. Light shone through their translucent surface in a manner that made them practically invisible.

"It's a walkway!" Taff exclaimed. He bent down to touch a clear netting tautly suspended across the tips of the stalactites. Its strands were as thin as fishing line.

"No way that's strong enough to hold us," Kara said.

"Impossible things." Lucas shrugged and stepped forward. The netting dipped beneath his weight, causing him to gasp in surprise, but held fast.

"See," he said, smiling nervously. "I knew it would work."

Kara and Taff made their way onto the netting—so clear that it was like walking on air—and dashed between the stalactites. The hall below them was empty. They passed through a narrow opening in the wall and entered the next hall, which was dedicated to a large metal vehicle with legs like a centipede. There was no one here either.

Everyone was in the third hall.

Given its size and grandeur, Kara suspected that this was the main entrance to the Museum of Impossible Things. Hundreds of men, women, and children stood in perfect rows, like an army about to march into battle. Kara crouched behind a metal sculpture suspended from the air, shielding herself from sight, and the two boys squeezed in behind her. Peeking out, Kara saw that the crowd's attention was fixed on a woman standing on a raised platform almost directly below them.

Rygoth.

The platform, Kara now saw, was the flat shell of what looked like a mammoth tortoise. It lay subserviently still, its face puckered with boils and half-formed scales; Rygoth, knowing that she would be using the pitiable beast as little more than a stage, had put the barest of efforts into its creation. Standing on either end of the shell, the twins sneered down at the cowering crowd.

Xindra lay sprawled at Rygoth's feet. She wasn't moving.

"I hope I have made it clear," said Rygoth, as two witches dragged the curator's body away, "that I am truly disappointed."

A line of black-cloaked witches provided a human barrier between Rygoth and the assembled Kuttians. The witches held their grimoires close to their chests like sheathed swords, their expressions devoid of any human emotion. All stood save a kneeling girl whose hands were manacled together.

Safi, Kara mouthed to Taff, pointing in their friend's direction.

Her face was puffy on one side, as though she had been recently struck. A wooden block had been fastened around her ankles. *What have they done to you?* Kara wondered, gripping the railing tightly in order to calm red thoughts that might be like an alarm bell to Rygoth. She turned to her brother and saw no anger in his face, only concern for his friend. Kara nodded at the unasked question in his eyes.

We'll save her. I promise.

Kara searched the witches for Bethany. She was nowhere to be found.

"I came to this horrid cesspool expecting two simple things," Rygoth announced, enumerating with the fingers of her gloved hand. "My grims. And the girl. You have managed to let both slip through your fingers."

Safi grinned, clearly enjoying Rygoth's frustration, and Kara realized that in resisting the Spider Queen for so long her friend had found a new source of strength.

Rygoth couldn't break you, Kara thought admiringly. *You beat her!* The young witch's triumph rejuvenated Kara's sagging spirits.

If Safi can stand against Rygoth, then so can I.

"It's not too late for redemption though," Rygoth continued, "and to demonstrate my mercy I'm going to give you all a chance to help. Together you are going to comb every inch of this building for the girl and bring her to me. But time is of the essence, my friends, so allow me to offer you some encouragement. For every minute that passes, I shall send one of your children into the Clinging Mist. Perhaps you will allow them to return and spread your marvelous plague. Or perhaps you will turn your backs on them while they die out there in the darkness, their little hands pounding on the glass, calling your names. Tough decision. I'm honestly curious what will happen."

Upon hearing this pronouncement, the crowd rumbled and shook like a great beast awakening from its slumber. *Yes*, thought Kara, thinking that Rygoth's threats might finally be enough to spur them into action. *Help us! Together we might have a chance!*

Kara's hope of an alliance was short-lived, however, for the moment the witches threw open their grimoires the crowd fell silent, the fires of its rebellion doused by fear.

"Let me be perfectly clear," Rygoth said, staring down at the people of Kutt with a pitiless gaze. "Some of you can die, or all of you can die. It doesn't matter to me. I will leave here with what I came for either way."

Dozens of black-cloaked figures shoved through the

horrified crowd, snatching children at random. Screams and sobs filled the hall. Breaking with tradition, a young mother held her son close, refusing to relinquish him. A bolt of red lightning sent her flying across the room.

Kara watched it all, knowing what she had to do.

"You two head through those slits in the wall and back to the surface," she told the boys. "Now. While everyone's distracted. I'll catch up later."

"No way!" Taff exclaimed.

Lucas nodded in agreement. "That's not going to happen."

Kara drew them close. Even with the chaos below them she couldn't risk raising her voice.

"If I don't give myself up, people are going to die," Kara said.

"You can't," Lucas replied. "She'll kill you."

Kara shrugged with feigned bravery.

"She's tried it before. It hasn't worked yet." She lay a hand on Lucas's satchel and met his eyes. "You *must* get as far from here as possible. Everything depends on it."

Lucas shook his head. "There has to be another—"

"There's not," Kara said. "And we've no more time to discuss it." She bent down next to Taff and brushed the hair out of his eyes. "Find Father," she said. "Stay with the graycloaks until—"

"No," Taff said. "We're supposed to stay together. You and me. *Always.*"

"Don't worry," she said, tapping him playfully on the nose. "I have a *plan.*" She looked up at Lucas. "My brother's life is in your hands. Keep him safe."

Lucas, close to tears but fighting it, straightened at Kara's words. He bowed slightly.

"I will," he said, his voice cracking.

Acting quickly, before he could change his mind, Lucas dragged Taff backward across the netting. The smaller boy fought him the entire way, kicking fiercely.

"Shh," Lucas whispered in a calming voice. "We have to trust her. She'll be all right. You know your sister. She can handle anything."

Lucas met Kara's eyes for one final moment, and then

the two boys slipped through an air gill and into the unknown reaches beyond the museum.

They'll be safe, Kara thought. *They have to be.*

She stepped out of her hiding place behind the sculpture, ready to announce her presence, when a new voice cut through the chaos below.

"My Queen!"

With head held high, Grace made her way through the parted crowd and strode up the ridged tail of the tortoise. Kara froze, uncertain what to do.

Grace knelt before Rygoth.

"Here are your grims," she said, offering the satchel with two hands. "I have succeeded"——her eyes skewered the twins—"where others have failed. Do you know that these two fools tried to kill Kara in the farmhouse, my queen? They would have ruined your entire plan. Probably would have killed me too."

"Is this true?" Rygoth asked, glaring at the twins. "You were only supposed to create the appearance of danger in order to put our white-haired witch in the *wexari*'s favor."

That's why Grace warned us at the farmhouse, Kara thought, putting it all together and feeling foolish that she had not seen it from the start. *It was all planned from the beginning to make me trust her. Grace is right, though—despite their orders, the twins did not intend to let us survive.*

"They're jealous, my queen," Grace said, smiling with unabashed pleasure now. "Of me. The seer. Kara. Anyone you see as more important than them. Poor things don't realize that they're little more than guard dogs."

Bristling at Grace's words, the twins shouted in their strange, sibilant language, completing each other's sentences as though they were two halves of the same creature.

"Enough," Rygoth said, raising her hand. "Your transgression will be dealt with later." She bestowed a smile upon Grace and the girl beamed with pleasure. "You've done well," she said, reaching into the satchel and withdrawing the red chest. She plucked a white hair from

Grace's head, which she transformed into tiny worms that ate through the lid in seconds. "The spine of the *Vulkera!*" Rygoth exclaimed in triumph, withdrawing a narrow flap of leather embossed with a rose. "The smallest of the grims, but no less essential."

Grace reached into the satchel and presented a rope-bound bundle.

"And the pages, my queen," Grace said proudly, with the tone of a student trying to impress a schoolmaster. "From the ruins of Dolrose Castle. I retrieved them personally for you. A great battle that only proves——"

"Yes, yes," said Rygoth, untying the rope impatiently. "You can impress me with your fascinating tale when——"

Her multifaceted eyes turned as cold as ice.

"What. Is. This?"

Rygoth tossed the pages into the air. They were not blank, as expected, but rather covered with Taff's earliest sketches of Topper, before he had run out of paper and was forced to use the floors and walls of the farmhouse for his designs. Kara had saved the sketches as a memento, never guessing the use to which she would put them.

Mouth agape, Grace watched the pages fall.

"Kara switched the grims," she said, with a slight smile of admiration. "I guess she didn't trust me as much as I thought she did."

That's right, Kara thought. *The real grim is in Lucas's satchel.*

They had made the switch just before the Swoop ride. Kara had seen it as a failure on her part, wanting to trust Grace but being unable to do so completely. Now she was relieved that she had been so cautious.

"FOOL!" Rygoth screamed. "How could you permit her to trick you like this?"

"I'll get it back," Grace said, trying to sound confident. Behind her, the twins snickered, relishing her discomfiture. "This is just a minor setback, my queen. We're so close! You already have three of the grims."

"Two," barked Rygoth. "Your information about Auren

was incorrect. There was no grim there."

Grace swallowed nervously, feeling the heat of Rygoth's fury. She was on dangerous ground and knew it.

"But Kara said—"

"At one point, yes, the grim was stored there. But it was moved centuries ago and now I *don't know where it is!*" With a snarl of rage, Rygoth shoved Grace hard enough to send her flying across the tortoise shell. When the girl looked up, Kara could see the first glint of true terror in her eyes.

Rygoth pulled downward on her gloves, calmer now, her need for violence temporarily sated.

"However, my trip to Auren was not a total waste," she said, walking toward Grace. "Those aggravating gray-cloaks were there, searching for the grim as well. I was able to stamp them out once and for all."

Father, Kara thought, a claw of panic squeezing her chest. *If Rygoth caught him again, who knows what she did?* Unbidden, a series of gruesome images flashed through her mind. *No. He has to be all right. He has to . . .*

"And so now that is two times you've promised me a grim," Rygoth said, looking down at Grace, "and two times you've failed. I knew I was right about you, broken girl. You're weak."

With every word, Grace seemed to shrink like a wilting flower.

"You told me I was special," she said quietly.

"Special?" Rygoth asked. "Ha! A middling witch, at best. The only thing remotely special about you is that you happened to know the *wexari*. I had hoped to use that relationship to my benefit, but it looks like you couldn't even do that right."

Grace winced at the insults as though they were physical blows. Tears ran down her pale cheeks.

"There is a way you can regain my favor," Rygoth said. "Think carefully before you answer, for I will only ask this once. Where is Kara Westfall?"

"I don't know," Grace said, shaking her head.

"How unfortunate for you."

"Please, my queen. If you give me a little more time I'm sure I can—"

Grace gasped in surprise.

From her new vantage point half-lying on the surface of the shell, she found herself looking upward at Rygoth. The angle brought her eyes directly in contact with Kara's.

No, Kara thought, ducking behind the hanging sculpture just before Rygoth turned around to see what had caught Grace's attention. *No, no, no.*

Kara waited a few seconds and then peeked out again. Grace started to speak, her voice halting and uncertain.

"My queen," she said. "I know where . . . I know . . ."

She stopped. Considered. Looked down at her hands.

When Grace looked up, once again finding Kara's eyes, she looked more certain of herself but somewhat bemused, as though she had made a decision that surprised her.

She rose to her feet and spoke, looking Rygoth directly in the eyes.

"Kara conjured some kind of creature that I had never seen before," Grace said, the lie told in the same sweet voice that she had once used to wrap all the villagers of De'Noran around her pretty little finger. "A bat twice the size of a man. It folded its large leathery wings around Kara and the two boys, and they all vanished. My guess is she's far, far away from here." Grace waved dismissively toward the crowd, who were watching the proceedings with horrified fascination. "Not worth your trouble to hurt these sheep anymore, my queen. Might as well forget about them and go."

Rygoth stared at Grace for a long time, rage rising within her like a gathering storm.

"*Forget?*" she finally asked, slowly removing the glove of her right hand. "A truly powerful word. I will, as you suggest, *forget* all about these people and leave them in peace. After all, what use are they to me now? But your failures, ahh, I'm afraid I can't *forget* about those. In fact, it's now your turn to *forget* something." She touched Grace's forehead with a single fingertip and whispered: "How to breathe."

Grace clawed at her throat, a look of utter bafflement on her face. She did not gasp for air. She had forgotten how. She fell to the ground, her skin turning blue. Her eyes remained fastened on Kara's the entire time. Without thinking, Kara found herself doing something she had never done before—building a mind-bridge to a human being. With the clarity of desperation, she realized what Grace wanted more than anything else and sacrificed a memory of the De'Noran crowd reveling in the Shadow Festival, the joy of a community. Grace snatched at it eagerly, and they were together.

Kara, Grace thought. *What's happening to me? I can't . . .*

I'm here, Kara said, doing her best to ease Grace's panic. *You're not alone.*

She built a world for Grace from one of her earliest memories. Two small girls—one with black hair, one with white—as they sat in the village square and drew shapes in the earth with their pudgy fingers, giggling and

whispering almost-words to each other. In a few moments
the white-haired girl's father would drag her away and
punish her for her choice of playmate, but for now there
was nothing but the uncomplicated joy of not being alone.

I wish it could stay like this, Grace thought. *I wish . . . I
wish . . .*

The mind-bridge vanished. Grace slipped away into
the dark.

BOOK THREE
THE BALANGE

"The greater the spell,
the greater the cost."

—Minoth Dravania
Final Sablethorn Lecture

SEVENTEEN

The passageways beyond the museum started as a close-fitting maze of twists and turns until finally opening up into a tunnel large enough to stand in. Kara saw Lucas's glorb lantern hovering like a glowfly in the distance.

"Taff!" she called out in a whisper-shout. "Lucas!"

She figured that the boys would simply wait for her until she caught up, but the moment they heard her voice they sprinted back in Kara's direction. She met them halfway. Lucas spun her in his arms, laughing with relief, and a few moments after that she felt Taff's comforting weight as he hugged her from behind.

"That was quick," Lucas said. "What happened?"

They stood in the darkness while she told them about Grace's final moments. Lucas and Taff listened in stunned silence.

"So she could have told Rygoth where you were and she *didn't?*" Lucas asked, baffled. "She lied to save you? Why?"

Kara shrugged, surprised to find that her eyes were damp with tears.

"I'm not sure that even Grace herself would be able to answer that."

"It's because she turned good," Taff said. "I knew it all along."

Kara wasn't convinced it was that simple. She thought that Grace's last act might have had more to do with spiting Rygoth than saving Kara. The Spider Queen had hurt Grace's feelings badly, and it was in her nature to get even.

Then again, maybe I'm wrong and Taff's right. Maybe Grace really did change at the end.

Either way, she wasn't about to diminish the glow on her brother's face by voicing her doubts.

"She turned good," Kara told him, sliding her thumb along his cheekbone. "Just like you said. Isn't that something?"

"We need to go," Lucas said softly, touching her shoulder.

They ran through the tunnel, the wind snapping their clothes like flags. Kara tried not to think about the Clinging Mist that lay just above them, the rock and dirt that could collapse on her at any moment. She imagined instead the sun's warmth on her back, the smell of flowers after a spring rainfall. As they pressed onward the wind grew in strength, slamming into them like a hurricane. Kara's legs were throbbing with exhaustion when they finally came to its source: a massive fan built into the center of the tunnel. It reminded Kara of the Windmill

Graveyard near Nye's Landing, though the blades in that place had been rusty with disuse, while these sliced through the air with deadly efficiency.

Dead end, Kara thought. *There's no way around it. And even if we managed to get past the fan, the wind would suck us back into the blades.* Her merciless imagination supplied her with a mental image to accompany that particular scenario, and Kara felt her stomach heave.

She leaped in surprise when Lucas squeezed her arm.

"There!" he screamed, indicating a metal door in the wall of the tunnel.

They managed to get through the door and pull it shut. There was no wind here, only a muffled wailing behind the wall. A musty-smelling passageway threaded through the darkness. Water dripped from the ceiling. Kara's legs grew wet as she splashed through large puddles.

"Why didn't you tell me that you had switched the real grim for a fake one?" Taff asked.

"Grace was always around," Kara said apologetically. "I never got a chance."

"Was Rygoth mad?"

"*Beyond* mad."

Taff grinned.

"I wish I could have seen it."

"Don't worry," Kara said. "We're not done making her mad. You'll get another chance. And we're going to save Safi. I promise."

"I know," Taff said. "We're the good guys. And the good guys always win."

Kara smiled encouragingly. She thought that in the darkness it might have even been convincing.

"So Rygoth has the grims from Lux and Kutt," Lucas said, speaking out loud to get it all straight in his head. "And we have the pages from Dolrose Castle. What about the one from Auren?"

Kara shook her head.

"Turns out it wasn't even there."

"But when we went back in time," Taff said, "we saw Minoth give it to that man from Auren, the one with the visor over his eyes. Maska? Mazden?"

"Mazkus," said Kara. "The grim started in Auren, but according to Rygoth it was moved at some point."

Taff nodded, the idea making sense to him.

"That Maka guy didn't seem to want it very much. If he had a chance to get rid of the thing, I think he would have done it in a heartbeat."

"All right," Lucas said. "Where do we look first?"

"Auren," said Kara.

Lucas and Taff exchanged a confused look.

"But you just said that—"

"Father went to Auren, just like I told him to," Kara said. "There was a battle between Rygoth and the gray-cloaks. She won."

"Oh no," Lucas said.

"Father?" Taff asked, squeezing the single word through a throat clenched with tears.

"Rygoth didn't say a single word about him," Kara said, "and that makes me believe that Father is just fine. She wouldn't have passed on the chance to brag about killing the great Timoth Clen, especially in front of an audience. But we still need to go to Auren and make sure he's all right. He might be hurt. He might need our help."

"Plus," Taff said, brightening, "we need to get *our* grim as far away from Rygoth as possible, and since she thinks we'll be looking for the last section of the *Vulkera* . . ."

". . . Auren is the last place she'd expect us to go," Kara finished.

At the end of the passageway they were deposited back into the main tunnel. The wind had grown weaker; they were past the danger zone of being sucked into the blades. This was only a brief respite, however, the wind growing violent again as they came to a second fan. The children passed through another metal door. This passageway was virtually identical to the first one, including the puddles, and for a few minutes all Taff could talk about was the exciting idea that the fans might be powered by water.

By the fifth fan, however, even Taff had grown quiet.

Though their initial plan had been to sleep only after

they had reached the surface, exhaustion caused them to collapse just inside the windless passageway. Kara curled up, not caring about the water dripping on her boots, and fell instantly asleep.

She awoke with a start. Someone was knocking on the metal door.

It started out gently—politely, even—a neighbor asking to borrow a cup of flour, but gradually rose in volume to an insane pounding that shook the hinges of the door.

How could I forget? Kara thought with blinding terror. *Querin. He's come for Taff. The Khr'nouls must have gotten hungry, and he's here to collect his payment.*

She begged herself not to open the door, but her shaking hand was moving of its own accord, turning the knob . . .

There was no one on the other side.

"You don't really think you can save him, do you?" asked a familiar voice behind her.

She spun around. Rygoth was bent over Taff, a single

finger pressed against his forehead. Taff jerked awake. He gasped for breath, hands clawing the air, eyes wide with fear.

Kara woke up.

A nightmare, she thought, curling next to Taff, who snored peacefully. She brushed back a lock of his hair—*Need to cut it*—and kissed him on the temple.

I have to protect him. No matter what.

The next day was more of the same, but finally, after three more fans, the children saw light in the distance and ran toward it, forgetting their exhaustion, forgetting their fear, and then leaping with great joy into a newborn morning and the welcoming warmth of the sun.

Rygoth's witches were waiting for them.

They stood ankle-deep in swamp water and looked very unhappy about it—until they caught sight of Kara. Then the apparent leader, older than the other two witches and with a flat face that looked like the result of some unfortunate ironing accident, cackled with glee.

"Our queen was right, of course," the witch said, opening her grimoire. "The white-haired traitor was a foul liar who deserved even worse than what she got. You never left Kutt. She knew that there was only one way out, and that if we just guarded this passageway you'd pop your little head out like a filthy *rat* that needs to be—"

Rattle—who had remained in the area, waiting for Kara's return—now landed on the head witch and flexed her magnificent wings, sending the other two women airborne.

The rustle-foot rattled with pleasure, a playful look in her eyes.

"You have truly excellent timing," Kara said, scratching Rattle's flank, "but I think you'd better get us out of here as quickly as possible."

Rattle's landing had not gone unnoticed. Kara could hear shouts in the distance, hooves pounding wetly through the muck. Rattle ran along the tips of her wings until she found a clear spot to take off and then shot into the air. As they left the ground, a group of witches riding creatures resembling gold-plated ostriches burst through the trees.

"You're too late!" Taff exclaimed, waving both hands with glee. "Bet you wish you could—"

The ostriches leaped into the air.

They didn't fly, exactly, but climbed higher in a series of giant jumps, as though the sky were composed of landings that only they could see. Just below Rattle, one of the golden ostriches ran at blinding speed along ground that wasn't there. Kara noticed that its two-toed feet, black at the start of its leap, were now the precise blue of the sky—either an intrinsic part of its magic or a meaningless side effect. The ostrich bent its thin, powerful legs and vaulted to another invisible landing, its brethren right behind it.

Running on thin air should have been impossible. But these were Rygoth's creatures, and the laws of nature were not for them.

Lucas turned so he was facing backward and aimed his glorb-bow. His first arrow missed, but the second one took an ostrich in the neck. The strange bird and the witch on its back fell in two different directions.

"Higher, Rattle," Kara said. "Maybe we can get out of their range."

As though anticipating this plan, one of the witches read from her grimoire. The clouds above them turned dark. Lightning cracked across the sky, followed by a great peal of thunder. A torrent of rain drenched Kara's hair.

"I got another one," Lucas said with a flat, pragmatic tone that made it clear he took no pleasure from the act. He reached for a new arrow. With a sinking feeling, Kara saw that there were only three remaining in his quill.

"I'll get help," Kara said, reaching out with her powers. *There are some vultures in the distance—good fighters, but too far. I need someone closer. Maybe those sicklejays. Not as strong, but they can be here in—*

Rattle suddenly reared in pain.

Kara struggled to hold on, feeling Rattle's rising panic as she continued to jerk and twist frantically in midair. *What's going on, girl?* Kara asked. And then she saw. One of the ostriches hung upside down from Rattle's torso, its claws sunk deep. The rustle-foot was desperately trying to shake the creature free. The witch on the ostrich's back smiled with malicious glee as she withdrew a serrated dagger from her cloak and raised it above Rattle's stomach.

"Can you tell her to stay still for a moment?" Lucas asked, leaning dangerously over the side while drawing back his bow. "I can't get a clear shot if—"

The witch plunged her dagger home.

A screech of pain filled Kara's head. Rattle shook more violently than ever.

The ostrich fell. The witch fell.

Lucas fell.

Kara threw herself across the rustle-foot and managed

to grab his satchel before it vanished out of sight. Lucas's weight jerked her forward, and Taff wrapped his arms around her, pulling back with all his strength. Kara peered over the edge. Lucas was dangling with both hands grasping the satchel, his legs kicking empty air.

"Hang on," Kara said. "I'm going to pull you back up."

"No!" Lucas exclaimed. "It's too dangerous! You'll fall!"

Rattle, delirious with pain, was climbing upward toward the black clouds. Kara tried to send the rustlefoot calming images but could not think of any right now. It was taking all her concentration to hold on to Lucas. Just beneath him Kara saw the last two ostriches, running on their invisible platform. The first one leaped at Lucas. He saw it just in time and stomped down, his boot striking its neck with a satisfying *thwack*. The animal tried to land, but the sky below it, blue when it leaped, had turned black, and the color of its feet no longer matched. It tumbled through the sky, striking one invisible surface after the other. The witch on its back screamed as they vanished out of sight.

One more left.

Grunting with effort, Kara pulled Lucas a few inches higher. The clouds grew preternaturally dark, a black fog making it difficult to see. Wind whipped her hair. Lightning flashed.

Stay still, Rattle, she pleaded, feeling the lifeblood pour out of the creature, her panicked thoughts a swirling maelstrom to match the sky. *Please.*

Somehow, Kara's calming words made it through to the creature. Despite her agony and fear, Rattle managed to steady her flight.

Thank you, brave friend, Kara thought.

She pulled Lucas higher, his hand just beyond her reach now, and heard a tearing sound: the strap of the satchel.

NO!

"Kara," Lucas said, his face suddenly calm. "Stop pulling. It's going to break. If the grim falls, Rygoth will find it. We can't risk that."

"It won't break," Kara said, even as the satchel slipped lower, the weak fibers holding it together tearing apart. "Just hold on . . ."

"You're the only one who can stop her," he said.

Lucas let go.

Kara screamed as he vanished into the dark mists.

"Lucas! Lucas!"

Desperately she called out for help—*Someone catch him!*—but her thoughts were too chaotic to create a workable mind-bridge, and her loss instead became an incoherent shriek of pain felt by all the animals of Sentium. In the forests of Auren, owls jerked in their sleep, beset by unexplainable fears; Luxian piglets cuddled closer to their mothers; beneath the Windmill Graveyards of Ilma a single gray wolf howled in sorrow.

"Rattle!" Kara shouted, sitting up, forcing herself to remain calm. "Down! As fast as you can! Down!"

Kara felt the brave rustle-foot, weak and dazed as she

was, gather her senses, ready to rocket toward the ground like an arrow and catch the falling boy, when a bolt of lightning struck her wing. The creature's body went lax as she lost consciousness and fell lifelessly through the air. Kara clung desperately to her neck, Taff beneath her, holding tight. "Don't let go," she whispered in his ear. While spiraling downward, Kara saw white pages fluttering through the darkness and realized that she had lost her grip on the satchel.

They continued to fall, in blue sky once more, the ground approaching far too fast.

Kara closed her eyes.

EIGHTEEN

She awoke to find a one-eyed bird staring back at her.

"Watcher?" Kara mumbled, not believing her eyes. Her head was pounding fiercely, and her left shoulder felt swollen and out of joint. The ground beneath her was strangely rough and warm.

Where am I? What happened? She tried to recall, but her mind felt empty. All she wanted to do was go back to sleep.

She closed her eyes.

Watcher pecked her hand.

"Ow!" Kara exclaimed.

The bird's single eye rolled out of sight and was quickly displaced by eyes of various other colors, reminding Kara, as always, of marbles on a track. The subtle variations in hue each represented a different word or feeling; it was Watcher's way of communicating with her.

Up! Fast! Bad witches come soon!

Kara should have reacted with horror to this news, but instead she was overwhelmed by the marvelous fact that she could *understand* what Watcher was saying. She hadn't been in possession of her powers the last time she had seen the bird, rendering its colors a language she no longer spoke.

"I've missed you," Kara said, her voice trembling. "I didn't mean to hurt you that time in the Thickety. I'm so sorry. Please . . ."

I forgive you, Witch Girl. Cry later. Brother need help.

Those last three words, conveyed with the brown of burned butter, jerked Kara to life as effectively as a smelling salt. Ignoring her pain, she pushed herself up and realized that she was not lying on the ground at all.

"No!" she gasped.

Kara reached out with her mind, but Rattle was gone; the rustle-foot had used her own body to break their fall, sacrificing her life to save theirs. *Noble protector*, Kara thought, the tears coming freely now. *Until the very end.*

Taff, groggy but unhurt, had managed to sit up. There were tears in his eyes as well.

"Rattle?" he asked. Kara crawled over and took him in her arms.

She started to remember. Their flight from Kutt. The lost satchel.

Lucas.

Her initial reaction was to blame herself. *If I had acted calmly, been in control of my powers, I could have saved him.* But Kara knew that there was nothing to be gained from that sort of self-pity. The true fault for every misfortune that had befallen them was Rygoth. She pictured the *wexari*'s face, as cruel and beautiful as marble, and molten rage gushed through her veins.

I hate you, she thought, knowing that mindless anger led nowhere but choosing, for just this one moment, to bask in it. *I hate you, I hate you, I hate you.* In her mind's eye she saw Lucas fall, heard his last words: *You're the only one who can stop her.*

I will, she promised.

"We need to go," Kara said, forcing back any further tears. Once she started to grieve for Lucas she wouldn't be able to stop, and right now she needed to get Taff to safety. "They'll find us if we stay here."

Taff buried his face in her shoulder. His tears dampened her neck.

"I'm so sorry about Lucas," he said.

"We need to go," she repeated.

Kara helped him to his feet and together they slid off Rattle's body. They had landed in the middle of the swamp; the marshy ground rose up to her ankles. Low-growing trees provided cover for now, but Kara was certain the witches would find them soon enough.

"Why's Watcher here?" Taff asked. A long gash ran beneath his left eye and along the side of his nose. It wasn't bleeding much, but it was certainly going to leave a scar.

"I don't know," Kara said, awkwardly using her left sleeve to clean the wound; her right arm hung uselessly at her side. She faced the one-eyed bird, who was perched on a nearby branch. "How did you find us?"

A flash of colors: *Always find you. Kara. Watcher. Connected.*

"Because we're friends?"

Connected. I am part of you. You are part of me.

This line of inquiry was only making Kara's head hurt more, so she tried a different angle.

"Why are you here?"

Take.

Watcher shook its left claw. Kara saw that a small pouch had been tied to it.

Take. Use.

"Kara," Taff whispered. "I think I hear someone coming."

Watcher hopped up and down.

Quickly! No time!

Kara reached out, intending to unhook the pouch, but Watcher stepped back.

Not for you.

The bird swiveled to face Taff.

With the sounds of their enemy now undeniably close, Taff quickly pulled the pouch off Watcher's foot and opened it. Inside was a simple wooden whistle. Taff brought it to his lips.

"Don't," Kara said. "They'll know exactly where we are!"

"Don't worry," Taff said, grinning. "This can only be from one person."

He blew the whistle.

It didn't make a sound, not that Kara's ears could hear,

at least, but she felt an almost painful sensation in her teeth and the fetid vapors of the swamp were replaced with the comforting smells of sawdust and burning peat. Taff blew the whistle again, harder this time, his face turning red and his cheeks puffing out. The smell of burning peat strengthened—Kara could even feel its heat on her skin!—and then the swamp vanished altogether.

They stood in a small workshop.

A thin layer of smoke hazed their surroundings: peat burning in the stone fireplace. Tools hung from the wall and hundreds of jars lined the shelves. These were filled with all manner of colored beads, springs, pegs, cogs, tiny bells, and wheels of every size. All sorts of wooden toys, some only half finished, stuffed the shelves to overflowing: finely carved animals, boats, play food, dolls, and more whistles than Kara had ever seen. The workshop, as a whole, did not appear to be overly organized, but Kara had the impression that its owner would be able to find anything she wanted.

Watcher, who had made this impromptu journey with them, sailed out a window just as a door opened and an old woman with short gray hair rushed into the room.

"It worked!" Mary Kettle exclaimed, throwing her arms around the children. "I wasn't certain. Risky thing, transporting you here with magic, but I had to chance it. There was no need for you to be risking your lives one moment longer, now that we——" She drew back and took in their faces. "It's so *good* to see you. You both look so much older. Taff, I'm cutting your hair *tonight*."

Mary was crushing Kara's bad arm, sending slivers of pain down her shoulder, but she didn't care—the pain meant she wasn't dreaming. They had first met Mary Kettle after fleeing the villagers of De'Noran and entering the Thickety, though Kara had heard about her long before that, the legendary witch who used children's souls to enchant her wicked toys. At first Mary had lived up to her evil reputation, but in the end she had overcome the darkness within her and saved their lives.

She looked at Kara now with deep sympathy.

"There's sorrow draped across those beautiful eyes of yours," she said. "What happened?"

"I lost someone."

"I'm sorry to hear that," Mary said, "but hold those tears at bay just a little bit longer, if you can. Right now you're expected. Come."

She opened the front door.

"Whoa!" exclaimed Taff.

Kara's legs trembled, the breathtaking beauty of the forest overwhelming to behold. Leaves of all colors—pumpkin orange, apple red, brilliant hues of gold—complemented one another in autumnal harmony. A crisp breeze caressed her cheeks, carrying with it the smells of honeysuckle and cinnamon.

Exhaustion, both physical and psychological, drained from her body. She felt instantly and totally at peace.

"Kara," Taff said, smiling. "Look!"

Dozens of animals were approaching them, some as small as chipmunks, others as large as elk. Most bore wounds that had been imperfectly sealed over with scars or misshapen fur. Though many were fierce-looking, with long fangs or sharp talons, Kara knew they were not dangerous—not to her, at least.

"This is a big day for them," Mary said. "They've been waiting a long time for your return."

Kara bent down and allowed the nearby creatures to nuzzle her hand.

"What is this place?" she asked in wonder.

"Haven't you figured it out yet?" Mary asked, laughing. "It's the Thickety, my dear! Welcome home."

As Mary led them past rows of huts and awe-struck villagers, Kara gathered as much of the story as she could. After she had used Niersook's venom to strip Sordyr of his powers, and thus turn him back into a man, the curse on the Thickety had been lifted. Over the past year and a half the forest had returned to its original state. Black fronds transformed into colorful leaves, poisonous flora withered away, and the animals shed the evil influence that had infected them. Safi's home village of Kala Malta, along with several other communities scattered throughout the forest, had banded together. Mary had recently been elected as their leader.

"I used to have nightmares about this place," Kara said, petting a bulbous-eyed paarn walking by her side. "Seems hard to believe now."

"There's good in all places," Mary said. "People too."

"Do you really believe that?"

"I do."

"Then why is there so much evil in the world?" Taff asked.

"Because it's easy," Mary said. "Easier to destroy than to build. Easier to blame than forgive. Evil corrupts. Tempts." She waved her hand dismissively. "*Anyone* can do that—Rygoth's nothing special. But good? Good heals.

Redeems. That's hard." She looked at Kara. "That takes someone truly remarkable."

Kara shook her head, unwilling to accept the praise.

"I'm happy to see how things have changed, of course," she said. "But let's not forget what else happened. When I undid the curse on this place, I freed Rygoth. She's hurt so many people since then. Was it worth it?"

"You did what you thought was right," Mary said as they reached a large hut in the center of the village. "We can only control our actions. The results?" She shrugged. "What happens, happens. And who knows? Even bad things may happen for a good reason."

She opened the front door.

"Father!" Taff exclaimed.

William Westfall stretched out his arms and Taff leaped joyously into them, Kara right behind him. They stayed that way for a long time, until Mary snapped her fingers and said, "Psst! Graycloaks coming!"

Father pushed the children away.

"They still believe I'm Timoth Clen," he whispered. "Forgive me for this."

Two graycloaks entered the hut. Father's kind face hardened into a mask of severity.

"My lord," the first man said, kneeling. "We've completed our rounds, and—"

His mouth fell open when he saw Kara.

"That's the witch of De'Noran!" he said, raising his bow-staff. "What's she doing here?"

Father stepped between the graycloak and Kara.

"As you know," he said, with Clenian arrogance, "this witch fought Rygoth herself and saved my life. She is a useful tool, and I will wield her as I see fit."

"Forgive me, my lord, but I don't understand," the man said, his head bowed. "'Magic is the vilest of sins, beyond forgiveness.' It says that in the Path itself."

"The Path also says, 'Magic can be wielded for the greater good.'"

The graycloak looked confused.

"I don't remember reading——"

"Do you claim to know the holy book better than me?" Father asked, stepping forward.

"Of course not, sir."

"Leave us. Now."

The two men scampered out of the hut. Taff stared at his father with shocked admiration.

"You lied about the *Path*!" he said.

"Shh," Father said, kissing him on the forehead. "Hopefully he won't look it up later." He smiled at Mary. "Thanks for the warning. Do you think you could linger just outside, make sure we're not interrupted for a little while?"

"My pleasure," Mary said, slipping through the door.

"Sit," Father said, indicating a small table laden with bread and fruit. Taff immediately grabbed a handful of berries and shoved them into his mouth. He grinned with blue teeth. "Hungry," he said.

"I have so many questions," Kara said. "I don't even

know where to begin." Father watched her tenderly, as though he couldn't believe she was actually here. His beard had grown fuller since they last met, brown salted with white. Kara liked it.

"Just ask the first question that pops into your head," Father said. "Don't worry about the order. We'll figure it out together."

"How do you know Mary?"

"We arrived here a few weeks ago. After Mary determined that my graycloaks posed no threat to her people, we became fast friends. She knew that I wasn't really Timoth Clen from the start. Sharp old lady." Father scrunched his brows. "Well, when she *is* old, that is. Her age changes from day to day, you know."

Taff grinned. "We know."

"I'll never get used to this magic of yours," he said. "Anyway, she told me how you fought the Forest Demon and saved the Thickety. I wish your mother was here to see the great heroes our two children have become."

"We didn't really do *that* much," Kara said, blushing.

"She's just being modest, Father," Taff said. "You should have seen it! We were *amazing!*"

Taff immediately dove into a spirited retelling of their adventures in the Thickety and Sentium. He was a gifted storyteller, skimming over the nonessential parts and focusing only on the most important details (with the exception of signing his name on Querin Fyndrake's door, which he skipped altogether). Though none of these events were news to Kara, she listened intently, reliving them through her father's proud eyes.

When Taff reached the part about Lucas's fall through the clouds, Kara kept her gaze firmly on the table, refusing to cry.

Later, she thought. *When I'm alone.*

"I'm so sorry," Father said, folding his large hands around hers. "I know how much he meant to you. And I was fond of him myself, truth be told. I came to think of him as a second son."

Knowing that she wouldn't be able to stop crying once the dam was breached, Kara shifted the conversation away from Lucas.

"You received my letter about the grim being in Auren, right?" Kara asked. "Did you find it? Rygoth said it wasn't there, but I thought maybe you had just beaten her to it and—"

But Father was already shaking his head.

"Sorry," he said. "We did get there first, but the grim was already long gone. It *had* been stored in the Silent Vault at one point—you were right about that. But after a thousand years of being told that magic was nothing but superstitious nonsense, the Aurians stopped believing that the grim held any sort of power. It was just a worthless artifact, nothing more. So they sold it."

"To who?" Taff asked.

"A religious cult whose antiquated ideas had fallen out of favor. They swore that they would protect the grim from witches, the greatest evil in the world. The Aurians didn't believe a word of it, of course, but the Fold's coin was good, and they were happy to rid themselves of—"

"They sold the grim to *the Fold*?" Kara asked in disbelief.

Father nodded, smiling slightly.

"Once I learned that, I got an idea about where the grim might really be located," Father said. "But Rygoth's forces reached Auren before we could leave. It was a devastating attack. I lost over three-quarters of my men."

Kara heard the sadness in his voice and realized that although Father was only pretending to be Timoth Clen, he legitimately cared for the soldiers in his charge.

"I led those of us who survived to Nye's Landing, where we hired a ship to take us to De'Noran," said Father.

"The Children of the Fold brought the grim here!" Taff exclaimed, his brain racing. "Of course! That might have even been the reason they picked De'Noran as their home in the first place. So far away from the rest of the world, a cursed forest—no one would ever want to come here. It's the perfect hiding spot."

"My thoughts exactly," Father said, mussing Taff's hair. "I think that the existence of the grim was a secret passed down from fen'de to fen'de."

"Have you started looking for it yet?" Taff asked. His eyes glowed with a sudden thought. "Maybe Fen'de Stone left behind a *treasure map* with riddles and clues to—"

"I already found it," Father said.

"The map?"

"The grim."

"Oh," said Taff, clearly disappointed.

Kara shook her fogged head, wondering if she had heard Father correctly.

"You have the grim?" she asked. "Are you sure?"

Father nodded. "It's under guard, night and day—though my graycloaks believe that they're protecting our stockpile of coin, not the most dangerous object in the world. The less people who know, the better."

"Where did you find it?" Taff asked.

"Buried beneath the Fenroot tree."

Taff and Kara exchanged a look of gape-mouthed surprise. The Fenroot tree had been the epicenter of their village. They had passed it dozens of times a day, sat beneath its limbs during Worship.

All those hours spent bewailing the evils of magic—none of us had any idea what was buried just a few feet away.

"We have to keep the grim safe," Kara said. "Rygoth already has the other three. If she finds out—"

"She won't," Father said.

"Someone from Auren could have told her about the Fold," Taff said. "She could figure it out, like you did."

"There were only two men left who knew the truth, and they both died in the battle," Father said. "I saw it happen. The secret is ours alone. And Mary Kettle's. I feel like I can trust her, for some reason."

"You can," Taff said.

"This is a place of nightmares for Rygoth," Kara said, thinking it through. "She spent two thousand years trapped beneath the dirt here. She won't return without a reason."

"Exactly," said Father. "Without the final grim, Rygoth will never be able to assemble the princess's grimoire. It's the best ending we could have hoped for."

Kara considered other ways that Rygoth might learn about the grim's location. *Not Safi—even if she had a vision, she's already proven that she would never reveal it to the Spider Queen. Querin Fyndrake is a possibility, but if Rygoth knew of the Hourglass Tower she would have already gone there.*

Father was right. The final grim was safe.

"So what's next?" she asked, feeling a foreign sense of relief.

Father looked at her strangely.

"Nothing," he said.

"Nothing?"

"We stay here. Protect the grim. Live our lives. I'm sure you've noticed, but this isn't the Thickety of old. We can make this a home. Be a family again."

Kara couldn't believe what she was hearing.

"We can't just sit here and do nothing while Rygoth lays waste to Sentium."

"We don't want to do anything that risks drawing attention to ourselves. That will only increase the chance of Rygoth finding the grim. Sometimes doing nothing is the best course of action."

Kara stood up, knocking her chair backward.

"Not when people are dying! We need to fight!"

She stared at him fiercely, black eyes blazing, daring him to contradict her.

Father smiled.

"You look exactly like your mother when you're angry," he said, and despite her anger Kara felt a glimmer of pleasure at the comparison. "Just hear me out, please. One question. And answer honestly. Promise, Moonbeam?"

He indicated Kara's chair. She reluctantly took a seat.

"I'm too old for that name," she said, crossing her arms peevishly.

"You might be right about that," said Father. "So I'm going to treat you like an adult and tell you the hard truth of what's going to happen. In a few days' time, leaders from all over Sentium will be gathering at Penta's Keep."

"Yes!" Kara exclaimed. "Instead of trying to fight Rygoth on their own they can band together, form a common army . . ."

Father shook his head.

"I think this is hard for you to appreciate," he said, "because you have magic at your command. But imagine what it's like for a common soldier. Rygoth can conjure monsters out of nothingness. Her witches can control the weather, befuddle minds, make inanimate objects come to life. What use are swords and bows against power like that? We're like children kicking at dragons. All we can do now is try to save as many innocent lives as possible."

"What are you saying?" Kara asked, a sick feeling in her stomach.

"These leaders are not meeting to figure out the best way to fight Rygoth," Father said, unable to meet her eyes. "They're meeting to prepare their formal surrender."

"No," Kara said. "They can't do that. It's a mistake."

"I agree," Father said. "I warned the leader of Auren when she told me their plan. They shouldn't trust Rygoth, even for a moment. But it's not up to us. They're going to proclaim her the Supreme Ruler of Sentium and swear their loyalty to—"

"NO!" Kara shouted, slamming both of her hands down on the table. "If they do that, she wins!"

"She's already won!" Father exclaimed. "It's just a matter of how many more people have to die before we concede victory. The best we can do is keep the grim out of her hands so at least we still have a world to live in."

"What about Safi and Bethany?" Taff asked quietly. "Are we just going to forget about them?"

Father inhaled deeply and scratched his beard.

"I will let the leaders know about your friends," he

said, almost—but not quite—meeting Kara's eyes. "Perhaps their freedom can be negotiated when they meet with Rygoth. But I won't have you two gallivanting off on some foolish rescue attempt. The risk is too great." He took them in his arms. "You've done enough. *More* than enough. This is your life now, children. You're home at last."

NINETEEN

T he village doctor used her gnarled fingers to pop Kara's shoulder into place and offered her herbs for the pain, which Kara refused; she had a lot to think about and didn't want her brain fogged by medicine. What she needed more than anything was some time alone, away from people—and so she hurried to the paddock that Mary Kettle had told her about, just outside the main village.

Shadowdancer was waiting for her.

Kara leaped over the fence and wrapped her arms around the mare's neck. Shadowdancer told her the story. She and Darno had tracked down the graycloaks, as planned, and the mare had been welcomed into the cavalry. The scorpion-wolf followed them at a distance, and when Shadowdancer had boarded the ship that brought them here to De'Noran, Darno snuck into the cargo hold.

Reaching out with her powers, Kara felt the wolf crashing through the undergrowth of the Thickety, joyously free. Though she missed his companionship, she did not call him to her side.

He's happy. Let him be.

Kara nuzzled her face close to Shadowdancer.

"You up for a ride, girl?" she asked, though she already knew the answer. The paddock, despite its lush grass and freshly painted wooden fence, was no more than a prison to the speed-starved mare.

They galloped west to what used to be the village of De'Noran. Overgrown with fields of vibrant wildflowers, it bore little resemblance to Kara's childhood home, but she was able to recognize enough landmarks to find what she was looking for: a small hill overlooking what used to be a schoolhouse.

Kara sat down, brushing the silken grass with her fingers. Forest creatures peeked between branches and out of dens, eager to comfort their queen but sensing her need for solitude.

At last she allowed the tears to fall.

Lucas.

She had known loss before, but never like this, a physical force that drained all the strength from her body and left her feeling numb, as though death itself had tunneled through her veins and made a home of her heart. Kara's grief was tinged with guilt, not only because she hadn't been a good enough *wexari* to save her friend, but for the memories of Lucas that she had sacrificed to magic. It seemed inconceivable that she had thought a spell—any spell—could be more important than a moment with the boy she loved.

If I had known he was going to be taken from me, I wouldn't have parted with a single memory.

Kara had hoped that a return to their hill, the scene of so many happy times together, might help her recall some of these lost moments. She squeezed her head between her hands, willing herself to remember, but it was pointless; the gaps in the fabric of her mind remained, as immutable as the darkness between stars. For the first time, Kara understood the extent of the sacrifice demanded by *wexari* magic, for memories are the building blocks of life. *They make us who we are*, she thought. *They guide us, teach us, and act as a comforting blanket when days are cold. Without our memories, we're barely even human.*

This thought planted itself in her mind and, as great ideas often do, grew unnoticed until blossoming into an epiphany during her ride back to the village. Kara slowed Shadowdancer to a crawl, turning this unexpected revelation over and over in her head.

Could it be true? she thought.

Only one man could tell her for sure.

After getting directions from a young graycloak too afraid to meet her eyes, Kara journeyed to an area of the

Thickety that hadn't yet changed from the dark forest of old. A thick canopy blocked the light of the sun, and tree limbs reached for them like dangling claws. Shadowdancer didn't like this sudden change in their environment, but Kara found it surprisingly comforting.

"Relax," she whispered in Shadowdancer's ear. "There's nothing to fear here."

Kara could sense her creatures nearby, more monstrous than those found in the brighter part of the forest but every bit as loyal. There was no need for mind-bridges; they knew who she was, and they welcomed her like family. Kara basked in the glow of their simple affection and shared her affection in return.

They're starved for a kind thought, Kara thought. *If there's one thing all monsters have in common, it's that they haven't known enough love in their lives.* She was reminded of the faenix, who had only wanted a companion during its lonely hours in the dark, and Grace, desperate for her father's approval.

These thoughts led to Princess Evangeline.

What did you want? What made you into a monster?

Kara suspected that might be the key to everything.

She found the massive old tree that the graycloak had told her about and knocked on the door built into its trunk. When no one answered, she opened the door and entered a room-size tree hollow. There was very little furniture, just a simple cot, a pair of stools, and a long table covered with vials and jars of herbs. Shells of sunflower seeds littered the floor like a rodent's bedding. Kara approached the table and looked through a magnifying glass propped over a large brown seed. It had been cracked open with incredible precision and stuffed with what appeared to be bird feathers.

"Leave that alone," a voice said. "It's not finished yet."

Kara spun around to find Sordyr standing in the doorway. His brown hair had turned almost completely gray since she last saw him, but his eyes remained the same piercing green.

Watcher fluttered through the door and perched on a roost in the corner.

"What are you doing?" she asked, indicating the seed.

"Nothing. Just an experiment to pass the time. It probably won't even work."

"I thought you couldn't do magic anymore."

"I can't. This won't need magic until the very end. I'll ask Mary to enchant it if I actually think there's a chance——" He crossed the room and threw a scrap of linen over the dissected seed. "It's not important."

"Did you know I was back?" Kara asked.

Sordyr nodded.

"I would have come to see you, but . . . I'm not exactly welcome in the village. Oh, they say the right things, but I see them whisper when I pass. They can't look at me without remembering what I did."

Sordyr had been one of Sablethorn's most promising *wexari* until Rygoth had transformed him into a Forest Demon. In this guise, he had infected the Thickety with evil and forced the residents of Kala Malta to construct the grimoires that now wreaked havoc throughout Sentium, retaining just enough of his humanity to keep Rygoth imprisoned on the island. It was a status quo that Kara had unwittingly destroyed.

"Do you want some tea?" Sordyr asked. "I should have asked that straight off. I don't have guests often, so I'm afraid I'm out of practice with my niceties."

"Tea sounds wonderful," Kara said. "As long as it's not Clearer tea. My friend Lucas had to drink that stuff to cleanse his body from the Fringe weeds they burned. Worst thing I ever tasted. He used to dare me to drink it."

Kara thought that the memory might make her sad, but it didn't. She was happy that she still remembered it.

"It's just regular tea," Sordyr said.

"Perfect."

She watched him hang a kettle over a small fire carefully contained within a circle of stones. *It's hard to believe that this is the man who once struck terror in my entire village.*

He kept looking in her direction, smiling uncertainly, as though to make sure she wasn't going to leave. *He's human again, and lonely out here all by himself.*

Though she was anxious to ask her questions, Kara waited patiently until the tea was ready, taking a hesitant sip from the steaming mug and then a longer one. It was bitter but delicious.

"I like it," she said.

"I'm glad."

Kara put the mug on the table.

"I have some questions for you."

"I suspected you might." Sordyr shook his mug gently, swirling his tea. "Are they about . . . her?"

Kara didn't believe that Sordyr avoided saying Rygoth's name because he was frightened, but because it still pained him to think about her betrayal. She had once been his friend, maybe even more.

"I was actually more interested in Princess Evangeline," Kara said.

Sordyr pulled up a stool with interest.

"I told you everything I remembered in my letter. She was an unhappy little girl, and I never should have given her the grimoire. She took to its dark power all too well."

"But why was the grimoire evil to begin with? And so powerful? Minoth told me you designed it as a bauble, nothing more."

"How in the world do you know that?"

Quickly, Kara summarized her encounters with the Sablethorn headmaster, both in the Well of Witches and in the past. Sordyr hung on every word, thirsting for news of his old mentor.

"You've been busy," he said, chuckling to himself. "Truth be told, I don't know why my gift to Evangeline contained such power. Or such darkness. But the fault must be mine. I made it. I was so eager to impress Rygoth, and I never should have attempted something so—"

"What about the other grimoires?" Kara asked. "The ones that the people of Kala Malta produced in the Bindery? Were they made a different way than the *Vulkera*?"

"No," Sordyr said. "I changed the process a little so the grimoires could be mass produced, but the primary method remained the same."

"Then why aren't they as powerful?"

"Think of magic as a raging fire. The other grimoires are warmed by its heat. The *Vulkera* is the fire itself. The source."

"I thought the Well of Witches was the source of the grimoires' power," Kara said, confused. "Unless"— *thoughts inscribed across paperlike ground, parchment sky, borders like leather-bound walls*—"is the Well of Witches *inside* the *Vulkera*?"

"No," Sordyr said. "The physical Well of Witches is where Phadeen used to be, the place where Minoth would train *wexari*. Much easier for the *Vulkera* to corrupt a preexisting magical reality than to create a new one. The *Vulkera*—its role in this is a bit harder to explain, and this is only my theory, mind you——"

"The Well is the body, the *Vulkera* is the soul. If the *Vulkera* is bad, all the grimoires are bad."

Sordyr tipped his mug in her direction. "A little simplistic, but probably as close as we're going to get."

"Except that's impossible," Kara said.

"Why's that?" asked Sordyr with interest.

Kara smiled, surprised to find that she was enjoying their conversation immensely. *Was this what it was like in Sablethorn? Students debating the various intricacies of magic?*

She would have loved it.

"Once Evangeline cast her Last Spell, the *Vulkera* became a direct link to the Well of Witches, which makes it more powerful than any other grimoire," Kara said. "That all makes sense. But if it's the Well that gives the *Vulkera* its power, how did the *Vulkera* have enough power to create the Well in the first place? That's not the type of magic it should have been capable of."

"Ah," said Sordyr, nodding in appreciation. "Like the

chicken and the egg. You're right, of course. That's always been the weak point in my little theory. I could never really come up with a satisfactory explanation." He noted Kara's wide-eyed expression. "But it looks like you might have a theory of your own to share."

Kara stood up and stretched her back. Her shoulder was beginning to throb like mad, but she blocked out the pain and focused on the matter at hand. Answers that had eluded her for far too long finally felt within her grasp, and yet she hesitated, questioning the wild ideas that had seemed so feasible in her head.

Am I even thinking clearly right now? Will Sordyr laugh at me? Only one way to find out.

"Princess Evangeline was *wexari*," Kara said, and Sordyr's eyes widened with surprise. "Her father knew it, but he wasn't a supporter of Sablethorn and the last thing he wanted was his beloved daughter becoming one of *them*. So he built Evangeline a castle way out in the middle of the desert, where her powers could remain a secret. My guess is that somehow Rygoth learned of the girl's talents. That's why she traveled to Dolrose Castle to become the king's adviser after she was expelled. If Sablethorn didn't want her, Rygoth would just start her own army of witches. Only there was a flaw in Rygoth's plan. According to those who met her before Rygoth's arrival, Evangeline was a happy little girl. There was no darkness in her. So Rygoth changed that."

Sordyr started to take a sip from his tea and noticed that his mug was empty. He went back to the kettle and refilled it. Kara hesitated a moment, waiting for him to tell her that she was being ridiculous.

"Go on," he said instead.

"Rygoth stole Evangeline's memories. Not all of them, mind you. Just the happy ones. Imagine what that would be like. If all of a sudden you had no memory of any hugs or laughter or kind words—of anyone having ever loved you. I don't think Evangeline was evil at all. I think Rygoth tore that poor girl's mind apart until there was nothing left but a dark, empty shell."

"How do you know for sure?" Sordyr asked.

"Princess Evangeline's spirit still resides in the *Vulkera*," Kara said, wrapping her arms around her chest. "When I touched a section of it, I felt what it was like to be her. It was terrible, like being swallowed by darkness. Her presence became even stronger when I brought two grims close together. She spoke to me."

"What did she say?"

"'Who are you?'" Kara said, hearing the girl's haunted voice in her mind. "I didn't reply. I was too scared."

"I doubt she would have heard you anyway," Sordyr said. "To actually communicate with her spirit, I think you'd need to restore the *Vulkera* completely."

"So I'm right?" Kara asked with rising excitement.

Sordyr mulled this over. He brought the mug to his lips, his hand shaking slightly. Then he dumped the tea on the ground and filled the mug with liquid from a flask inside his cloak.

"Do you know why Rygoth is more powerful than other *wexari*?" he asked.

The question, seemingly off-topic, caught Kara unawares.

"She was born with a gift," Kara said. "Well, a gift for her. A curse for everyone else. I didn't think it went deeper than that."

"It does," Sordyr said. "And to truly understand Rygoth, you need to understand the source of her abilities." He paused a moment, as if unsure where to begin. "One of the first things you're taught at Sablethorn is the importance of the Balance. You must give a piece of yourself in order to cast a spell. That's how nature guarantees that no one *wexari* grows too powerful. For some it's a physical sacrifice. Each spell costs a headache or an upset stomach, minor ailments like that. It gives *wexari* limits, keeps them humble." Sordyr held out his two hands, perfectly level. "Balance. Cast an overly ambitious spell, and magic will dig its fangs into you and take all it can. Many *wexari*, overestimating their own skills, have lost the ability to walk or see. The greater the spell, the greater the cost. Balance."

Kara remembered what it was like when she created Topper, the memories spilling out of her like a punctured sack of grain.

"It isn't always a physical sacrifice, of course," Sordyr continued. "Other *wexari* trade minutes from their life, their ability to think and reason. And some, as you know, trade their memories. One of the most dangerous exchanges, in my opinion."

"What about Rygoth?" Kara asked. "What does she exchange?"

Sordyr turned away from her. Candlelit shadows flickered against his back.

"Rygoth is a special case," he said softly. "The rarest. And the most powerful. Each time she casts a spell she exchanges a piece of her soul. I doubt there's anything human left in her by this point, but she *was* good once."

He smiled sadly. "That must be so hard for you to believe."

Kara shook her head. "I know how magic can change a person."

With a weary sigh, Sordyr sat back down and indicated that she should do the same.

"Your theory about Evangeline being an unidentified *wexari* is definitely possible," he said. "If that were the case, her talent certainly would have augmented the power of the grimoire. And I also agree that Rygoth was probably stealing her memories. Corrupting others to suit her needs is how she operates—I think we can both appreciate that. But now I have a question for you. What does it matter if Evangeline was evil to begin with or another of Rygoth's victims? It doesn't change what happened. What's done is—"

"Did you make it so that grimoires could only be used by girls, or did that happen after Evangeline?" Kara asked.

Sordyr stared at her, utterly baffled.

"I don't understand why that matters."

"Just answer the question. Please."

"I have no idea why only girls can use grimoires," Sordyr said. "I've never understood it."

Kara clapped her hands with excitement.

"So that was Evangeline's doing too!" she exclaimed. "I knew it! That *proves* I'm right!"

"I'm a little lost," Sordyr said, running a hand through his unkempt hair.

"Minoth told me that magic wasn't evil," Kara said. "He said that it was sick—and that I was the one meant to heal it. I think I finally know how."

"Tell me."

Kara explained her plan. Sordyr listened carefully. In the end, he agreed that there was a possibility that it might work—a *minor* possibility—but that the risks were far too great.

"Even if everything else in your mad idea comes to pass, the last spell that you're suggesting has never been attempted before. It's not the type of magic that you walk away from unchanged—if you walk away at all."

"But if it works . . ."

"It won't. Such a spell would take a master *wexari*—I don't even know if Minoth Dravania himself could—"

"But *if*—"

"You'll die, Kara!" Sordyr exclaimed.

Silence shrouded the room.

"The Balance, right?" Kara finally asked. "I understand. It doesn't matter. It has to be me. I feel like everything in my life has led to this point. This is why I was given these powers. This is what I was born to do." She poked Sordyr's chest with a single finger. "Don't you tell my father or brother what I'm planning! You understand me? I'll turn you back into a Forest Demon, I swear it. I mean, I have no idea how to actually do that, but I'll figure something out. . . ."

Sordyr bowed gallantly.

"You are a true *wexari*," he said. "I realize that might not mean much, coming from me, but it's what I believe."

Kara touched her hand to his cheek.

"It means a lot," she said. "And no matter what people might think, you are *not* a monster. You never were. The Forest Demon was just a prison that Rygoth trapped you in. This is the real you . . . my friend."

Kara went outside. Night had fallen, and the canopy leaves glowed with stored light, casting the forest in a greenish hue. She mounted Shadowdancer, pausing just a moment to nod to Sordyr in the doorway. He nodded back. It might have just been her imagination, but Kara thought he stood taller than before.

TWENTY

The morning after speaking to Sordyr, Kara pulled Taff aside and gave him a basic outline of her plan. First, they would convince Rygoth to come to De'Noran. Then they would steal her grims. Finally, Kara would cast a spell from the completed *Vulkera* powerful enough to destroy the Spider Queen forever.

Taff could barely contain his excitement. There was no doubt in his mind that they were going to defeat the Spider Queen and save Safi.

He believed in the plan. He believed in *her*.

It made the fact that Kara was lying to him that much worse.

I don't have a choice, she told herself. *Taff would never go along with this if he knew the risk I was taking.*

Kara assuaged her guilt by focusing on the fact that *most* of what she had told her brother was the truth. She really did plan on stealing the *Vulkera* from Rygoth. She just hadn't worked out how to make this happen yet.

"I need your help," Kara told Taff. "I can't match Rygoth's power, so it'll be best if we keep her off-balance, confused. What we need more than anything else are *complications*."

She had never seen Taff smile so wide.

In two days he had worked out a plan, which he gleefully explained through the use of maps, illustrations, clay models, and several sock puppets. There were even more complications than Kara had anticipated, and though her instinct was to simplify matters, she didn't change a thing.

I have no idea how long it will take to cast this spell, and the extra confusion may buy me a few precious minutes.

Once the plan was settled, they brought it to Mary and Father.

"I have a task for each of you . . . ," Kara began.

Mary agreed without hesitation and marched off to her workshop, anxious to get to work. Father was more reluctant. He still viewed De'Noran as a sanctuary where they could build a new life. Once Rygoth discovered their location, that chance would be lost forever.

"We have to risk it," Kara said. "This is the only way to stop her for good."

"By leading her straight to the last grim?" Father asked. "That's madness! We must remain hidden. That's the safest plan."

"Not for the innocent people that Rygoth murders while we do nothing!"

Father winced, her words striking a nerve.

"We need to be patient," he said weakly, as though trying to convince himself. "When Rygoth accepts the treaty that the leaders—"

"Oh, please," Kara said. "Once those cravens bend their knees to Rygoth, do you really think she'll stop searching for the final piece of the *Vulkera*? The Spider Queen doesn't care about being in charge. She only cares about the magic. We'll *never* be safe. Not as long as she's alive."

Father met Kara's eyes. At first his expression was defiant, as though he were readying a counterpoint to her argument, but then his eyes suddenly welled up with tears.

"I only just got you back," he said. "The thought of losing you again . . . and Taff . . ."

It's not that he doesn't want to stop Rygoth, Kara suddenly realized. *He's not afraid for himself at all. He's frightened for his children.*

"I don't need you to protect me," she said, pressing her head against his chest. "I'm *wexari*."

"You're my daughter," Father said. "I'll always want to protect you. But I also know that you're the only one who can put an end to this." He held her close and sighed with resignation. "What do you need me to do?"

Kara sketched out Father's role in their plan, and then went to see the last person whose help they required: Breem. Safi's father had once been a giant of a man, but he had lost weight and gained wrinkles since they last saw him. His eyes were haunted by the loss of his only child, and though he was too kind-hearted to admit it, there was little doubt that he blamed Kara. Nevertheless, Breem was eager to do anything that might return Safi to his arms, and quickly agreed to their odd request.

After that, all Kara could do was wait until these initial tasks were completed. Long, empty hours stretched into weeks. Her shoulder healed. The pain of losing Lucas did not. She spent her days hiking the beautiful trails of the Thickety, thinking of him while reaching out to animals all over the island.

Be ready, she told them. *I'll need you soon.*

At long last, just when Kara thought she might go mad from impatience, the tasks were finally completed.

Now it was her turn.

She stood alone in an abandoned hut, staring at the only piece of furniture in the room: a full-length mirror, its frame fitted with long candles. Kara checked her reflection in the nimbus of light. She was wearing a cream-colored nightdress and no shoes. Her hair was purposefully mussed and there were quarter-moon shadows beneath her eyes. She looked like a girl who had lost all hope and was unable to sleep.

Perfect.

Back in the Hourglass Tower, Rygoth had claimed that Kara would one day come to her after realizing that there was no use resisting anymore. For this to work, it was important for Rygoth to believe that she was right.

I'm ready. I've thought of everything. There won't be any surprises.

Someone knocked at the door.

Kara jumped at the unexpected sound. She had given specific directions to the graycloaks posted outside the hut that she was not to be disturbed under any circumstances. More bewildered than upset, she crossed the room and turned the doorknob, only realizing at the last moment the horrifying possibility that Querin had come for payment at last.

No, Kara thought, her heart racing as the door swung open and began to reveal a small figure in the shadows. *Not now, not now . . .*

It was only Taff. Kara gasped with relief.

"Sorry," he whispered, and behind him the two guards shrugged, as if to say: *What could we do?* "I didn't hear any voices, so I figured you hadn't started yet."

"What is it?" Kara asked.

"I need you to do something for me," he said, slipping into the room. Kara closed the door behind them. "It was supposed to be Mary's job, but Mary is a toddler right now, so I think I better do it. Only my mind keeps racing, jumping from one thing to another, and I'm so afraid that I'll forget. And that would be *really bad*."

He handed her a small sticky ball that looked like partially chewed taffy. It was a familiar shade of red.

"Mary tried to make it the same exact color as the *Vulkera*, so Rygoth wouldn't notice it. I mean, I'm sure she'd find it eventually, but I figure everything will happen so fast . . ."

"This goes on our grim, right?" Kara asked, turning the taffy in her fingers. "Any special way to do it?"

Taff shook his head.

"Just smoosh it on there. Thanks. I'm just so worried that I'll forget, and then my part won't work at all——"

Taff started toward the door and then smacked himself in the forehead.

"Oh!" he exclaimed. He tore off half the taffy in Kara's hands and stuck it in his pocket. "Almost forgot. See what I mean? I can't think straight. I'm so worried that I'm going to mess up. You're counting on me and I don't know if you noticed this but I'm only eight and——"

"You'll be brilliant," Kara said. "Like always."

"I'm really scared. More scared than I've ever been in my entire life."

"I'm scared too," Kara said, "but here's the good news. You've been absurdly brave for so long now—you only have to keep it up a little longer. After this, I give you permission to be a coward for the rest of your life. Seriously. No one will think any worse of you. Speaking for myself, I plan to whimper during thunderstorms and sleep with a hundred candles burning every night. I've earned it!"

Taff grinned.

"I'm going to scream silly at the sight of snakes," he said. "And run away from my own shadow."

"That's the spirit!" Kara exclaimed. "Though snakes are actually rather nice." She kissed him on the cheek. "Try and get some sleep."

Taff left the hut with a renewed spring in his step.

Kara returned to the mirror. While picturing Bethany's face, she pressed two fingers against the glass. Roiling mist slammed so violently against the other side of the mirror that Kara was certain it would crack.

The mist dissipated. Bethany appeared.

Her face was streaked with dirt and tiny scratches. Instead of the black cloak embroidered with a double-fanged spider, she now wore a filthy gray frock.

Her left ankle was chained to a stake in the ground.

"Bethany," Kara said. "Are you all right? What has she done to you?"

Bethany touched the surface of the mirror in wonder.

"At last," Bethany said, scratching at a clump of matted hair. "Rygoth said I had to wait right here next to my grimoire until you contacted me. I tried to escape at first, but . . . since then, I've done only as she's asked. I've watched. And waited."

"I'm sorry," Kara said.

Bethany clasped her hand over her mouth.

"I'm not allowed to talk to you," she said. "Rygoth was very clear about that." She cupped a hand to her mouth and called out, "Guards! Guards!"

Kara heard footsteps approaching in the distance.

"Stay strong, Bethany," Kara whispered. "I'm going to get you out of there. Safi too. It won't be long now."

Bethany met her eyes and gave the slightest of nods. Then the grimoire was lifted into the air and carried for some time—carefully angled upward so that only the night sky was revealed—before being positioned before Rygoth.

Tonight the Spider Queen wore an emerald-green gown beneath a sheer layer of black lace. Her obsidian throne glimmered in the moonlight. Kara could hear Rygoth's followers talking and laughing just outside her field of vision.

Rygoth raised her hand and all talking stopped.

"I knew it was only a matter of time," she said. "Have you finally accepted the truth?"

Though Rygoth's arrogance made Kara burn with anger, she tried to look as downtrodden as possible.

"You were right," she said. "I thought I could defeat

you. But after what happened at Kutt—I know it's point-less to keep fighting. I'm not powerful enough. You're a far greater *wexari* than I can ever hope to be."

Kara instantly regretted that last sentence. *Too much*, she thought. Rygoth was vain enough to believe Kara's sudden obeisance, but not if she made the turnaround *too* drastic.

The Spider Queen, however, showed no sign of sus-picion, nodding at Kara's words as though they were expected.

"I'm pleased to hear that you've finally learned your place," Rygoth said, and Kara quickly looked down, hid-ing her anger beneath feigned servitude. "But I'm not sure what you hope to gain by telling me this. Soon the *Vulkera* will be mine. If you're seeking clemency in the new world to come, I'm afraid you've switched sides too late." She crossed one leg over the other. "This might come as a surprise, but I'm not exactly the forgiving sort."

Rygoth's cronies burst into obsequious laughter. It reminded Kara of the baying of wolves.

"I have the last grim," she said.

The laughter stopped.

Rygoth sat up in her throne and pointed a single finger at the mirror.

"Prove it," she hissed.

Kara, who had anticipated this request and thus taken the grim into the hut with her, pressed the flap of leather against the mirror. Upon seeing it, Rygoth's beautiful features contorted into those of a petulant child.

"What are you doing with that?" she asked. "That's *mine*."

"Not yet," Kara replied. "It can be. But there's something I want in exchange."

"What?"

"My friends. Safi and Bethany."

Rygoth waited, assuming that this couldn't possibly be the sum total of Kara's request.

"That's all?" Rygoth asked. "The seer and a common witch?"

I'm not asking for enough, Kara thought. *She's going to sense a trap. . . .*

"And I also want your solemn vow that you will allow all of us to live our lives in peace afterward. Not just Safi and Bethany, but my family and me, too. Do what you want to the world, but leave us alone."

"What happened to the good little witch who always put others before herself?" Rygoth asked.

Kara looked away, as though embarrassed to admit the truth.

"I grew up. The world doesn't care about me. Why should I return the favor?"

Rygoth spent a long time staring at Kara before finally nodding with approval.

"I agree to your terms," she said. "Where are you?"

"Swear on it," Kara said.

"I could say the words," she said, "but why would you

believe me? You'll just have to hope I'm telling the truth. Don't worry. Once I have the *Vulkera* in my hands, I'll forget about you and your friends completely. I have no interest in revenge."

The lie was so obvious that Kara had to bite back a laugh.

"I understand," Kara said. "I can't keep hiding forever. You'll find me eventually—I know you will. At least this way I have a chance." She bowed her head in deference. "I pray that you'll be merciful."

"Yes, yes," Rygoth said, her patience growing short. "Where *are* you?"

Kara took a deep breath. This was the point of no return.

"The Thickety," she said.

The Spider Queen raised her eyebrows.

"Is that some kind of joke?"

"It's the truth," Kara said. "Auren sold their grim to the Children of the Fold, who brought it to De'Noran. It was buried beneath the Fenroot tree at the center of my old village—which has since been overtaken by the Thickety itself."

The details fit, and Rygoth knew it. Kara had been waiting for an opportunity to share this information, hoping that her honesty here would make her earlier claims more believable.

As Grace had once said, lies went down smoother with a spoonful of truth.

"Are you in that cursed place right now?" Rygoth asked.

Kara was gratified to hear the slightest trepidation in the Spider Queen's voice. It was clear that she had no desire to return to the Thickety, where for two millennia she had been trapped in the body of a giant spider and imprisoned underground.

Good, Kara thought, remembering what she had told Taff: *We have to keep her off-balance, confused.*

"I'm here with the graycloaks," Kara said. "What's left of them, at least. They have no desire to fight you, but . . ." Kara shifted from foot to foot and wrung her hands, trying to look as nervous as possible. "I think their presence can only make things . . . I just think it's important . . . that others . . ."

"You're too frightened to face me alone," Rygoth said, smirking.

Kara covered her mouth in shock, as though stunned that Rygoth had figured out the truth.

"But why would the graycloaks help you?" Rygoth asked. "Surely they realize that the grim is not worth the lives of two measly girls."

Kara, having anticipated this question, had a response ready.

"The graycloaks believe that this is a peace treaty between us," she whispered conspiratorially. "In exchange for the grim, they think you're going to leave Sentium forever."

"Is that so?" asked Rygoth. "They're not going to be pleased when they find out you've lied."

"I can handle a few angry graycloaks," Kara said,

shrugging dismissively. "There's a village near the center of the Thickety. Used to be inhabited, but it was overtaken by notsuns. You know it?"

"I do."

"That's where we'll be. How fast can you get to De'Noran?"

"A few days," Rygoth said. "Maybe longer."

It'll be tight, Kara thought, *but that should give our new arrivals time to prepare. They need to learn the terrain of the Thickety, and also how to work together——*

"Oh!" Rygoth exclaimed, furrowing her brow as though she had just remembered something. "There is just *one* thing."

The Spider Queen rose from her throne and glided toward the mirror with an elegant stride. Beyond her limited field of vision Kara heard dozens—maybe hundreds—of her followers rise to their feet as well.

Rygoth kept coming closer until her face filled the entire mirror.

"On the off chance that you might be planning some sort of childish trick, I want you to know that I will not hesitate to kill your friends."

"Safi and Bethany remain unharmed," Kara said. "Or I'll make sure you never—"

"Not the girls," Rygoth said. "Your other friend. The handsome boy who fell from the sky."

For a few moments, Kara forgot to breathe.

"Lucas is alive?" she asked.

"You didn't know?" Rygoth asked in mock surprise. "One of my witches snatched him in midair. Didn't even break a fingernail, lucky boy."

Lucas is alive!

Warmth and energy flowed through her body as the colors of the world grew sharp again. She felt as though she had been returned to life.

"Look at you," Rygoth said with a thin smile. "So happy. That's good. That means you'll listen closely to what I'm about to say." Rygoth's variegated eyes grew as hard as crystals. "I don't trust you. And if I sense, even for a moment, that you are trying to trick me in some way, the first thing I will do is tear that boy open from head to toe. You think it was hard to lose him once? Imagine what it will be like to lose him again."

TWENTY-ONE

Rygoth arrived the next morning.

"No!" Kara exclaimed when Father came to tell her the news. "That's not possible. She said it would take her days to get—"

"She lied," Father said.

Of course she did, Kara thought, amazed at her own foolishness. *Why would she tell the truth about anything?*

This thought led to another, like a crash of thunder after lightning.

Is Lucas really alive? Or was that a lie too?

She couldn't allow herself to think about that now. She needed to remain focused.

Don't get distracted. Stick to the plan.

While Father organized the surprised soldiers as best he could, Kara and Taff rode Shadowdancer up a path that wound even higher than the trees. From here they had a clear view of the shore. Even from this distance they could see the mountainous beast that had landed in the ocean, flooding the beach with its impact.

"Niersook," Taff said.

The creature was perhaps Rygoth's greatest creation. A drop of its venom could steal a *wexari*'s magic, and it was capable of transforming into anything from a wagon to a tent. Today, Rygoth was using the carmine-scaled leviathan as a means of transport. Niersook's spiny head rested on the sand, like a dog on its owner's knee, and an endless stream of men, women, and monsters marched out its open mouth and joined their allies already standing in the sandy muck.

"There's so many of them," Taff said, his voice trembling. "We don't have anywhere close to that—"

"I know," Kara said.

Taff had recently received a spyglass from Father, and he now raised the handheld scope to his eye.

"Who are *those* people?" he asked, pointing down at an entire squadron shoving and arguing with one another. They wore the same black cloaks as the witches but bore swords and axes instead of grimoires. "Why are they helping Rygoth?"

"Father warned me this might happen," Kara said, borrowing the spyglass for a look of her own. "They're mercenaries. They fight for whoever pays them."

"But Rygoth's *bad*," Taff said. "I don't understand."

"Neither do I."

More mercenaries were exiting Niersook's mouth now, these in padded armor, as though Rygoth's numbers had swelled to such an extent that she had run out of cloaks. Their faces were scarred and tattooed with strange symbols; their eyes glowed with violent anticipation. Kara did not fear them. The graycloaks were accomplished soldiers, and she was certain that they could hold their own against such ruffians.

What worried her were the monsters.

Rygoth had been hard at work, and her manufactured army slunk, slithered, and flew onto shore. Kara had monsters of her own, of course, but the recent changes in the Thickety had gentled many dispositions, and truly fearsome creatures were few and far between. Rygoth's creations, on the other hand, had been engineered for death. Claws hooked like scythes. Wings lined with razor-sharp feathers. Gaping eyes that could swallow as well as blink.

"This isn't so bad," Taff said. "The graycloaks can fight the mercenaries. The monsters can fight one another."

"Which means all we have to worry about is the most powerful *wexari* in the world and her army of witches."

"Exactly," said Taff. "Besides, this isn't about winning

a battle. We just have to hold them off long enough to get the *Vulkera*. Surprise is our weapon."

Kara nodded, though she wondered if they were truly fooling Rygoth. *What if she has already anticipated our plan? What if she didn't even* bring *the grims? How many will die today because of me?*

She knew they should head back—for there was much to do and little time in which to do it—but she kept watching, refusing to return the spyglass to Taff despite his efforts to snatch it away. Finally she saw Safi, her hands manacled to a single long chain that allowed the twins to drag her through the muck. She saw Bethany, too, flanked by stern-looking witches.

"Kara," Taff said. "We *really* have to go."

It was the desperation in her brother's voice that brought Kara back to reality. *He's right.* She handed him the spyglass and pulled herself astride Shadowdancer without looking back.

It doesn't mean anything, she thought as they rode away.

There were still people coming out of Niersook. It doesn't mean that Rygoth lied.

And yet there was no reason to believe that she had told the truth, either. All Kara had to go by right now was a single, terrifying observation.

She had seen Safi. She had seen Bethany.

She had not seen Lucas.

Sordyr was the one who had chosen the notsun village as the rendezvous point. "It's about as far inland as you can get," he had explained. "Even if Rygoth lands on the nearest shore, the narrow paths are going to make traveling in such large numbers extremely difficult. It'll slow her down, maybe even slim her numbers a bit."

So far, Sordyr's plan seemed to be working. Watcher tracked the approaching army carefully, giving Kara constant updates on their torturous progress. The witches stayed close to their queen, but the mercenaries were less focused and tended to wander off. Sometimes they never came back.

The Thickety was not so dark and scary anymore, but its inhabitants still had to eat.

Two days had passed by the time Rygoth's army finally arrived, filing into the clearing just outside the village. They were tired and hungry and in bad spirits.

Kara's army was waiting for them.

She had sent her call for assistance throughout the Thickety, and all manner of creatures had responded: two-headed snakes with acid-bleached fangs, tall bears with long slashing tentacles instead of claws, tiny balls of venomous fur that floated along the wind like dandelion puffs. Hundreds of birds circled above them, ready to swoop downward and sink their talons into Kara's enemies. Beneath the ground, razor-toothed worms dug tunnels in preparation for the coming battle; Kara planned to use beetles and fire ants and wanted a clear path.

Behind Kara's animals the remaining graycloaks stood

in six perfect rows, their ball-staffs clenched across their chests. Some of them rode gnostors, big-bellied beasts that threw their weight from side to side to remain balanced. They were silly-looking but deceptively fast.

Kara herself sat on Shadowdancer, with Taff astride Darno. Father, Mary Kettle, and Sordyr were right behind them on mounts of their own. All of them wore gray cloaks. Kara hadn't liked donning the attire of her former enemy, but it was necessary for their plan to work.

"When should I release this?" Mary asked.

She held a kite in her hands whose magic was controlled by a wind-spun needle that would stop at one of four pictures. Taff called the kite his "favorite complication."

"When the fighting starts. We want things to be as chaotic as possible."

Tightly packed trees created borders to either side of them. The clearing was immense. It would take an hour's walk to traverse it, and yet the distant figures of Rygoth's army still managed to stretch from one end to the other, in more rows that Kara could count.

They were badly outnumbered.

For now, Kara thought.

A black flag bearing a double-fanged spider rose high over Rygoth's forces, flapping madly in the wind.

"How come we don't have a flag?" Taff asked.

"Next time," Kara said. "How close do you have to get to do your part?"

"A lot closer than this. On the other side of the field."

"I'll get you there," Kara said. "You're only going to get one chance, so make it count."

"Don't worry. I've been practicing!"

"Father," Kara said, glancing over her shoulder, "did Breem give all the graycloaks—"

"They're ready," he said. "As ready as they're going to be, at any rate."

"When I put my hood up," Kara said, looking at Sordyr now. "That's when you give the signal."

Sordyr patted the horn by his side. It was long and curved, carved from the hip bone of some gargantuan creature.

That's it, Kara thought. *The plan is set. There's nothing more you can do.*

What she hadn't anticipated was the raging fear in her stomach, the frantic pounding of her heart. Trying to keep her face as impassive as possible—*Don't show weakness!*—Kara rode Shadowdancer a few paces forward. On the other side of the field, Rygoth sat astride a white horse that looked surprisingly unmagical.

She spoke directly into Kara's mind.

Interesting choice of allies. Graycloaks and monsters. Are you sure you're on the right side?

Surprised at this mental intrusion, Kara immediately began setting up protective walls in her mind, like Sordyr had taught her.

Rygoth's laughter roared through her head.

Don't bother. I've no desire to control your mind. I'd rather do this the old-fashioned way. Witch versus witch.

Kara feigned surprise she did not feel.

I don't want to fight, she thought. *We're going to make an exchange. That's what we agreed on. The grim for my friends!*

No, foolish girl! I'm going to kill everyone here. And yank the grim from your cold dead hands!

Rygoth clasped her fingers into a fist and the mercenaries charged.

Kara could feel the ground rumble beneath the hooves of armored horses. She glanced at Taff, who nodded slightly. *We both knew that Rygoth would never go through with an exchange.* Of course, anticipating the attack was one thing. Seeing your death in the eyes of hired killers was something else entirely.

Cold sweat dribbled down Kara's back. She felt removed from herself, out of place.

I was raised to be a farmer, not lead a battle. Is this really me?

"Mary," Kara said, eyeing the kite. "It's time."

She knew the risk she was taking. *Rygoth said that the*

moment she sensed a trick she would kill Lucas. But what if that was just a cruel lie to keep her in line? She hadn't *seen* Lucas. How could she know for sure that he was truly alive?

He's not, Kara thought, her voice hard and practical, a remnant from her years in the Fold. *He's dead and you know it. And even if he was alive—he'd want you to do everything you could to stop Rygoth. This is bigger than all of us.*

Mary unwound the spindle, allowing the string a little slack. The kite rose a few feet above them. Its needle spun madly, refusing to stop at a single picture.

Father held out a hand.

"Wait," he said. "Let them get closer first. This way our men can flank them and split Rygoth's forces."

Kara watched with increasing trepidation as the mercenaries charged closer. In some ways, they were even more frightening than Rygoth's creations. The violent instincts of monsters made sense to her, but seeing such lust for death in human eyes was truly unsettling.

"Now!" Father exclaimed.

Mary released the kite. It caught the wind and sailed high into the air. Just before it rose too far out of sight, Kara saw the spinning needle settle on the drawing of a storm cloud.

It began to rain.

Water raged down in an angry torrent. Thunder boomed and startled horses kicked into the air, tossing the mercenaries on their backs. This chaos, however, was short-lived. In less than a minute, Rygoth's forces regained their composure. They marched forward, slower this time, their faces set with determination. A little storm wasn't going to stop them.

Except the storm wasn't just a storm.

It was also a signal.

From out of the thick woods to either side of the clearing charged hundreds of soldiers.

These reinforcements were the result of Father's role in their plan. Pretending to be Timoth Clen, he had sent messages to the four regions of Sentium, calling their armies to De'Noran for one final battle against the Spider Queen. Kara had doubted that anyone would come, but after several weeks of nervous waiting the first ship had arrived, this one from Ilma. The others soon followed.

They hadn't come because of the Clen. They had come because of Kara.

They had all heard stories of the young witch who had freed the village of De'Noran from evil, defeated the Forest Demon, saved the children of Nye's Landing, exorcised the evil spirit of Dolrose Castle, and wounded Rygoth at the Battle of Clen's Graveyard. Rumor had it that even vicious beasts were humbled by the goodness in her heart.

They called her Kara the Kind.

She was their only chance of stopping the Spider Queen, and they now fought in her name, their weapons revealing their region of origin. Those from Ilma fired glorb-arrows with deadly accuracy. The knights of Lux wore crystal armor and wielded beautiful swords that looked like glass but never shattered. Aurian warriors fought with only their bare hands and tiny bells that they would ring in their adversaries' ears, making them fall to the ground in agony. The contingent from Kutt was smaller and wore black masks, like the ones that Kara had seen on the Swoop, connected by clear tubes to metal canisters worn on their backs. They hung at the fringes of the fighting and tossed glass spheres into the larger groups of mercenaries. Upon breaking, these spheres released clouds of gas that caused anyone in the immediate vicinity to scream in pain as blisters and boils exploded all over their body.

The mercenaries grew fewer in number but continued to fight fiercely, delivering death on well-honed blades.

"Father," Kara said.

Raising his ball-staff high into the air, Kara's father charged into the fray, and the graycloaks followed. Their whirring weapons struck heads and knees with sickening speed, and the mercenaries, trapped between two enemy forces, began to show the first signs of panic.

High above them the spinner on the kite changed position. The rain stopped with the suddenness of a tightened spigot, and a blazing sun sent the temperature soaring. The Luxians quickly utilized this unexpected advantage, expertly tilting their cry-swords to blind the enemy with the sun's glare.

More mercenaries fell. Some fled into the Thickety.

Rygoth set her monsters loose.

Kara did the same.

Beast met beast just north of the main battle. Kara could see only the larger animals past the clashing soldiers, but she *felt* all of them, their violent instincts throbbing deep within her bones. Every animal sound imaginable, and some that were not, muffled the clang of weapons: roars and bleats, growls and hisses, screeches and snorts. Other noises—torn flesh, spraying blood—sent lightning bolts of pain through Kara's body. She suffered as her creatures suffered. Kara had learned how to diminish this link between them, even sever it altogether, but she chose not to. Those in her charge had offered their lives, and it would have been the highest form of disrespect not to share their pain.

"Are you ready?" she asked Taff.

He nodded bravely, tightening his little hands around Darno's neck.

I won't let him fall, the scorpion-wolf told her.

I know you won't, Kara said. She shifted her thoughts to a different animal. *Shadowdancer! Go!*

The mare shot off like a cannonball, Kara holding tight and keeping her head low as they danced past mercenaries and monsters. Near hits abounded. A bearded man charged with a raised ax but fell when an arrow took him in the chest. An eagle with quicksand eyes slashed Kara's back but was snatched in midair by her sledgeworm before it could attack again.

As they reached the center of the field, the chaos

closed around them like a vise. The two main battles had spilled into each other; a graycloak fought for her life against a mist-like creature, while a group of mercenaries fended off Kara's sickleowls. Shadowdancer whinnied and turned, every path blocked. Two snarling bodies crashed into the mare's flank. She nearly toppled over but somehow managed to maintain her balance.

Too many, Darno said, turning his body to sting a sable-toothed gorilla before it reached Taff. *We need help or we won't make it.*

Kara stretched out her mind until she felt the blood-red thoughts of her old enemy. *I need you!* she shouted. Immediately two low-riding gra'daks exploded through the mob like rampaging bulls, sending the bodies of both man and beast flying through the air. These gra'daks were larger than the one who had bitten off Lucas's fingers but had the same five mouths, which they used now to make short work of some squishy squid-like thing with fanned plumage.

"Go," Kara said, patting Shadowdancer's neck.

The gra'daks took the lead, creating a path by barreling through any man, woman, or creature stupid enough to get in their way.

Shadowdancer and Darno followed on their heels.

Soon they had passed through the main conflict. The open field spread out before them. Kara could see Rygoth clearly now, still astride the white horse, giving orders to the witches around her.

The sun vanished. Hail pelted Kara's body.

As one, the witches marched forward while opening their grimoires. Kara couldn't hear the words they spoke, but she could sense the oncoming threat as dark magic rose over them like a tidal wave. There was no time to scream a warning. Suddenly the sky was awash with colors: mauve lightning and streams of blue fire and a swirling yellow vortex that sucked three Luxian soldiers into its depths. Kara's allies had been doing well up until this point—perhaps even winning—but this barrage of magic instantly turned the tide of battle.

Get Taff into position, she told Darno. *This next part is going to happen fast.*

The scorpion-wolf dashed away, Taff clinging to his back. Kara met her brother's eyes as he departed and saw the worry there. It was not for himself.

Nightseekers, she commanded. *Attack!*

It was Father who had brought the innocuous-looking dogs to the Thickety, having used them to hunt witches as Timoth Clen. At first Kara had been reluctant to use the animals—for one had nearly blinded her when she was a little girl and that fear had never completely dissipated—but finally she had built a mind-bridge and made them her own. For the entire battle, following her command, they had been slinking unnoticed through the trees. Now they rushed at the witches from behind, already changing form and rising up on two legs as translucent needles extended from their paws. Kara saw several witches go down, grimoires flying out of their hands as they desperately tried to fend off the beasts.

The attack created a break in the witches' lines that revealed Safi and Bethany, tethered to the ground by chains. Kara reached out to a shy raccoon with pincers strong enough to snap a sword in half and sent it an order.

Free my friends!

Before Kara could signal to Safi and Bethany that help was on its way, a cold voice frosted the passageways of her mind.

What do you hope to accomplish here?

Though a good distance still spanned the ground between them, Kara was now close enough to see the expression on Rygoth's face. By this point in the battle, after dealing with such unexpected losses, Kara had hoped to see at least an inkling of worry in the Spider Queen's eyes——maybe even panic.

She looked bemused.

I could end this entire fiasco in a heartbeat if I desired, but the practice is good for my witches. Look—they've already regained the upper hand.

Rygoth was right. Nightseeker bodies, battered and broken, lay strewn across the field. The witches had continued their march toward Kara's forces, casting spells as they approached. The body of a Kuttian soldier shot high into the air and plummeted into the trees. Graycloaks writhed in pain as invisible forces whipped their bodies. A brave knight in the process of swinging his sword simply vanished.

Kara saw the twins read from the grimoire they shared. The ground grew grass teeth and swallowed a soldier whole.

We don't have a chance against so much magic, Kara thought.

A dozen voices screamed in terror as a cloud-colored hand reached down from the sky, grabbed the last of Ilma's troops, and squeezed. The caster of this Last Spell, a tiny witch no older than eight, was dragged shrieking through an open portal in her grimoire. The Well of Witches awaited her.

"I grow bored," Rygoth snapped in Kara's ear. "Give me the grim."

Kara jerked in surprise. Just a moment ago, Rygoth had still been across the field. Now she was close enough to touch.

The horse teleports, Kara thought. *It's magical after—*

She noticed that there was a dagger in Rygoth's hand.

The blade slashed Kara's shoulder, cutting away the strap of her satchel and sending a searing line of pain across her arm. Rygoth caught the satchel. Kara slipped off Shadowdancer's back and struck the ground hard, biting her tongue. The taste of blood filled her mouth.

The hail stopped. The sun blazed down once more.

Rising shakily to her feet, Kara saw Rygoth remove the grim from the satchel and examine it with reverence. Luckily, she did not notice the sticky substance flattened to the underside of the leather square, its color a perfect camouflage against the rose leather.

Where are you? Kara called out to Darno, frantically searching for the wolf among the chaos of the field. *Get Taff here now!*

Laying the back cover of the *Vulkera* on her lap, Rygoth reached into her saddlebag and produced the other three grims. She placed the sixteen pages in a neat stack on top of the back cover and then pressed the spine into place. The moment she added the front cover there was a terrible hissing sound, like the opening of a tomb sealed for centuries, and a blinding ray of blue light speared the grimoire. It looped quickly through the spine, over and over again, acting as needle and thread to bind the book together.

The *Vulkera* was complete again.

"At last," Rygoth said. "Now you will all see *true* power!"

With a gloved hand trembling ever so slightly, Rygoth opened to the first page. Her eyes widened at the spell awaiting her.

"Oh yes," she said. "Why don't we start there?"

Her mouth formed the first word. It did not make a sound in the traditional way but rather slid down Kara's throat like rancid meat. She gripped her stomach, fighting the urge to vomit. Rygoth spoke the second word. The sound of this one turned Kara's ears numb, as if she had just rubbed them with snow.

Rygoth never made it to the third word.

The *Vulkera* flew out of her hands and attached itself to a spinning object whistling through the air, the taffy on its back cover magically bonding to its counterpart on the boomerang. The toy continued its forward trajectory a few more feet before reversing direction and landing halfway across the field—in Taff's outstretched hand.

"NO!" Rygoth shrieked.

Taff pulled the *Vulkera* from the boomerang and handed it to Sordyr. The former Forest Demon nodded to the Spider Queen, as though they were acquaintances meeting by chance in a crowded square, and then raised the curved horn to his lips.

A blaring sound like the call of some aquatic beast rose over the sounds of battle, signaling the graycloaks to action.

Each of them withdrew a grimoire.

The idea had been Taff's, but Safi's father had played the most important role. By utilizing his years of experience working in the Bindery, Breem had been able to make the books to Kara's precise specifications.

They all looked exactly like the *Vulkera*.

Keeping these grimoires in full view, the graycloaks donned their hoods and set off in every direction. Sordyr lifted his own hood into place and vanished into their numbers. In moments he was indistinguishable from the others.

Rygoth scanned the battlefield, desperately searching for the true *Vulkera*, now lost in a sea of duplicates. Her face, frozen in a rictus of rage, was no longer beautiful.

"Where is it?" she screamed. *"GIVE ME MY BOOK!"*

Hissing like a cornered cat, she flicked her wrist forward and killed the nearest graycloak with a handful of black butterflies, and then slid off her horse to examine the bloodstained grimoire in the poor man's hands.

Kara didn't wait to see what happened next; her destination was on the other side of the battlefield, and there was no time to waste. She raised her hood and ran, leaping over fallen bodies and weaving around monsters locked in battle. It would have been faster to ride Shadowdancer, but the mare was too recognizable and would have revealed her identity. Her loyal creatures always knew where she was, however, and subtly cleared a path out of harm's way. Kara kept her head down and ran as fast as she could—until she found herself suddenly falling to the ground, her feet yanked backward as though by invisible hands.

She looked up and saw the twins staring at her.

They looked both surprised and thrilled by this unexpected gift. The sisters exchanged a glance, and the meaning was as clear as if they had spoken aloud.

After we kill this one the Spider Queen will finally love us best!

In unison they began to chant a spell from the grimoire they shared between them. Kara heard the air crackle and felt magical energy gather around her. The twins raced toward the end of the spell, their eyes gleaming with mad delight.

Before they could finish, a beam of purple light sent them flying.

Kara turned and saw Safi standing behind her. There was an open grimoire in her hands.

"Taff told me the plan," she said, helping Kara to her feet. "Go!"

The twins, already standing, eyed Safi with murderous intent.

"Can you handle them on your own?" Kara asked.

Safi smiled brightly as she turned to the next page of her grimoire.

"Absolutely."

Fat flakes of snow had begun to fall. Forcing herself to ignore the vicious exchange of spells behind her, Kara sprinted to the shadows of the trees, where Sordyr was waiting. His breath misted the suddenly frigid air.

"Cast well, Kara," he said, and handed her the *Vulkera*.

TWENTY-TWO

Upon touching the completed *Vulkera* a desperate need to use it flooded all of Kara's other thoughts and senses. This was more than just a simple desire to cast a spell. It was as though her very soul had grown teeth and developed a ravenous hunger for magic.

The voice she heard in her head was not quite her own.

With this spellbook you can be far more powerful than Rygoth, it said. *Why make it hard on yourself? Just speak a few words and you can end this battle in a heartbeat.*

Kara realized, in a distant way, that she had opened

the grimoire to the first page. Words of startling power inscribed themselves before her eyes.

Think of all the good you can do. End the battle. Keep Taff safe from Querin Fyndrake. And why stop there? You can reverse death! Lucas. Your mother. Both can be returned to you.

You've suffered so much. Saved so many. You deserve this.

Just speak the words.

Speak the—

Kara slammed the *Vulkera* shut.

"No!" she exclaimed. "Your magic is tainted." Talking out loud fueled her anger, allowed her to think clearly again. "I'll try to do good, but it won't last. You'll change me. That's what true evil does—it brings darkness into the world through others and *I've had about enough of that*! It's time someone changes *you* instead!"

She coiled her *wexari* powers around the *Vulkera*, seeking purchase. *It's just another animal*, she thought, *only it uses spells to hurt its victims instead of claws and fangs.* It would have been impossible to connect to an ordinary grimoire in this manner, but the *Vulkera* was different.

There was a human being trapped in its depths.

Cold emptiness flooded Kara's heart. It was far worse than when she had touched a single grim near Dolrose Castle. At that point, Kara had barely been scratching at the surface of Evangeline's despair.

Now she was drowning in it.

She sensed the true girl like an island in the desolation, floating in an abyss of dark thoughts and sadness. *I need to build a mind-bridge so I can communicate with her directly*, Kara thought, struggling to retain her own identity. *What type of memory would build the strongest link? What does she want the most? Warmth? Companionship?*

With a sigh of resignation, Kara chose one of her favorite memories. She had avoided using it for other mind-bridges because she treasured it so much, but she needed to act fast and could think of nothing stronger.

Taff is a little over a year old, she thought, using each image as a brick in the mind-bridge. *He's lying in his bed*

while I play peekaboo with him—just another night, really—
when he speaks his first word.

My name.

It's more "Karu" than "Kara," but I don't care. I lift him joy-
ously into the air and kiss his little nose. He sneezes. For that one
perfect moment I forget that our mother is dead and the towns-
people hate us. There's just me and Taff and this bubble of love
shielding us from the cruelties of the world.

The bridge snapped into place and Kara lost the memory forever. She closed her eyes and crossed into Princess
Evangeline's mind, feeling the terrible loneliness pressing
down on her like a physical weight.

Poor child. What did Rygoth do to you?

Kara opened her eyes. She was no longer on the battlefield.

Shelves packed with leather-bound volumes extended
to the high ceiling of a triangular room. At the center of
this library, a small girl sat in a simple wooden chair. She
was wearing a formal black gown with a stiff high collar.

Her dark hair was long and straight.

"Princess Evangeline," Kara said.

The girl nodded, unfazed by the sudden appearance of a stranger in her library. She was younger than Kara had anticipated, perhaps eight or nine, and her feet dangled a few inches off the floor. The thin line of her mouth was set in a perpetual frown.

"Hello, Kara Westfall," Evangeline said.

"How do you know who I am?"

"I recognize you. From your thoughts. I was sad that you didn't stay in my Well longer. You caused all sorts of trouble. It was interesting."

Kara examined the volumes of the library more closely. They looked like grimoires. Girls' names had been sewn into their spines with black thread. Kara took the nearest one—*ANNIE*—and flipped from the back until she found words writing themselves before her eyes:

". . . got another strip yesterday. Started thinking about my husband, trying to remember whether his eyes were blue or green, and my mind wandered when I was supposed to be cutting down a tree for the Spellfire . . ."

Kara closed the book and slid it back onto the shelf.

"When someone has a thought in the Well of Witches, it's scrawled across the ground," she said, remembering her own experience with this phenomenon. "But it's also recorded in these books, isn't it?"

"Yes," Evangeline said. She lifted a thin volume from the top of the tall pile sitting by her side. "This one's yours. Do you want to read it?"

Kara shook her head and knelt in front of the girl.

"Is this what you've been doing this entire time?" she asked, taking the girl's hand. "Just sitting here, reading other people's thoughts?"

Evangeline trembled at her touch.

"I don't mind," she said. "They're my friends."

"Let me be your friend," Kara said. "A *real* friend."

"No!" Evangeline exclaimed, shaking her head. A single book fell from a top shelf. "You can't. I'm a monster. I made this place and . . . I hurt people. I deserve to be punished." She yanked her hand away from Kara's. "How did you even *get* here?"

"That doesn't matter," Kara said. "The important question is how *you* got here."

The girl shook her head wildly.

"I don't want to talk about that."

While Kara spoke to Evangeline, she remained cognizant of what was happening back in De'Noran, like a dreamer who's aware that she's dreaming. She saw herself kneeling in the dirt of the battlefield as though in prayer, the *Vulkera* clasped to her chest. A dozen Thickety creatures encircled her, standing guard.

It's only a matter of time before Rygoth realizes that I have what she wants. I have to hurry.

"If you don't want to talk about it," Kara said, "then I'll tell *you* what happened—my best guess, at least. Let's start with Rygoth." Fear clouded Evangeline's face, and several more books plummeted from the shelves. "She was supposed to teach you how to control your *wexari* powers, but instead she stole all your memories of love and happiness, and a terrible darkness took root within you. You became—through no fault of your own—just a shell of a person."

Evangeline tried to cover her ears, but Kara wouldn't let her. If her plan was going to work, it was important that the princess accepted the truth.

"And then a man named Sordyr gave you a spellbook," Kara continued, "and you used it to do terrible things. *Awful* things. And yet at the end you must have remembered the real you, at least a little bit, because your Last Spell wasn't evil at all. . . ."

"Of course it was!" Evangeline exclaimed, pushing Kara away. "I created the Well of Witches!"

"Not intentionally," Kara said. "Your Last Spell was far more innocent than that, wasn't it? You wished you weren't lonely anymore. Only the *Vulkera* was so corrupted by darkness at that point that it twisted the spell all around, creating an entire system of magic that would trap 'friends' for you and allow you to read their thoughts."

An entire bookcase crashed to the floor.

"I don't want to hear anymore," Evangeline said, knocking her chair over as she backed away into a corner. "Just leave me and go! I *killed* people. This is my fault! My punishment. You don't understand!"

"I *do*!" Kara exclaimed. "I grew up in a place where *everyone* despised me. And I took a life, just like you did. The only difference between us is I was able to cling to those who loved me. If I hadn't known such love, the darkness would have swallowed me whole—as it did you." Kara took the girl's hand and this time she didn't pull away. "What happened wasn't your fault, Evangeline. But even if you can't remember it, you need to know that your mother and father loved you deeply."

"I know," she mumbled, and her body fell as lax as a rag doll.

How? Kara wondered, but sensing that it would be a mistake to push the girl, she remained silent and gazed toward the real world. The circle of creatures surrounding her had grown in size, a living shield facing an overwhelming number of opponents. Bolts of pain rattled Kara's bones as creature after creature fell dead. Bethany read from her grimoire and the entire group was encased in a series of mirrors that reflected the magical attacks.

It wouldn't hold long.

"After I cast all the spells except the last one," Evangeline said quietly, "I found my father. He had tried to protect my mother, but she died in his arms. He was almost dead himself. I sat down next to him, expecting to hear how much he hated me, for I had no memory of even a single kind word. But with his dying breath, Father took me in his arms and whispered that he loved me, and I realized that I had made a terrible mistake."

Tears stoppered for centuries rushed freely from Evangeline's eyes.

"His words were like a splash of cold water, waking me up, and I could finally think for myself again," she said. "I wasn't sure how long it would last, though. I wanted to make sure that I used the last page of the grimoire before I lost myself again and hurt someone else." Evangeline reached out with her fingertips, as though imagining an open tome spread out before her. "It was more powerful than all the other pages combined. I could sense it."

"Your Last Spell," Kara said. "The one that created the Well of Witches."

Princess Evangeline bowed her head in shame.

"That was never my intent," she said, shaking her head. "I could sense that the Last Spell would be more powerful than the others, and I thought about trying to bring my parents back, only I was too ashamed to face them after the things that I had done. Plus, I knew that they would come back wrong somehow. The grimoire had grown dark and violent because of the things I did, like a pup trained to hunt and kill and never knowing the touch of a kind master. I knew that I couldn't trust its magic, and so I decided to cast a spell that—I foolishly presumed—couldn't possibly harm anyone. I ordered the book to give me some friends, other girls who had mysterious powers and would understand what that was like. That's all I wanted. But the grimoire twisted even this and made the Well of Witches instead, trapping girls like flies in a spider's web." Evangeline stared at Kara with pleading eyes. "I never meant for that to happen! I never meant to turn all grimoires bad. I just wanted some friends."

"Only girls?" Kara asked.

Evangeline offered the barest hint of a smile.

"I don't like to play with boys," she said.

Kara started to laugh, thinking of Taff's reaction when she told him the reason why grimoire magic was limited to girls, when she felt a stabbing pain in her side. She touched her hip and her hand came away wet. In the battle raging outside, one of Rygoth's minions must have managed to slip through her defenses. The wound wasn't deep, but it would be the first of many if she didn't finish here quickly.

"What's wrong?" Evangeline asked, noticing Kara's pained expression.

"I don't have time to explain," Kara said. "But there might be a way for you to stop Rygoth from hurting anyone else."

Evangeline raised her chin, looking very much like a princess.

"Tell me what to do," she said.

"Your grimoire was a blank slate," Kara said. "It wasn't good or evil. But it grew from the soil of your mind, which, thanks to Rygoth, never knew love or compassion. This darkness was like an infection, and it carried over into all the other grimoires. But they're just the leaves. You and the *Vulkera*—you're the roots. If we can undo Rygoth's damage, I think we can change things."

"You mean give me back the memories of my mother and father?" Evangeline asked with heart-wrenching hope.

"I'm sorry," Kara said. "No one can do that. But

perhaps I can do the next best thing. I gave you a memory, just before I entered the library. Do you remember?"

"The little boy?" Evangeline asked, her lips twitching in an almost-smile. "He knew my name. It made me . . ."

She struggled for the word.

"Happy?" Kara asked.

Evangeline nodded, the hint of a blush touching her cheeks, as though happiness were something to be ashamed of.

"I'd like to feel that again," she said.

Kara placed her hands on the girl's shoulders, wishing there was another way to do this, knowing there was not.

"Then close your eyes," she said, "and remember what it was like to be loved."

Lifting the floodgates of her memory, Kara gifted her past unto the girl. Her mother's nose pressed against a bouquet of wildflowers. The stubble of her father's beard as it scratched her cheeks. The way Taff gurgled contently when she sang him a lullaby. Kara saw a smile fill Evangeline's face, the memories flowing into her fast now, a sweeping tide of images. *Taff skipping stones. Wind tousling Lucas's hair. Mother and Father sharing a kiss when they think we're not looking.* Soon Kara was losing more than just happy memories but also the arguments and tragedies and even the moments of tedium, for love was threaded through them all, and only love could change the tide of darkness.

Kara realized, just before she forgot her mother's face forever, that she had lived a very fortunate life.

"Thank you," Evangeline said, her face beatific, "for helping me remember what it's like . . ."

Around them books rained from the shelves until the shelves themselves crashed to the floor and the walls of the library fell away, leaving Kara in a field—

She opened her eyes.

The snowfall had escalated into a blizzard that made seeing more than twenty feet in any direction impossible. Other than the sound of a kite flapping in the white sky, the afternoon was eerily silent. Witches stared strangely at their grimoires as though seeing them for the first time.

The whole battle had come to a standstill.

"What did you do?" Taff asked, helping Kara to her feet.

"I'm not sure," she replied.

The mind leeches had arrived like sharks to bloody water, and Kara was too weak to send them away. They devoured her past in indiscriminate chunks. Memories. Faces. Snatches of conversation. There was nothing she could do to stop it.

I have to hurry, she thought.

Two girls holding grimoires stepped to Kara's side. One had dark skin and the other one was older, with frizzy hair. It took Kara a moment to remember their names, and even then she wasn't quite sure who they were—only that they were her friends.

"Do you feel it?" Bethany asked, raising her grimoire.

Safi nodded as though a great weight had been lifted off her shoulders.

"It isn't trying to get me to do bad things anymore," she said. "It's just a spellbook. I can use it however I want."

This was beginning to occur to the other witches as well. They now split into two distinct factions, an unspoken truce granting them the time to resolve this unexpected complication. Some witches backed away, their loyalty to darkness a matter of personal choice, but most shrugged free of their black cloaks and slipped uneasily into Kara's ranks, eager to change sides.

With their numbers now greatly diminished, Rygoth's forces retreated, stepping around two girls with identical features who stared lifelessly into the falling snow.

Kara's allies cheered in triumph.

"You did it!" Safi said, throwing her arms around Kara's neck.

"Not yet," she replied.

Kara pressed her hands against her temples, struggling to halt the loss of her remaining memories, but it was like stoppering a broken cask. They continued to leave her at an alarming rate. To her right an older woman reeling in a kite paused to give Kara a look of concern.

"What's wrong?" she asked.

"I'm fine," Kara said, wondering if she and the woman were somehow related. *She's so worried about me! Could she be my mother? No—my mother is dead. At least, I think she is.*

Her mind was coming apart at the seams. She had to act fast, before she forgot everything.

"I need to," Kara said, trying to remember. "I need to . . ."

The gray-haired woman pulled the kite onto her lap and the blinding snowstorm vanished, revealing the figure that had been lurking only a stone's throw behind them. Witches opened their grimoires and soldiers unsheathed their blades.

"Give me my book," Rygoth said.

Her gloved hand clutched the arm of a young man trying to look brave, which was difficult to do considering the serpent coiled around his chest.

"Lucas!" Kara exclaimed, recalling his name without hesitation.

Her heart swelled with joy. Lucas was imperiled but gloriously, completely *alive*.

"I hid this one away, just in case," Rygoth said. "And here we are. Shall we trade?"

"Don't do it, Kara," Lucas said. "Don't—"

With lightning speed, the serpent opened its mouth and pressed three fangs against Lucas's neck. He gritted his teeth, beads of sweat rolling down his temples.

"My pet is quite venomous, in case you're curious," Rygoth said. "It will be a slow, painful death."

"You can have it!" Kara exclaimed, holding out the *Vulkera*. "Just don't hurt him!"

Slowly, she started walking toward the Spider Queen. Kara's allies looked at one another in astonishment, unsure what to do.

"Everyone lower your weapons," Kara announced. "And close your grimoires."

Reluctantly, they followed her orders.

"You can't, Kara," Safi said, blocking her path. "You know what will happen if—"

Kara laid a hand on her arm, and a look passed between them: *Trust me.* Safi moved out of her way. After walking forward for a few more steps, Kara slipped her fingers between the pages of the grimoire, as though getting ready to open it.

"STOP!" Rygoth shouted. "Put the book down or the boy dies right now!"

Kara laid the *Vulkera* open on the ground.

"You think I'm a fool?" Rygoth asked. Her eyes, which had always courted madness, had now wedded it completely. "You hope to use its power against me. I will not be tricked again by you, witch." She smiled wickedly as her eyes settled on Taff. "Send your brother instead."

Kara nervously handed the grimoire to Taff and hugged him tight. She whispered something softly in his ear and he looked up at her with disbelief.

"Now!" Rygoth exclaimed. Her forces, emboldened by their master, had reassembled behind her.

Soldiers and witches parted, creating a path for the

boy. The grimoire looked huge in his hands. He shifted it in his grip, struggling to maintain his hold.

"Faster!" Rygoth exclaimed.

Taff quickened his pace and the book slipped out of his hands. It spread open on the ground in front of him. He bent down to pick it up, and the moment his hands touched the surface he looked back at Kara and grinned.

"You were right!" he said.

Without a moment's hesitation Taff read the words that had appeared on the page before him. It was a strange language that had never been spoken by a boy before, for only girls were allowed to use grimoires. At least, that *had* been true while they were under Evangeline's spell.

Things were different now.

"WHAT ARE YOU DOING?" Rygoth screamed. "YOU CAN'T USE—"

Two black fangs exploded from her mouth, rendering the rest of her words unintelligible. Rygoth watched in growing horror as segmented legs covered with tiny hairs burst through her white gloves in the place where her hands used to be. She fell to the ground as four more legs grew from her body. Kara had one last look at Rygoth's multicolored eyes and then they cracked like a shell, the pieces falling into the grass as two new orbs—these black and glossy—pushed their way to the surface.

The Spider Queen was a spider once more.

Rygoth's troops fled into the trees of the Thickety. Releasing its hold on Lucas, the python followed suit.

Meanwhile, the spider began to shrink. First it was the size of a child, then a small dog, and then a tarantula. Eventually it would be no bigger than any other spider, at which point it would be able to escape into the grass with ease.

Lucas stepped on it before that could happen.

There was a lot of shouting and celebration after that. People hugged her and a bearded man lifted her high into the air and twirled her all around, and the boy who had stepped on the spider kissed her on the lips, which was strange but nice. She was confused but not unhappy, because obviously these people cared about her and she must have cared about them in return. It was only hours later, when she was alone with the little boy who had cast the last spell, that she finally asked the question that had been plaguing her all night.

"Who am I?"

The boy put his arms around her and began to cry.

EPILOGUE

The Shadow Festival would begin in just a few hours and Taff couldn't wait. He stared at his reflection in the mirror: red eyes and an elongated snout set over thick black fur. The paper-mâché mask had taken him weeks to make and he was proud of it.

"Scary," Safi said, peeking over his shoulder.

"You *sure* you don't want to come?" Taff asked. He took off his mask, freeing unruly blond hair. "You've never attended a Shadow Festival before. You knock on people's doors and they *have* to give you candy." He threw up his hands in exasperation. "Why would anyone want to miss that?"

"There'll be sweets at the dance, too," Safi said, smiling. "And I've had enough of monsters. Even the make-believe kind."

At thirteen, Safi was a year older than him and more interested in fancy dresses than childish costumes. She had grown tall and elegant, and though she was still beset by the occasional nightmare, Safi's green eyes had returned to their playful, twinkling form. Taff saw the way other boys' heads turned when she passed. He wasn't jealous—absolutely not—but the idea of one of them dancing with his best friend tonight twisted his stomach into tight knots.

Am I too old for this? Taff wondered, looking down at the mask in his hands. *Should I go to the dance too?*

"Next year," Safi said, reading his thoughts as always. "I know how much you've been looking forward to this. You should enjoy it." She nudged him playfully. "And save a few houses for me. I'll meet up with you later."

"Great!" Taff exclaimed, beaming. He already knew one house he would definitely reserve for her. A young woman who had recently settled on the island had turned her cornfield into a maze, and she made cider dumplings that were, if rumor could be believed, as good as Widow Miller's had been.

Taff was about to tell Safi all about it when there came a knocking at the door.

"It's probably Lucas," Taff said, crossing the room. "He wants everything to be perfect and there are tons of last-minute details to—"

Taff opened the door. The rest of his sentence froze on his lips.

"I've come for what's mine," said Querin Fyndrake.

The master of the Hourglass Tower had not changed much in the intervening years. His clothes were still lavish, his beard well oiled. His eyes still twitched from side to side like a pendulum.

Safi looked down at the small man in disgust.

"He's exactly how you described him," she said.

"Handsome?" Querin asked. "Magnificent?"

"Monstrous."

"Ah," Querin said, glaring at Safi. "What's *your* name?"

"Why? Want me to carve it into your door?"

"If you'd like," Querin replied, grinning. "The Khr'nouls have been particularly hungry lately, and I'm always on the lookout for fresh sacrifices."

Taff's legs wobbled, and he leaned against a nearby table in order to remain steady. He had been expecting this moment for the past four years, but now that it was actually happening he felt woefully ill-prepared.

I need another week, he thought. *Even just a few more days . . .*

"Come on, boy," Querin said, stepping aside to allow him room to pass. "Let's get this business over with. I've experiments to attend to."

"He's not going anywhere," Safi said.

"The boy agreed to a magical pact," Querin said, "and there's nothing that you, him, or I can do to change that."

He reached forward, intending to grab Taff by the arm and drag him outside, but his hand smacked into an invisible wall.

"What's this?" Querin asked, clutching his hand with pain.

"A spell I put on the house," Safi said. "No one can enter without being invited first. I got the idea from a bedtime story my father once told me about bloodsucking creatures who lived forever. Reminded me of you, for some reason."

Taff drew the slingshot from his belt and aimed it at Querin's face.

"Really?" asked the man with growing impatience. "A magic slingshot? I am *immortal*. You can't hurt me with invisible pellets."

"I know," Taff said. "But that was my other slingshot. This one's new."

Bending down to create a better angle, Taff shot over Querin's head and into the sky. A trail of purple light blazed from his slingshot, like a shooting star in reverse. It rose above the beautiful trees of the Thickety and then exploded with a thunderous noise that shook the entire island. Colored light fell like rain and evaporated into a blue mist that hovered just above the ground.

Querin, who had fallen to the ground during this unexpected display, stared back at Taff in confusion.

"What did you do *that* for?" he asked.

Taff felt no need to reply, for the answer to his question was already here. He simply waited for Querin to turn around and see it for himself.

Witches.

Upon seeing Taff's signal they had come immediately. Some rode fantastic beasts. Some flew on one enchanted contraption or another. Some just appeared out of nowhere.

They all carried grimoires.

Within moments the clearing was packed with

women, men, and children eager to defend a boy they all loved dearly. Taff saw Lucas and his grandfather West, Bethany and Mary Kettle, Sordyr and Breem. At the head of this welcome procession rode Father.

The sight of his friends bolstered Taff's spirits, and he spoke to Querin with renewed courage.

"Perhaps you haven't heard," he said, "since you've been trapped in your little tower all this time, but after the Spider Queen was defeated there were a lot of witches looking for a home. Not just the ones who had fought in the final battle, but those in the Well of Witches too. See, when Princess Evangeline's spirit was freed, the Well changed back into Phadeen—the paradise that Minoth Dravania had originally created for the students of Sablethorn—and all the witches who had been imprisoned there were free to reenter the world."

"They were confused at first," Mary added. "But we gathered them here in the Thickety and did our best to ease their transition, help them understand what had happened. Some chose to stay in Phadeen and start new lives there. Others remained with us. The Thickety became their sanctuary."

"And so, with Sentium's blessing, we decided to rebuild Sablethorn and train these witches properly," Sordyr said, indicating the giant pyramid nestled beneath the trees behind him. "I asked my mentor Minoth Dravania to reclaim his old position as headmaster, but he chose to remain in Phadeen. Mary and I share leadership of the school, while my friend William Westfall here runs things on the island."

"And all three of us," Father said, "order you to leave my son alone."

As their leaders spoke, the witches had gathered into a large circle that completely surrounded Querin. Now they opened their grimoires. Pages flapped in the late autumn wind.

If Querin was the slightest bit unnerved, he hid it well.

"Look at all these marvelous witches you've assembled,"

he said, a mocking curl to his lips. "At one point, I might have even been intimidated. But I've watched from my tower, and I know that things are different now. Back when these spellbooks got their power from the Well of Witches, they could do truly remarkable things. But without the darkness at their core—what are they good for? A few tricks, nothing more. You think you've saved magic? You've only weakened it."

He was right, of course. The grimoires were no longer evil, but they wielded less power. In Taff's opinion, this was a more than fair exchange, but he was disappointed that their enemy knew the truth.

Shaking his head, Querin pulled out a gold pocket watch on a chain and checked the time.

"Enough," he said, snapping the lid of the watch closed. "This conversation is meaningless. I cannot undo the boy's pact—it is with the Khr'nouls. I am simply here to deliver him. If I do not do so in time, the Khr'nouls will come for him themselves. You *really* don't want that to happen. They will destroy everyone on this island to get to their prize. There's no magic in this world that can stop them!"

Looking at something past Querin, Taff smiled.

"We'll see about that," he said.

The witches parted and a tall figure rode past them on a black mare. She was seventeen and achingly beautiful, with long hair that flew freely in the wind. Her dark eyes settled on Querin and he seemed to shrink beneath her gaze.

"So you're him," Kara said. "I must confess, the memory of your face was not one I minded losing."

Querin looked up at her, baffled.

"Impossible," he said. "I saw what happened to you. Magic wiped your mind completely clean."

"True," Kara said. "And were I not surrounded by people dedicated to rebuilding those lost memories—with patience, compassion, and long stories by firelight—I might have been lost forever. But even when I didn't recognize their faces, I felt their love—and that was what saved me. Since then I've replenished my lost memories with plenty of new ones. Life has been kind."

"Until today," Querin said, regaining his composure. "Your brother carved his name into my door. I will have what's mine."

Kara slid off Shadowdancer's back. She knelt in front of the man until they were face-to-face. Her black eyes seemed to grow even darker. Querin swallowed nervously and a bead of sweat ran down his temple.

Taff loved his sister more than anyone in the world, but even he had to admit that she could be a little scary sometimes.

"Do you really think that I will let you take my brother?" she asked quietly.

"You don't have a choice."

Darno trotted lazily into the open circle and took a seat behind Kara, his scorpion tail raised high in the air.

"There's always a choice," Kara said. "For me—and

for you. Leave this island. Go in peace. This needn't end badly."

"Enough!" Querin exclaimed, stomping his foot down like a petulant child. "*There's nothing you can do to save him!* Even if you somehow manage to kill me, the Khr'nouls will come for the boy anyway. But let me take him to the Hourglass Tower, where the sacrifice can be completed safely, and no harm will come to anyone else."

"And if I refuse?" Kara asked.

"Then I summon the Khr'nouls here right now," Querin said. "Everyone dies!"

Taff saw Sordyr shift uneasily in his saddle. The library from the old Sablethorn had been moved here, and Sordyr had spent months reading everything he could about the terrifying Khr'nouls. They were ancient gods that could only come when summoned, and only a fool or one attempting to gain great power would do so. Querin had been the latter. In his youth, he had called forth the Khr'nouls, thinking that he could control them, and they had destroyed his entire city in a single hour. Tens of thousands of people had perished. The only reason Querin had been spared was his promise to provide his new masters with food for centuries to come.

"For the last time!" Querin exclaimed. "Give me the boy, or I will summon the Khr'nouls right now!"

Kara rose to her full height and breathed deeply, enjoying the crisp air.

"Go right ahead," she said, stretching her arms high as though awakening from a long nap. "We've a lovely island, and I've never had the pleasure of meeting their kind before."

Querin stared at her with disbelief.

"So be it," he said.

Falling to his knees, Querin clasped his hands and raised them into the air. Beneath his breath he mumbled a complicated string of words that turned his lips dark red and then black. Taff turned to Safi, hoping to hold her hand, but she had taken her place among the other witches.

I hope Kara knows what she's doing, he thought.

The blue sky suddenly solidified, as though frozen in place. Cloud shards showered the trees, and a crack split the sky. Two gargantuan fingers with knuckles like mountain ridges pried their way into the world. Their mottled skin was comprised of colors that Taff had never seen before, and they filled his mind with strange, violent thoughts.

He looked away.

Pages ruffled as some of the younger witches, and many of the older ones, began to shake in fear. They turned to Kara and drew confidence from her calm demeanor. Taff watched Safi take the hand of the little blond-haired girl next to her, and this girl linked hands with an old man particularly good at levitation spells. The old man held hands with Bethany . . . and on and on it went, hands clasping together until the circle was closed.

The grimoires floated in front of the witches, waiting to be read.

"Together!" Kara exclaimed.

She closed her eyes. Taff could tell, from the strain on his sister's face and the rapid flickering of her eyelids, that she was attempting to build a mind-bridge to the Khr'nouls. It would have been an impossible feat, even for a *wexari* as powerful as Kara. She was, after all, just a single witch.

Only she wasn't alone anymore.

In unison, the witches began to chant from their grimoires, and Kara's face relaxed as new power surged into her, augmenting her spell. Querin whirled in confusion, unsure what to make of this unexpected development.

A single grimoire is no longer as powerful as it used to be, Taff thought. *Querin was right about that. But what he didn't realize is that witches can now link their magic together, creating spells more powerful than ever.*

Kara no longer wielded the power of a single witch. She was guiding an army of minds joined together in their desire to drive evil from the world.

"Leave . . . my brother . . . alone!" Kara exclaimed.

From behind the parted sky came a teeth-grinding

wail of fury, and then the fingers withdrew in defeat. The sun returned to its rightful place in the sky, shedding light on Kara's smiling face.

"Return to your tower," she told Querin, who was now looking at her with something approaching awe. "Live out the last of your days. Don't bother trying to make any more sacrifices to the Khr'nouls. They will not come again."

"Why not?"

Kara leaned forward and whispered in his ear.

"Because they're afraid of me."

Querin's eyes widened. He fumbled with shaking hands for the watch in his pocket, finally managing to set it free, and pressed a button on the top. He vanished.

They never saw him again.

That night, the inhabitants of the Thickety were in a celebratory mood. Fireworks rose high above the new Sablethorn. The town square rumbled with music and dancing. Costumed children paraded through the streets, filling their sacks with sweets and their minds with memories.

Kara stood on the edge of the crowd and waited for Lucas.

She was wearing a red dress embroidered with black swirls, a gift from Mary Kettle. Around her neck she wore her mother's wooden locket with the seashell crest, and in her hair she wore a neat bow tied with red ribbon. It was the only thing she remembered of the girl named Grace Stone, and though they might have been enemies, it felt right to have a piece of her here tonight.

Kara caught sight of Lucas approaching through the crowd. He was wearing dark breeches and a pressed white shirt. His eyes met hers, and Kara's heart fluttered with excitement.

"I was wondering, miss," Lucas asked, bowing, "if I could have the first dance?"

Kara curtsied shyly.

"You have my sincere promise," she said. Kara took his hand and gazed across the town square in wonder. "I still can't believe you did all this for me."

Lucas shrugged as though it had been nothing, but Kara knew that months of planning had gone into tonight's celebration.

"The Shadow Festival was the one thing about the Fold that I actually liked," Lucas said. "I just wanted you to experience it again."

"Feels like the first time for me."

"Well, you only ever did the little-kid stuff," Lucas said. "You never attended the dance. So that *will* be a first." He held out his arm. "Shall we?"

"Soon," Kara promised, touching his lips. "There's something I have to do first. The dance doesn't start until later. I'll meet you there."

Though Lucas was clearly disappointed, he did not ask her what could possibly be so important. His absolute trust was one of the things that Kara loved best about him.

She wrapped her arms around his waist.

"We're going to be together forever, Lucas Walker," she whispered.

"How can you be so sure?"

"Because I'm a witch, silly," Kara said, kissing him. "I know these things."

She found Taff and they rode Shadowdancer to a quiet field flooded with moonlight. Watcher perched on a nearby branch, its eye the color of a ripe nectarine: *Curious.* Sordyr claimed that the one-eyed bird had no idea of the important role it had played in tonight's enterprise. Kara wasn't as convinced.

"Do you think it will really work?" Taff asked, his voice trembling with excitement.

"Stranger things have happened," Kara said, "especially to us."

She unclasped her locket and removed the seed.

Its hard casing was midnight blue, and it made a soft

whish whish sound when Kara shook it. For as long as she could remember—which was, admittedly, not very long at all—the seed had been a constant presence in Sordyr's lab, a secret project he could never seem to perfect. Finally, he had made some sort of breakthrough, and only then did Mary Kettle imbue the seed with the necessary magic.

They gave it to Kara on her seventeenth birthday and explained what it did.

She knew that Mary and Sordyr had meant the gift as a kindness, and appreciated the love and effort behind its creation. Nevertheless, Kara found herself hesitant to use it.

The magic isn't permanent, she thought. *Will it cause more heartache than happiness?*

For the last eight months she had been carrying the seed around in her locket, considering that same question. But now, with the threat to Taff gone, she felt that the time had come at last.

"You want me to plant it?" Taff asked, holding out his hand for the seed. "You don't want to get your dress dirty."

"Let's do it together," Kara said.

They dug until their hands were black with dirt, dropped the seed into the hole, and covered it up. Sordyr had told Kara that the seed didn't need to be planted deep, only "watered by moonlight." He was right. Stems shot up from the ground and unfolded into strange peonies that gave off a soft silvery glow. Sordyr called them "moonflowers," and soon Taff and Kara were standing in a small garden of them.

"Children!" exclaimed a voice behind them, thick with emotion.

Father had often told Kara that if she wanted to remember what her mother looked like she need only look in the mirror. But while it was true that Helena Westfall shared her daughter's dark hair and eyes, there was a certain mischievous energy in her general demeanor that was all Taff.

"Mother?" Taff asked.

She leaped forward, her arms extended. Kara was worried that she might pass right through them like a ghost, but her body was warm and solid. Kara could even smell sandalwood in her hair.

"The things you've done!" she exclaimed, her beautiful face glowing with pride. "*My* children!"

"You saw?" Taff asked.

"Most of it," Mother said. "Before they captured me that night, I used my grimoire to cast one last spell, just in case the worst happened. It allowed me to move my spirit into the nearest animal." She looked over at Watcher. "Luckily this little fellow was in the trees above me."

"Watcher was you this entire time?" Taff asked, mouth agape.

"Not exactly," Mother said. "Mostly my spirit just lingered and watched, like a passenger on a ship. But I might have provided a little influence when I could."

"Like when Watcher led me into the Thickety that first time," Kara said.

"I knew you'd need a grimoire in the battles to come," Mother replied. "And I was confident that you were strong enough to overcome its darkness. You are my daughter, after all."

Sordyr had been the one who figured out that Watcher was more than just a bird. That's why he had placed a piece of its feather inside the seed, providing just enough of Mother's spirit to make the spell work.

"Let's go," Taff said, grabbing Mother by the hand. "Come back to the village with us. We've made such interesting friends! I can't wait to introduce you!"

Kara felt her heart tear a little. In all his excitement, Taff had forgotten her repeated warnings about the limitations of the spell. It was why she had hesitated to plant the seed in the first place—and why Father had refused to come.

Beneath her feet, a moonflower died, its wilted petals drifting to the earth.

"I'm so sorry," Mother said. "I can't leave the garden.

And once the last flower dies I have to go. Forever this time."

Another moonflower wilted.

"But that's not enough time!" Taff exclaimed, tears rolling down his cheeks. "This isn't fair! We just got you back and——"

"Hush," Mother said. "Any time with those we love is a gift, son. The trick is to use it well. Besides, this isn't an ending. I live on, in you and Kara. I might have been a competent witch, but nothing I could cast or conjure could ever compare to you. I've left my mark on the world in the most astounding way, and I didn't even need a grimoire to do it!"

She drew them close.

"You, children, are my Last Spell," she whispered.

And so, no longer looking at the moonflowers, the three figures talked quietly in the dark. They spoke of the past and present but mostly of the future that stretched before the children like an undiscovered forest. Taff, inspired by the architects of Sablethorn, hoped to design even bigger buildings one day. And Kara imagined a quiet life of caring for animals and teaching witches how to use magic properly. Their mother barely spoke, preferring to listen in awed fascination, every word a revelation.

No one noticed when the last moonflower died. One moment their mother was there and the next she was simply gone, leaving the smell of sandalwood in the air.

The siblings sat in silence for a long time.

"Are you okay?" Kara finally asked.

"I'm not sad, if that's what you mean," Taff replied, sounding surprised at his own reaction. "I'm glad we saw her. I always knew that Mother loved us, but it's different, actually seeing it in her eyes. Now I know for sure. I wouldn't trade that memory for anything in the world."

"You made her so proud," Kara said.

Taff grinned madly, looking for just a moment like an eight-year-old boy again.

"Not just me," he said. "Both of us."

Kara smiled, recalling the look of pride in her mother's eyes. *I have a memory of her again*, she thought. *One that I can keep forever.* A warm bloom of joy filled her chest. Sordyr had indeed given her a gift beyond compare.

Taff turned toward the village.

"We should get back. Lucas will be waiting for you."

Kara raised her eyebrows. "Or maybe you're just worried that all the best candy will be gone if we don't hurry."

"Exactly!" Taff exclaimed, already starting along the path. "The Shadow Festival only comes one time a year!"

Kara began to follow him and then, after a moment's consideration, untied the wooden locket from around her neck and left it at the base of the tree. She took her brother's hand, and together the witch's children made their way toward the warmth and lights of home.

ACKNOWLEDGMENTS

When I first started writing *The Thickety*, I envisioned a sixty-thousand-word stand-alone novel that I could pound out in five months. Little did I know that it would take me three hundred thousand words, six years, and seventy-two thousand cups of coffee to reach the final page.

I could not have pulled this off without the following people:

My editor, Katherine Tegen, is clearly a time traveler who goes into the future, reads the published book, and bases her feedback on the differences between that and my initial draft. It's the only reasonable explanation for such startling insights.

Alexandra Machinist gives sagely advice and makes me laugh, often simultaneously. She is a good friend as well as a brilliant agent.

These novels would not be the same without the amazing illustrations of Andrea Offermann and design genius of Amy Ryan—thank you!

I also want to thank all the folks at HarperCollins/KT books, especially Kelsey Horton, who is painstakingly meticulous about making my books perfect, and Jenny Sheridan and Kathy Faber. They convinced countless independent booksellers that *A Path Begins* was worth checking out, and I think that has made all the difference in the world.

Thank you to my three sons—Jack, Logan, and Colin—for understanding why their dad has to lock himself in the basement with his laptop and can't always play Monopoly.

My wife, Yeeshing, is a never-ending source of patience, love, and inspiration. I don't deserve you.

And finally, thank you so much to the readers, both old and young, who have taken this journey along with Kara and Taff. I hope you've enjoyed the ride.